©2018 by James Bierce. All rights reserved.
jamesbierce.com

Published by Grays Harbor Publishing.
graysharborpublishing.com

Cover design by Clayton Swim.

Grayland (Grays Harbor Series: Book 2) First Edition

ISBN: 978-1948714037

This book is dedicated to my cousin, Robie,
whose constant encouragement (along with
some nagging), is greatly appreciated.

I would also like to acknowledge the pessimists and naysayers out
there — for without your doubts and criticisms, the world would be a
wretchedly wonderful place.

— James Bierce

PROLOGUE
WESTPORT

According to the calender on the kitchen wall, which she marks at the beginning of every day, the date is Monday, September 24th, and it was exactly one week ago that twelve-year-old Amanda Williams murdered both her father and step-mother. Over the next couple of days, she watched from their house as the entire town evacuated to the south, where word was spreading that emergency shelters had been setup in both South Bend and Raymond — neither of which were showing any signs of being infected with the virus. After everyone was gone, and the beaches surrounding the city became quiet for the first time in over a century, Amanda decided to take a walk down the street to the beach access road, passing by the darkened lighthouse that towers above the sand dunes in the Westhaven State Park. She misses seeing the light, the glow of which she could often see from her bedroom window — but even the silhouette of the obsolete lighthouse wasn't enough to distract her from the perfect evening along the beach. There were no tourists or parents, no children screaming, no dogs barking as they ran through the surf — it was only her and the sliver of moonlight overhead. For the first time in her rather short life, she finally felt happy.

That feeling lasted for a single night, and her world changed forever when she went for a walk the following evening.

The first time that she saw someone else in town was right down

1

the road from her house, a woman that was sitting on a bench in front of the town drugstore. At first she didn't think much of it, but after walking down to the beach it began to bother her — an invader in her otherwise pure oasis of solitude. She decided to get rid of the woman on her way back, an easy kill by the looks of her — but after searching for over an hour, with no trace of the woman anywhere, she turned around and faced the street that led back to her house, and that was the first time that she saw them.

Staring back at her, with eyes that somehow looked dead and menacing at the same time, was a crowd of dozens of people — all of them slowly moving in her direction.

Although she managed to make it back to the house that night, it was also the last time she was able to wander into the streets after sundown. Her once perfect existence had been taken over by the infected souls that never left the town.

With the sun just barely under the horizon, Amanda can already hear the sound of someone moving outside of her bedroom window. Huddled in the corner of her closet, with her knife held tightly in her hand, she tries to cough as quietly as possible to clear her congested throat, fearing what might happen if someone were to find her. She can see them walking around after dark, often wandering with no obvious purpose or direction, and becoming more violent as each day passes. For days now she's been living like this — alone, hungry, and afraid, hiding in a house once occupied by the family that she murdered. The fact that it was her own family doesn't usually bother her, but on nights like this, when the streets are alive with the creatures that now occupy Westport, she finds herself missing them. While she doesn't necessarily regret killing any of them, she does miss the companionship and security that her father provided.

She hears a faint scratching at her window, followed by a voice whose tone seems calm and soothing — 'The Whisperer' she calls him. Amanda has learned the hard way not to listen to him, no matter how pitiful or reassuring he may sound. Soon, after ignoring him for too long, he'll grow impatient and desperate, and the gentle voice that only wants to come inside will turn into a vicious rage. She's never once seen him this close to the house at such an early hour. Normally he keeps his distance until much later into the night, when the light is dim, and the cold, damp air moves in through the streets from the ocean to the west.

As she tries to force herself to sleep, a feeling of terror suddenly comes over her as she remembers the candle burning in the living room. Although the people in town seem to be scared of daylight, they're strangely attracted to the lights at night — even to the subtle flicker of candlelight. She feels relatively safe behind the locked doors of her home, especially inside of the closet that she now sleeps in, but she also knows that if enough of them come to the window and see her moving around, they might be able to break through. With the knife held tightly in her hand, she carefully reaches out and pushes the closet door open, then slowly crawls out onto the floor beside her bed. She knows that he can't see her yet, but when she moves away from the bed and toward the door he might see movement through the semi-transparent curtains that cover the glass. Peeking around the bedpost, she glances up at the window, frightened that she'll see his grotesque face — or even worse, he might see her. To her relief though, only the quivering flame from the candlelight on her bedroom wall is visible.

After hurrying through the doorway and into the hall, she lies down on the hardwood floor and whispers underneath a door across from her bedroom... "Aaron, don't worry, I'll put it out before they see us..."

Her brother, Aaron, who was the only member of the Williams family to survive the massacre (besides Amanda, of course), had inadvertently locked himself in the basement of the house while hiding from her, in the mistaken belief that their father would be able to stop her. For the next several days, Amanda could hear him plead with her to let him out — but as his fists pounding against the door became weaker, and his once dominating voice shriveled to a gasping whisper, she stopped hearing from him altogether. Her routine, however, remains the same. After she finds herself something to eat, she slides a small amount of food under the door for him. After that, and until it's time for bed, she talks to him for hours, telling him all about the changes in the neighborhood — and the people that they once knew that are now dead, some of them by her own hands. As she turns and faces the burning candle, she stops and listens to the silence emanating from the basement below, feeling the cold, musty air blow across the floor from under the door.

"Aaron, are you there?"

Hearing no response, she crawls quickly into the living room, heading straight to the coffee table where the candle is lit. The room seems different after dark, more tranquil somehow — she rarely ever sees it this way. Ordinarily she spends every hour of darkness locked away in her own personal fortress of clothes, dolls, and her stepmother's butcher knife. In the nearly dark room in front of her though, she can no longer see the seemingly empty town outside the windows, or the blood splattered in the entryway, or her father's mangled body lying just outside the antique glass-paned front door where she left him. What she can see is her breath from the dry, cold air inside the house, which only gets worse as the brisk autumn winds move into the region.

She's angry with herself for leaving the candle burning, angry that she kept one lit in the first place. The skies the day before, however, were almost black, leaving the house dark in the middle of the afternoon.

Still on her stomach, trembling with fear and afraid that they might see her through the windows, she slowly reaches up for the candlestick.

Then she hears a familiar sound.

The doorknob on the front door starts rattling, ever so slightly. She quickly grabs hold of the candlestick and extinguishes the flame. Now surrounded by complete darkness, she waits for the sound outside to stop before she turns around to go back into her room, but it's soon replaced with yet another sound. This one is coming from another direction — from the kitchen behind her.

When it happens a second time, she lets out a quiet whimper as she finally realizes that it's coming from inside the house.

She waits on the floor, gripping the candlestick in one hand, and the knife in the other. The house is entirely dark, and silent aside from the graceless footsteps on the front porch. Then she hears it again, the sound of shuffling feet across the tile floor.

They're still in the kitchen.

She's frozen with fear, but somehow manages to slide her body against the front of the couch. She can only hear one of them, but however this one got in, others could soon follow. They'd been inside the house only once before, and it nearly ended tragically. She knows that the only chance she has is to somehow lure them out, and that means forcing her fear-paralyzed body to stand up and face whatever is in the next room. As quietly as possible, she stands up in front of the couch and listens to them. The steps are short, slow and uncoordinated. Wherever they're going, they don't seem to be in any hurry.

The only other door into the house is at the end of the hallway, and that leads her right past the kitchen. As she makes her way across the living room she can hear them breathing — a deep, rattling, congested wheeze that sounds painful. She can smell them too. They all give off what could only be described as every human stench imaginable. The smell stops her in her tracks, and for a moment she has to hold her breath and back up a few steps to keep from gagging — but then she covers her nose and mouth in the crook of her arm, and manages to start moving again. Feeling something at her feet, she realizes that it's the transition between the hardwood in the living room and the carpet in the hallway.

That means the kitchen, and the intruder, is right next to her.

She waits once again for any signs of movement. For all she knows they're directly in front of her, waiting for her to walk right into them — but when she stops to hear where they are, she can only hear the labored breathing a few feet to her right. As she steps onto the carpet, the weight of her frail frame causes the ancient floorboards underneath to creak, and from the next room she hears a frantic moan cry out. Loud footsteps are coming toward her, followed by the crashing of frying pans landing on the tile floor. Amanda quickly steps back onto the hardwood and back into the living room, the footsteps following right behind her, slowed only by the constant dragging of their feet. She doesn't want to run back to the couch in the middle of the room, afraid she might trip on something, so instead, she turns to her left and stands against the wall just inside the room. She closes her eyes, trying not to scream, with every muscle in her body clenched in fear.

Only seconds later the footsteps are right next to her — but they hurry past her and into the room beyond. She hears a stumble coming from the direction of the couch, then a horrible, sickly scream as they scramble to get up. Without hesitating, she opens her eyes, useless as they are in the dark room, then runs down the hallway toward the back door. When she reaches it, she's surprised to find that it's still locked.

This wasn't how they got in.

She turns around and faces the hallway again, the sound of the footsteps once again coming closer, along with the now desperate gasps for air. With her hands trembling, she drops the candlestick and feels the door for the deadbolt and handle. The footsteps are getting closer as she finally manages to open the door and make her way out onto the porch that surrounds the house — then she turns around and grabs the door handle, slamming it shut as she catches just a glimpse of the person chasing her. Only seconds later she can hear a loud thump against the closed door, and then a scratching sound as she sees a pale hand against the surface of the small glass window beside it.

Turning around, she can barely see the outlines of the craftsman-styled homes of downtown Westport from the faint sliver of moonlight overhead, giving everything a subdued blue tint that looks almost dreamlike. Tonight the town looks completely different than it had a year ago. The streets are dark, and so are the windows of the now empty homes and businesses. There's no traffic, no loud music coming from the neighbor's house, and no sounds from the harbor only a short walk from her house.

She looks around frantically at the dark buildings and streets, her bare feet now feeling numb against the cold wood decking of the porch, and her face burning from the icy winds coming off of the ocean. She doesn't know where to go, she hasn't been out at night since the people emerged from the shadows. Sometimes at night, while she was trying to fall asleep through the noise and chaos outside, she thought about where she would go if something like this happened — in fact her brother used to obsess over it after the news of the virus broke. He said their safest bet was the apartment above the Peterson Bar & Grill. It had a reputation for prostitutes and illegal liquor during prohibition, but it turned into a family restaurant in recent years. The owner had boarded up the staircase to the second story years ago, and the only way inside was now up a rusty fire escape in the alley out back. The only problem was getting there — it's on the other side of town.

She makes her way down the steps carefully, wishing that she'd slept with her shoes on as she reaches the landing at the bottom. Her bare feet were already feeling the effects of the rough planks on the porch, but the sidewalk leading to the street is sharp gravel. Hoping to save her feet, she jumps off of the landing and into a mud puddle in the lawn, splashing mud on her already filthy dress.

Immediately after landing she hears a loud crack, and then the creaking of the front door. She ducks into the bushes beside the porch and waits, and for a moment she can only hear the loud breathing — and then the groaning of the wooden steps leading to the sidewalk as they begin to move. For the first time she can see that it's a younger man, probably in his late teens or twenties. He stumbles down the graveled walkway, barely keeping his balance as he heads away from her hiding spot. He doesn't have any pants on, or shoes for that matter — the only thing that he's wearing is a soiled white t-shirt and boxer shorts. He's also drenched in sweat, with pale, clammy skin that's covered with bruises and scratches. At the end of her sidewalk he stops and looks around, making Amanda nervous that she might be seen if she hangs around for too long. One thing that she's learned is that the infected people she's seen in the past aren't completely stupid, some shred of intelligence has managed to stay intact. She tries to move silently behind the bushes, toward the alley that runs next to her house. If she can get there she can make her way to Forrest Street, which is only a couple of blocks away, and from there it's a straight shot to the restaurant.

Crawling on her hands and knees through the pine needle mulch of her stepmother's flower bed, which is the only place that's still completely hidden from the moonlight, she looks up and sees the man walking across the lawn, his hands reaching out toward her, and his blank eyes fixed on hers. She jumps out of the flower bed and starts running, hoping that she doesn't draw attention to herself from the other people in town.

Just as she enters the alley, with her pursuer only twenty feet behind her, she finds herself staring at another man ahead of her. He's standing, rather calmly, on the other end of the alley. She glances back at the young man chasing her, who has now blocked off the narrow space she's trapped in, then he stops when he sees the second man. Amanda looks ahead at this new guy, noticing a faint smile appearing on his face. He's wearing what looks like a brown suit, but it's ragged and stained, with holes ripped in the knees and elbows. Apart from the tattered outfit, the man looks rather distinguished until he opens his mouth to speak, and absolutely nothing comes out. He tries it again, this time with some effort, but it's obvious that there's something wrong with him. He stops trying, then simply smiles at her, a wide evil grin that sends shivers down her spine, then very slowly he moves forward, his footsteps far more coordinated than the first man. She backs up slightly and looks around for a way out, and sees that the neighboring house has a crawlspace opening, but she's afraid of getting caught under the house with no other way out. She clenches her knife, glad that she had the wherewithal to hold onto it. She'd used it before, but her victims were caught off-guard and never had the chance to fight back. This time, she turns around to face the weaker opponent, the one who can barely walk, or even breathe.

She walks slowly and deliberately toward the man who forced her out of her home. Her face is blank, and any fear or desperation she

9

had a moment ago has disappeared. The man just stands there as she plunges the knife into his stomach, leaving his t-shirt and her dress both soaked in his blood. As he crumples to the ground, his hands reach out at her, but she quickly backs away and glances behind her. The second man is walking toward her with his arms reaching out warmly, as if he means to give her a hug, his footsteps faster than before. She takes off running in the direction of her front door, figuring that if she can outrun him she might be able to get back into the house — but as she rounds the corner and makes it to the bottom of the steps she notices that the door doesn't look right. Then she realizes that the hinges have been partly snapped off, and the door is no longer functional. Not knowing where else to go, she runs around the other end of the house and continues making her way toward the restaurant.

After running a block and a half, she stops and tries to catch her breath, exhausted from the activity and the cold. A thick blanket of fog is rolling in from the beach, and she's having a hard time seeing the buildings in front of her. With another quick glance behind her, she sees the man is still following her, and seems to be gaining ground. He's moving faster than she thought any of them could, and with no sign of slowing down.

With her lungs screaming for rest, she begins running again, and finally reaches Forrest street just as the fog becomes so heavy she can barely see the pavement under her feet. She slows down some, afraid that if she continues at this pace that she might run face first into a building or a street sign — or even worse. Her only hope now is that the man following her can see as poorly as she does.

Confident that the restaurant is to her right, only two blocks north of her current location, she turns and walks down the sidewalk, hoping he doesn't realize that she's changed direction.

After only a couple dozen more steps the fog becomes unbearable.

Not only is it difficult to see through, but it's now managed to block the faint moonlight that's been her savior tonight. She's being forced to walk agonizingly slow, with her arms held out in front of her to guide her along, and after several minutes she begins to wonder just how far she's come, or even which direction she's facing. Desperate to find her bearings, she stops, hoping to see something familiar around her, or anything at all — and while she can't see anything, she does hear something in the distance. It's behind her, like hard shoes walking on the concrete sidewalk. The gait doesn't sound right though, like they're slightly dragging one foot. She's almost certain that it's not the same man, since she doesn't remember his shoes making any noise at all. Then there's more noise coming from even further away, a chaotic mixture of countless feet against the pavement, and the moans and groans of the infected that she's been hearing night after night outside of her bedroom window.

Still blinded by the fog, she searches for the curb, and for the street below it. Finding it, she walks to the sidewalk on the other side, her legs wobbly from the extreme stress and chronic lack of sleep, then she waits for a moment and listens. She can still hear them moving closer, but she can also hear something in front of her — the sound of graceless and unsteady footsteps, like a drunk that's close to passing out. Closing her eyes and holding her breath, she backs up against the building behind her — waiting for them to pass by. As the steps get louder, she wonders if she'll be able to continue holding her breath — praying that they'll move on before the crowd catches up. Just when she thinks she'll either pass out or gasp for a breath, she feels the air move as they pass by, and the low rattling sound of someone struggling to breathe. The smell is also familiar, it's the same putrid odor they all seem to have. After what seems like an eternity, they finally reach a distance where she feels safe enough to take a breath.

11

The building behind her is made of either concrete or stone, she can't tell which, with what feels like elaborate etching in the surface — she can't remember a building quite like this one in town. Seeing the fog start to clear between her and the group of people, she walks away from them, hoping that something next to her will feel familiar. About twenty steps later she can feel something, a doorknob. She still has no idea where these people go during the day, and whether some of them might stay behind at night. In the past few months she'd seen dozens of them in front of her house, and she can't imagine how many others are roaming the streets throughout the rest of the town. Beyond this door could be a crowded room, but right now that really didn't matter — if she stays out here she'll be dead by morning.

Giving the knob a twist, the door opens silently, and she almost lets out a sigh of relief when it does. She closes the door behind her and locks it, then feels her way along a wall. Tired and exhausted, she decides to lie down on the carpeted floor beneath her feet, closing her eyes and trying not to listen to the commotion outside. She tries not to think about Aaron, and the fact that he's now alone in their house with nobody to talk to. Within a few minutes she falls asleep, escaping into an unconscious world full of vivid nightmares and horrible memories — all of them preferable to her reality.

CHAPTER 1
COHASSETT BEACH: DAY 1

In the distance, past the dunes and crashing waves along the shore, Sarah can see yet another weather system approaching — its dark gray clouds churning as the high winds push the front closer to land. By nightfall it will be over them, leaving behind even more wreckage on the beach, and more difficulties for her family and friends as they struggle to stay safe in a home that's surrounded by tall fir trees.

Although she spent a fair amount of time camping with her family along the Washington and Oregon coastlines as a child, she keeps reminding herself that those trips were always in the warmer months of summer, when the occasional rain and dense fog used to roll in from the ocean on a gentle breeze.

Winter storms, however, are anything but gentle.

As much as she despised the cabin when they first moved into it, her respect for its structural integrity has steadily increased with every passing windstorm — many of which have toppled trees and sent branches crashing onto their roof as they tried to sleep through the roar of the gusts. She's wondered on more than one occasion why the original settlers stayed in such an inhospitable place, or the native tribes that were here long before them, where the constant cloud cover obscures a sun that's only around for a short period each day. To call this season depressing would be an understatement, but Curtis tells her on an almost daily basis that when spring comes, she'll understand why they're here instead of the warm, fertile grounds of the Willamette Valley which was waiting for them in Oregon. As the endless series of rain clouds move overhead though, filling each day with the same dreary color to the sky as the last, she's beginning to have her doubts as to whether even he believes it.

On more than one cold night, the wind has become too strong to have a fire burning in the wood stove, as gusts of wind drive the smoke back down the chimney and into the cabin, sometimes with such force that it actually puts the fire out. Even the short walks around the property, which have helped her avoid the madness of cabin fever, have proven to be difficult at times, with the torrential rains soaking through several layers of weatherproof clothing in mere minutes.

On the rare pleasant days, however, which are so few and far between that you can probably count them on one hand, she has to admit that there's likely no other place on earth with such beautiful scenery. It's on those days, for that briefest of moments, that she forgets the struggles and hardships that come with living on the coast.

It's been six months to the day since the Lockwood family first arrived at the cabin in Cohassett Beach — and as agonizing as those first couple of months were, the last few have been the most challenging of their lives. Having four people sleeping and living in the same cramped space was bad enough, but adding two more adults to the cabin in the middle of winter was starting to create an impossibly difficult situation.

Sarah can't help but feel resentful, of not only the world around her, but also the relative strangers that have invaded her home and her family. She knows it's not their fault, and she feels guilty for ever feeling that way about Larry, but she feels even worse for thinking so negatively of Beth. The two of them have become inseparable, learning to lean on one another on the most difficult days, both of them knowing full well what it feels like to lose someone to the horrors of this last year.

In her heart, she knows that her daughter, Annie, is likely dead — and in some selfish way, she's actually comforted by the idea of her being gone. The concept of living in a world without people seems terrifying to her, but knowing the gut-wrenching truth of their reality is even worse. The thought of Annie still alive, yet hundreds of miles away and surrounded by strangers, was too much for Sarah to bear — and although it went against all of her maternal instincts, her stressed out and burdened mind had grown used to the thought that Annie was no longer suffering like the rest of them. She also knows that the odds of the entire Lockwood family surviving a worldwide apocalypse would have to be astronomical.

The absolute worst scenario though, the one that hasn't entirely made it's way into her consciousness, is the thought that Annie could be one of the infected — her mind traumatized by the same virus that wiped out the rest of the human race.

She can see the same look of loss on Beth's face too, the look of someone incomplete and lost in the world around them. Larry has tried to be a comfort to her, but his loss is different — he knows exactly what happened to his wife. It's the mystery, the not knowing, that truly tortures you.

As Sarah walks down the pathway behind Beth, with the early light of the morning sun on their backs, she looks back at the cabin, feeling strangely guilty about leaving the place for the first time since being reunited with her husband and son — but she reminds herself that it was Curtis who convinced her to get out of the house and try to do something normal for a change, just as long as she was willing to take a gun along. Along with their guns, her and Beth are carrying small, narrow shovels that are made specifically for digging in the sandy shore, both of them looking forward to having razor clams out of season and without a license.

"Do you ever see anybody on the beach anymore?" Sarah asks, as she walks beside Beth.

"Sometimes, but not very often. Don't worry though, they always keep their distance."

"My family used to come here on mornings just like this," Sarah says, as they reach the top of the dunes and look out at the wet sands of the low tide. "You'd have to practically push your way through the crowd of people to find a clam, even this early."

"I remember that too. Not really a problem anymore I guess."

Sarah looks in both directions at the long stretch of beach in front of them, seeing only seagulls and the now familiar scene of shipwreck debris washed up on the high tide line.

"Have you ever dug for clams before?" Sarah asks, as they both reach the edge of the water line.

"Not since I was a kid."

"Just look for the dimples in the sand — the bigger the dimple, the bigger the clam.

"Do you face away from the water when you're digging?"

"Some people do, but it's also a good way to get caught by a sneaker wave. Trust me, you don't want that — there's a hell of an undertow here."

They place the fresh clams in a sack as they work their way down the beach, feeling the cold spray of saltwater that's carried by the wind from the ocean.

"Do you ever wonder what it's like in other places?" Sarah asks, as if the subject were smalltalk.

"You mean in other countries?"

"Yeah, or even other states. Do you really think everyone is dead?"

Beth stops digging and stands up, letting the clam she's digging for get away while she rests her back and stretches. "You guys haven't really seen much besides this area, have you?"

"Curtis saw Aberdeen, but that's it. Why?"

"How much did he tell you about it?"

"He told me everything."

"Even about the people?" Beth asks.

"Yes, we don't keep secrets."

"I'm sure that's true — but Curtis was also watching from across the harbor. He wasn't in the city."

"What was in the city?"

"I'm sure there's plenty of people around the world that are still technically alive, but if they're anything like the ones that I've seen along the coast, they might as well be dead."

"I know, I've seen a few of them up close."

"But you haven't seen the vast number of them. We've seen thousands, in Sequim, Port Angeles, Westport, Aberdeen — and yet the six of us, our small group of survivors, we're probably the only ones in all of those places who are truly still alive. I can't imagine what it's like in Seattle or New York…"

"So you don't think there's any chance of people rebuilding again?"

"Not after this amount of time, no."

"It's only been a few months."

"Yeah, it's been six months, with no signs of anything. No airplanes, no cars, no radio signals, nothing."

Sarah starts digging again, surprised at the negativity she's hearing from Beth. As odd as it seems, especially given their extremely close living conditions, the two of them have never really talked about the possibilities of life returning to normal again.

"So you don't hold out any hope at all?" Sarah asks, giving her one

17

last chance to respond with something other than pessimism.

"Hope can be dangerous, Sarah."

"I know, but not when you have kids." She looks up at Beth, trying to gauge her reaction, but it's obvious that something else has caught her attention toward the dunes.

"What is it?" she asks quietly, trying to keep her fear from showing.

"There's someone up there, on the other side of that nearest dune. I saw their head just a second ago."

Sarah watches, but sees nothing at first, then she notices a quick flash of black appear over the top of the sand. Leaving her shovel on the beach, Beth pulls her pistol from the side holster and begins walking in that direction. Sarah bends over and picks her shovel up, then follows her into the soft, loose sand of the dunes, where only the strongest of ocean currents ever reach. Her mind is conflicted as to whether or not she should have her gun ready as well, and as Beth starts climbing the first rise on her hands and knees, she finally places the shovels quietly on the sand and pulls out the .357 revolver that Curtis gave her before she left. Seeing Beth at the top of the mound, just lying there and watching whatever is on the other side, Sarah slowly makes her way beside her and aims her gun down into the ravine of grass and beige sand.

What she sees surprises her, since it's the first time in nearly four months that anyone has even gotten a glimpse of the girl that nobody likes to mention. They'd even questioned whether she was still alive — but here she was, wearing a heavy black winter coat and kneeling down away from them in the side of the next dune, letting her fingers run lazily through the soft ground in front of her. Then suddenly, she looks up, still facing away from Sarah and Beth, then turns her head partway in their direction before standing up and walking away — her movements carefree and relaxed as she casually strolls down the pathway to the north. Once she disappears from their sight, Beth starts sliding down the sand toward the area she was in.

"I'm guessing that was Amanda?" Sarah asks quietly as she follows her.

"Yeah, that was her."

"Aren't we going to follow her?"

"No, she'd just lose us anyway. I can't believe she's still alive."

"Do you think she saw us?"

"Definitely."

They come to an area where the sand has been heavily disturbed, piled up in an intricate pattern that contains strange symbols and a seemingly random arraignment of numbers and letters. Beth hands her gun to Sarah, then starts digging into the pile.

"Shouldn't we head back and tell the others?"

"Not until I see what she buried here."

Scooping away large handfuls at a time, Beth suddenly jumps back, startling Sarah enough to make her drop her own gun. As she reaches down to pick it up, she sees what scared Beth so badly. Buried just beneath the surface is a woman's face, with the name '*BEN*' scrawled out across her forehead in a crudely made wound.

"What the hell is that?" Sarah yells out, her body now shaking as her mind starts to absorb the shocking image.

"It's the crier."

"The what?"

"We call her the crier. We've seen her around the neighborhood before on dark days, and she's always crying."

"What is Ben's name doing on her face?" she asks, her voice on the edge of hysteria.

"Sarah, you need to calm down... I know this is scary, but we don't need anymore attention that we already have."

"Did she do this? Did Amanda carve that into her?"

"I think you already know the answer to that..." Beth stands up and looks around, wondering if Amanda is watching them from a distance. "Come on, we need to get back to the cabin, but we can't go back the same way."

"Don't you think she already knows where we live?"

"She probably does, but I don't want to risk it." Beth climbs to the top of the next dune and surveys the area with some binoculars from her pocket. She can see Amanda's footprints winding through the sandy ravines, then disappearing altogether in a large cluster of pine trees. "Do you still have the radio?"

"Yeah." Sarah climbs up and hands the radio to Beth. "Are you calling them for help?"

"No, I'm calling to warn them."

CHAPTER 2
COHASSETT BEACH: DAY 2

The beaches of Washington State have never been famous for their contrast in seasons, and judging from the weather alone it would often be impossible to guess what time of the year it actually is. The endless months of cold, wet conditions are only occasionally interrupted by the rare days of full sun in the summer, and the even rarer days of snow and ice during the winter. The locals, who have somehow managed to become accustomed to it, are well-known and quite proud of the fact that they view umbrellas as a sign of weakness — an object that should only be used by those with delicate sensitivities to an otherwise harmless natural phenomenon.

Amanda, herself drenched from the downpour of rain that's soaking through her winter coat, is standing next to a car beside the road. She recognized it as belonging to a friend of her father the moment she saw it, and she assumes that it's his partial skeleton still slumped over the steering wheel. Unlike most of the cars along the highway, this one had the passenger side door wide-open to predators, and the remains of his wife and newborn infant are scattered across the pavement only a few feet from the vehicle. Feeling the raw ache of hunger pains in her stomach, she quickly searches through the car, hoping to find something that's at least halfway edible. After finding nothing but clothes and mildewed diapers, however, she climbs out of the car and walks to a nearby house instead, her eyes constantly scanning the loose gravel in the driveway for signs of recent activity.

When she opens the door, the strong scent of mold and decay brush past her face and escape into the outside air — an unfortunate consequence of the house being closed up and unheated for several months. She stays on the porch and looks inside, but sees nothing but a darkened room full of furniture and knick knacks. The cold air against her bare skin makes her shiver as she steps inside.

The place isn't all that messy, but it's cluttered, and the walls are covered nearly floor to ceiling with someone else's memories, the faces in the photos staring back at her and leaving her with a strange feeling, as if all of them were watching her every move. She obviously knows that it can't be true of course, these people are probably already dead, or at least will be soon enough — but she can feel their eyes following her as she walks further into the house, their glares becoming even more menacing if she gazes at one of the pictures for too long.

Her breathing becomes even more difficult the further inside she goes, which isn't surprising considering the amount of mildew and black mold that's covering the curtains and rugs in the living room. She turns around and takes another look at the front yard, making sure that she's alone before continuing further.

The small two-story house sits right at the edge of the dunes, only a stone's throw from the Pacific Ocean — and although the neighboring homes look as though they've never been properly cared for, it appears that at one time someone took great care of this place. She can tell that the siding and trim were once painted bright white, something only the brave or foolish would attempt in the wet climate of the Pacific Northwest coastline. Today, however, wild evergreen blackberries are encroaching onto the meticulously crafted pathways and flowerbeds that lead to the entrance of the home, and the once manicured lawn is overgrown and full of weeds and rotting leaves from the maple trees above. This wasn't a summer home, this house was well cared for year-round by someone who clearly isn't around anymore.

Stepping over the threshold and into the living area, she sees a thick layer of dampness on everything, and smells a horrible, thick aroma hanging in the air. The antique hardwood floors are buckled and warped from the moisture that's accumulated, and the houseplants lay withered and dead on the tables by the back door.

Through the partially open window on the back of the house she can see the ocean beyond, the waves crashing high with the incoming tide, and she realizes that she can't hear anything except for the sound of her own heartbeat pounding in her ears.

For most, the atmosphere of the beach is filled with the rich sounds of crashing waves, screeching seagulls, powerful winds that seemingly never stop, and of course the melodic tunes of countless wind chimes hanging from every house and shop along the coast. It drifts in relentlessly through every door and window, open or not, and provides the tourists and weekenders with a level of calmness they can't manage to find anywhere else.

The natives who live here year-round, however, generally hear none of it — for them the sounds all blend together into a silent chorus of background noise that somehow disappears from their consciousness. It's only after they leave the coast behind and head inland that they realize how silent everyone else's lives really are.

Looking out the window at the rising ocean, Amanda realizes that she no longer hears those soothing sounds of the world around her. Truth be told, she barely remembers what she's trying so desperately to listen to in the first place. She can still hear people talking, hear their footsteps as they try to walk quietly through the woods, and she can still hear her blade as it rips through the clothing of her victims. What she doesn't hear though, is life, the little things like the leaves and branches blowing in the wind, or the high-pitched chirps of the squirrels and birds in the woods nearby. Her world is suddenly silent, without distractions, and she wonders now if it will always stay that way.

As she moves into the bedroom, she sees much of the same, an area filled with dead plants and moldy walls, and what appears to be the remains of a small dog lying on the bed next to a bulge in the covers. The girl walks up and tries to see who or what might be underneath, but the quilt is pulled clear over their head. She takes her kitchen knife and slowly peels back the covers, seeing a frightened face staring back at her, a face that's still very much alive. As she stares at the woman's sunken eyes and shriveled up lips, wondering whether the same thing might soon happen to her, she looks up at the window in front of her and feels her mind beginning to slip away into a trance — almost as if she's falling asleep, but she can still see everything around her. Whatever it is, it's happened to her before, and often at the most inopportune time.

Noticing Amanda's clear distraction, the woman slides a hand out from beneath the covers, and tries desperately to lift her fingers enough to reach the knife that the young girl is carrying — but just before she does, Amanda comes to again, and smiles coldly at the woman as she pulls her blade away from the bed.

It's not often that she manages to find another living person, sick or not, and when she does they're usually in relatively the same dismal shape. The woman in front of her is no different. Lying in bed, barely breathing, soft incoherent whispers coming from her mouth, her eyes pleading with Amanda for help. She looks down at the woman and tries to pretend that she feels something for her, whether it be pity or empathy, or even rage — but the only thought that's on her mind is finding enough food to ease the hunger pains. Feeling sorry for this woman won't help her with that. The woman, probably in her fifties or sixties, it's hard to tell for sure, raises her hand up when Amanda lifts the knife.

"Don't fight me." Amanda orders her.

The woman attempts to lift herself up into a sitting position, then quickly falls back to the mattress as she begins to violently cough. Amanda watches her for a moment, waiting to see if one of the gasps might be her last, but when she finally catches her breath the young girl thrusts her blade into the woman's chest, then casually wipes the blood off onto the quilt covering her body. She waits for a few minutes to make sure that the woman actually dies, since she's learned the hard way that sometimes they don't — then she turns around and walks into the kitchen, somehow comforted by the fact that she's the only person left alive in the house.

It's been over four months since Ben was reunited with his family and taken away from her, four months of trying to stay warm and scavenging for food alone while Ben enjoys the comforts of his family's cabin. Her only solace is knowing that the weather is finally starting to improve, and the cold rains of winter have changed to the slightly warmer rains of spring.

Active only in the day, she spends her nights hiding in different houses along the beaches of Cohassett, waiting for the sun to drive away the remaining people that still roam the area after dark. She's not really all that scared of them, most of them are too slow and mindless to be of any real threat — but in the darkness of night they travel in larger groups, making them more dangerous than usual. With that constant worry on her mind every night, deep sleep has become somewhat of an impossibility, perhaps only an hour or two each night — and even then, with no one else to watch her back, it's the only time she's truly vulnerable.

25

Her days are mostly spent watching the Lockwood cabin, looking for patterns in their activity, waiting for them to finally let their guard down long enough for her to make her move. She's spent weeks thinking of almost nothing else, the perfect way to deal with the people who have hurt her the most. Killing all of them at once had crossed her mind, but she knows she can't bring herself to do that, they deserve so much worse. She's finally decided that they'll die one by one, no more than one each day, and Ben will be the last.

As soon as she opens the pantry door she remembers searching this house once before, and finding nothing but stale chips and crackers that were no doubt left behind by the Lockwoods. Why she never noticed the woman in the bed last time is somewhat unsettling, considering that she carefully checks every house she enters. Maybe the woman doesn't live here, maybe she wandered in during the night and simply stayed — or maybe she hasn't been as careful as she thought. Whichever the case, from now on she has to be more cautious.

Still feeling the intense hunger pains, she starts dumping the contents of the pantry onto the floor, until she spots a half eaten jar of peanut butter hidden in the back. Ignoring the pull date, she unscrews the lid and scoops out a mouthful, gorging on it as she makes her way out of the house and down the driveway. When she reaches the mailbox she stops and lifts the flag up, a reminder that there's nothing of any use inside anymore. She turns around, looking down both directions of the highway for any other mailboxes without their flags up, but there aren't any, at least not in this neighborhood. Between her and the Lockwoods, they've pretty well cleaned everything out.

With her knife tucked away under her arm, she continues to eat as she heads south along the highway, her steps slow and light, her feet barely making a sound on top of the fallen leaves and needles on the pavement. A few hundred feet down the road she stops and watches a house, noticing that the front door is wide open. Hearing voices inside, she drops the jar of peanut butter on the ground and walks down the driveway, slipping quietly through the open door.

"I'm gonna check out back really quick," Larry yells out from the living room.

"Don't go far," Beth replies from the kitchen, hearing the sliding glass door open from the other room, and then the sound of crashing waves from the nearby ocean.

This place wasn't nearly as empty as some of the other houses they've searched. With fully stocked cupboards and no car in the driveway, Beth figures that whoever lived here must have left sometime after the outbreak, and apparently took almost nothing with them. Even though today's goal was to find toilet paper and bleach, which were becoming scarcer by the day, they couldn't pass up gathering everything else the place had to offer — in fact she even wondered if it might be a good idea for the group to move in here instead of the cramped cabin they've been living in for months, but she knew that would never happen. Curtis insisted that it was safer for them to live away from the beach where the sick seemed to concentrate, and that the cabin was in a perfect location, tucked back into the woods and out of sight from the highway. As much as she hated to admit it, he was right, the single bedroom shitty excuse for a house was probably their best chance of staying hidden from the rest of humanity, or whatever is left of it.

She starts loading anything that might be useful into a laundry basket that she found in the bedroom. Dry pasta, boxes of cereal, canned goods, even a few utensils they've been lacking. Just as she opens another cupboard and looks inside, she hears a thump from the next room.

"Larry?"

There's no answer from her brother, but the thump is followed by the sound of something scraping the wall between the kitchen and dining room next to her. The long, slow scrape almost reaches the doorway before it stops, then nothing.

"Larry, is that you? This isn't funny..."

She knows that he wouldn't joke around like this, not after everything that they've been through these last several months. She walks quietly into the dining room, noticing that the sliding door is still open in the living room — but both rooms are completely empty. Then she sees a mark about halfway up on the wall, where someone has sliced through the wallpaper, then gouged out a chunk of the drywall. She knows that wasn't there when she searched the room only a few minutes before.

"Who's in here? Come on out!" she yells out, hoping that Larry might hear her.

Still facing away from the kitchen, she hears the cupboard door behind her close, and instinctively she reaches down for the gun in her pocket, but she stops when she feels something sharp poking her in the back.

"Don't try it," says a small, frail voice. "Raise your hands, slowly."

Beth follows the order, then feels someone reach into her pocket and remove the revolver.

"Turn around."

She turns around to see what could be an attractive young girl, wearing a filthy, tattered dress that's nearly falling apart, and an oversized black coat. Her long black hair is tangled and dirty, and her face is covered in what looks to be specks of dried blood.

"Amanda?" Beth asks her, trying to hide the fear in her voice. The girl responds with a wicked grin and soft giggle that makes her shiver, then Beth glances toward the front door that's still open.

"He won't come," Amanda tells her, pointing the gun directly at her face. "Don't scream, you'll only make it worse."

CHAPTER 3
MENLO: DAY 2

"There are two kinds of dead people, the ones that move, and the ones that don't."

Christine's father had recently told her this, hoping that the warning would make the fifteen-year-old think differently about the people now infected with the virus — and even though the young teenager realizes that he didn't mean it literally, she's seen enough of them herself to know the similarities between the scarcely living and the dead. The 'moving dead' are obviously still very much alive, but the people they once were, their personalities and memories, seem to be entirely gone. She's watched people she once knew from her bedroom window, people from around the neighborhood, stumbling around at night and finding themselves trapped behind their very own unlocked gates. They were lost, and showed signs of being seriously ill, but otherwise they seemed harmless enough.

There are others, however, who aren't so benign. They move around with more dexterity, sometimes even in the daylight, acutely aware of their surroundings, and with an insatiable appetite for bloodshed and violence. Their existence alone has kept Christine's family prisoners in their own home — terrified of being seen by someone who will follow them home, then relentlessly pursue them with an unnatural obsession, staying awake for days on end while the hunt was on. They've only seen a few of the stalkers around town, terrorizing neighboring houses and wiping out the few people around them that survived the plague untouched. What they saw, and what they heard, was enough to keep them awake at night, haunted by the unthinkable acts committed right next door to them.

When the outbreak first began, they were in the small town of Adna, sheltered by the Boistfort hills in Western Washington, living only a short distance from the headwaters of the Chehalis river. In many ways it was an ideal place to start over — surrounded by forests, orchards, and rolling pastures that are filled with cattle, deer and elk. It also has memories though, many of them wonderful, but some far too painful to be reminded of.

Her mother had been fighting cancer for over a year when news of the virus broke, and doctors had been optimistic about her chances of ultimately beating it. As the world started to disintegrate around them, however, and the hospitals and local clinics closed down, her mother's treatment abruptly ended — and with it, so did any hope of curing the disease. Day after day, they watched her slowly slip away from them, dying from what was a treatable illness only a few months before. Her father, George, was devastated, slipping into a deep depression that nearly cost him his own life the day they buried her — saved only by the thought of his daughter being forced to live alone in this horrible new world.

The virus came to the town in mid-September, spreading through the schools and retail businesses first, and killing nearly every resident in less than a week. Besides the two of them, the only person left in the area is their neighbor and friend, David — and after discussing it thoroughly, the three of them decided to leave their homes, headed for a destination without crowds or pavement, where they could catch their breath long enough to figure things out. After talking over the list of possible places, they came to the conclusion that the continually temperate climate of the coast, with its stark population and abundant food supplies, would be the perfect location to start over. They would move slow, only traveling on bright days under the safety of the sun, resting behind locked doors and gathering supplies as they made their way down fifty miles of highway on foot. A car was unfortunately out of the question due to the conditions of the roads, which are now littered with vehicles and debris from the panic that ensued after the initial outbreak. Almost all of the cars are useless anyway, crippled with either dead batteries or destroyed circuitry, making the task of stealing them all the more difficult.

With the sun nearly gone over the horizon, and the darkness of night quickly approaching from the east, Christine watches as the last few rays of sunlight shine over the town of Menlo in the distance — the last few moments of peace before the madness begins once again.

When they first came to the Menlo area only a few days before, it was immediately apparent that the town must have survived the virus longer than most, since this was the first time they had seen an attempt to rebuild what was left of their town. Houses that were evidently presumed to be contaminated were burned to the ground, as were their belongings — and the highway leading in and out of town was purposely blocked by heavy equipment, with deep ditches carved into the ground to stop anybody from driving around the barricade. As they moved in closer, however, it became clear that none of those protections worked. The virus was already in their community, killing nearly everyone except for the unlucky few who were driven insane by the infection. Nobody was around to tell the full story, but every town they've traveled through so far has suffered the same ultimate fate — quiet, empty, and almost tranquil in the daytime, and terrifying under the cover of darkness.

Ready to move on once again, and mere miles from the coastline, Christine sits in the hayloft of a massive old barn that's perched on the side of a hill overlooking the valley below, her legs dangling out of the loft. The fog is already forming over the pastures, hiding the remnants of what must have been a horrible ordeal for the community, and filling the air with the salty smell of saltwater from the bay just to the west of here. She can barely make out the piles of corpses scattered across a nearby field, most of which are only skeletons now, picked apart by both wild animals and the formerly domesticated pets that are now left to fend for themselves. The fog also hides something else, something far more sinister than coyotes or wild dogs, and she can already see the mist moving as they make their way out of the buildings and into the fields not far from where they're staying.

"You should close the door," she hears her father say from behind her.

"I know, I was just about to." She stands up and closes the two wooden doors, then looks back at the dimly lit area they've been living in for the last few days, wondering if she'll miss it once they leave. The place has everything they could ask for — water, canned and dried food, a dry place to sleep, livestock still roaming the fields. Everything they could possibly desire in this new world is here — except for safety. Even now, hidden in a barn behind two locked doors, her dad still has to nudge David every time he starts to snore for fear of alerting someone to their presence — and the dust from the broken bales of hay he's sleeping on doesn't help. The people around here tried so hard to keep the chaos of the outside world from entering their small town, and ironically, they ended up trapping the chaos inside.

Hearing David coughing in his sleep on the other side of the loft, she sits down on the floor next to her dad and puts her head against his shoulder.

"His coughing is getting worse," he whispers to her.

"He's fine, it's just the dust." She looks up and sees the worried look on his face, and the fear in his eyes. He's right, David *has* been coughing more lately, but then he's always had a problem with allergies, and the mixture of barn dust and the extreme moisture outside has also caused her sinuses to flare up. "There's a lot more people outside tonight, I was thinking we should probably leave tomorrow."

"I was thinking the same thing." With the skies finally dark outside, he looks at the loft doors and sees the orange glow coming through the cracks and knotholes, something they first noticed several nights ago, apparently coming from a large fire in the west. "We should probably go around the towns from now on, maybe find a farm like this out in the middle of nowhere — and one that isn't on fire."

"...and doesn't have any of *them*, right?"

"At least not more than we can handle."

"Yeah." She lifts her head off of his shoulder, her body tensing up. The idea of killing another person, even if they were trying to kill her, seemed wrong to her on some level — but she also knows that the day is coming, and she knows that's exactly what he's getting at. "Do you think it's like this everywhere?"

He pauses for a moment, not really sure how to answer it. "I don't know, I really don't."

"I think it is. I'll bet there's people just like us all over, waiting for everyone else to just die and get it over with. There's probably somebody in Japan right now, thinking the same thing." She can feel the revolver in her pocket, pushing into her side, a constant reminder that it's there. "I really don't want to kill anybody, dad."

He can hear her start to cry. "I know, I wish you didn't have to." He reaches over and gently pulls her chin toward him, looking directly into her eyes, his voice suddenly stern, but still somehow comforting at the same time. "...but you have to sweety, it's either them, or it's us." She looks down and nods, the tears still running down her face. "You should get some sleep, I'll wake David up in a little bit."

She stands up and makes her way to the loose hay where David is sleeping, finding a soft place to lie down just a few feet away. He's moaning a little bit, which isn't unusual for him, but she can hear a slight ticking sound every time he breathes, which is something that she's never heard from him before. She listens to it for a few minutes before she starts to drift off, wakened only momentarily by the sound of the barn door downstairs rattling from someone trying to get in. A moment later she falls asleep, her mind unconcerned by the attempted intrusion. They do it every night.

Christine wakes up in a panic, her heart about to jump out of her chest. She can hear somebody downstairs, inside of the first locked door, yelling and throwing things around. She looks around, trying to see her dad or David, but the only light visible is the bright glow of firelight that's seeping in through the siding.

"Dad!" she whispers in a frightened tone.

"Shh, I'm right here."

She looks to her right, toward the door that leads to the stairs, and sees the outline of her father standing beside it with his gun drawn. She carefully stands up and starts to walk forward.

"Stay there, he might hear you..."

"Who?" She waits for an answer, but she doesn't get one. "Dad, where is David?"

She starts to move forward again, then she hears footsteps coming up the steps, each of the old floorboards creaking loudly as they get closer to the top. George reaches out and pulls her to his side against the wall, placing himself between her and the doorway.

He whispers quietly into her ear. "The door was open when I woke up, and David was gone. He's been screaming and trashing everything downstairs, yelling something about a noise — that's when I locked the door again."

"What are we gonna do?"

"I don't know, I think he still has his gun."

"I can hear you in there talking!" David screams from the other side of the door. "Open the door, George."

"You know I can't do that, I'm sorry."

David hits the door with a closed fist, rattling the heavy rusted hinges that look at least as old as the barn. "Christine can, can't you darling?"

"David, listen to me, you're sick — you have to know that."

"Christine..." he pleads, his voice suddenly gentle. "I'm not sick, I just panicked, that's all. Christine, they're coming, they're getting closer..."

"Who's getting closer?" asks George.

"I opened the door, for just a minute, and now they're inside. Christine, you have to let me in, they're coming up the stairs!" His voice is panicked and desperate.

"Dad..." whispers Christina. "It's David, we can't just leave him out there."

"Shh, listen... Do you hear anybody on the stairs?"

She listens closely, but aside from David beating on the door, it sounds silent.

"Open up, I'm not lying!" David screams as he begins kicking the door.

George can see that the barrel bolt that's holding the door closed is starting to come loose — David's kicking is tearing the nails right out of the wall. He barricades himself against the wood, trying to hold back the blows, but then he feels a sharp pain in his stomach just as David stops his assault. Immediately he senses something warm and wet running down his abdomen and leg. Then he sees the knife blade still sticking through the slats of boards in the door, and realizes that he's been stabbed by his best friend, the man he grew up with. He takes a step back as David starts beating against the door again, then he aims his gun at the door and fires it three times, hearing a thud from the other side only a moment later. George falls to his knees, in shock at what just happened.

"Dad, are you okay?" Christine asks as she sits next to him, trying to see the wound on his stomach.

"Quiet — I hear something."

Christine can hear it too, the unmistakable sound of creaking steps, coming up toward the door.

CHAPTER 4
COHASSETT BEACH: DAY 2

The night before, after everybody else had gone to sleep, Sarah had talked to Curtis about leaving the cabin and heading deeper into the wilderness. Having Amanda lurk around was bad enough, but Westport was also infested with people, or at least something that vaguely resembled people, and from what Larry and Beth had seen during their travels along the water, the other towns in the region were likely suffering the same fate. She knew that society as they once knew it was gone, and the perverted fragments that remain are wasting away and destroying what little is left. The only answer that she could come up with is to distance themselves from it completely, to live in one of the few remote places still untouched by humanity — but that also means ending their reliance on scavenging for food and supplies, which is something that none of them have been prepared to do. The houses around the outskirts of Westport have been their one and only source of sustenance for months, and although they've been stockpiling any usable goods they come across, all of them are aware that it won't last them forever. Sometime over the next several years, virtually every piece of canned food will become inedible, and the raw ingredients like flour and yeast will expire long before that — especially after being exposed to the dampness of the coastal air.

Curtis had to admit to Sarah that coming to the coast might have been a mistake in hindsight, considering that the climate isn't exactly ideal for growing crops like corn and wheat — but he was still against the idea of leaving an area that had kept them alive for this long. He explained that what it does have is an abundance of seafood and wildlife in the forest, which is a combination that worked well for the native tribes that once inhabited the area — long before we became reliant on the supermarkets and restaurants of the modern age.

They were planning on bringing all of this up to their sons today, and to Larry and Beth. Sarah wanted to argue that moving further south later in the spring, into the slightly warmer weather of the southern beaches of Washington or Oregon, would make it that much easier to plant a garden or harvest fruit and nut trees.

That conversation, however, never took place.

Larry and Beth had taken off on another scavenging trip early in the morning, and when they came back, it was clearer to her than ever that moving was now essential.

"Where were you during all of this?" Curtis asks, his tone more scolding than he meant it to be. He's looking right at Larry, who's sitting on a bed next to an obviously shaken Beth.

"I was out behind the house near the dunes, I couldn't hear anything."

"How long were you out there?"

"Apparently longer than I should have been," Larry snaps back, before regaining his composure. "I went out to have a quick look around, and then I saw a trail of blood on the pathway, and I guess curiosity got the best of me."

"What was the blood from?"

"It was a cat that we found this morning — we had it in a carrier on the front porch. I guess she must have used it as a distraction, or maybe she just decided to kill it, I don't know."

Curtis turns to Beth, who looks tired and afraid. "Then what did she do?"

"She left. She said that you had to die first, and that she would kill me later, and then she walked out."

"She said Curtis had to die first?" asks Sarah, who's been sitting on the other bed and trying to distract their sons, but has now spun around to face Beth.

Matt and Ben, still keeping up the facade that they're not paying attention by flipping through an outdated magazine, finally turn around as well.

"Yeah, she said we'll all die in order, with Curtis going first," answers Beth.

"Did she take your gun?" Curtis asks, seemingly unshaken by Amanda's threat by proxy.

Beth nods and starts to speak, then Larry interrupts. "We looked around for it, but she must have taken it."

Curtis walks to the window and pulls back the curtains slowly, looking out at the gray sky and damp ground from the nearly constant rain over the last week. He knows that she's probably out there somewhere, waiting for him. "We have to kill her, we don't have a choice anymore." He looks around the room, trying to gauge everyone's response to his solution.

"We're not going to hunt down a little girl," Beth manages to blurt out through the mixed emotions welling up inside of her.

"She pointed a gun at you, she threatened to kill you! You're actually defending her?"

"She didn't pull the trigger."

"Because I'm first, right?" Curtis shakes his head and looks at Larry, who now has his hand resting on Beth's shoulder, his face red with anger, more at the situation than anything — but he says nothing.

"I'm not an idiot," Beth says quietly, trying to control the tension. "I saw her, I saw how insane she is. I know she's capable of..."

"You have no idea what she's capable of," Curtis interrupts, trying to calm himself. "She's pure evil, and I'm not talking about the normal everyday psychopathic evil — that virus did something to her, it made her into something a lot more dangerous than the rest of them. Did you know she murdered her entire family? She told Ben all about it, every gruesome detail so that he wouldn't even think about leaving her."

"Yes, Larry told me about it, but..."

"There's no but... She's out there right now, plotting our deaths, and she's smarter and more sadistic than any of us."

"Why didn't she kill me when she had the chance? I was right in front of her..."

"Beth..." Larry says, finally breaking his silence. "She was toying with you."

"She's a young girl, she's not Hitler or Manson..."

"Look, I'm not saying we should kill her..." He looks up at Curtis, and sees him looking back disapprovingly. "...and I'm not saying we shouldn't either, but Curtis is right, there's something seriously wrong with her."

"So what's your idea? How should we deal with her?" Curtis asks him.

"Maybe we should move on, try to lose her on the way."

"No, that's a bad idea, the last thing we should do is move from here. We haven't had a single incident in weeks."

"Why is it a bad idea? What's keeping us here?" Beth asks.

Curtis looks over at Sarah, who he knows feels the same way, then he looks back at Beth. "Do you honestly believe that there's something better out there? Do you think there's some city or town that wasn't obliterated by this thing?" He pauses for a moment as he hears something moving outside, then sits down at the table when he realizes it's only the wind outside. "We're *it* guys, we're all that's left —

and until all those *things* outside are gone, I think we should stay exactly where we're at."

"I realize that we might be alone, but I'm not so sure that this is the safest place for us," Beth says. "Besides, I still have a husband out there."

"Yeah, a husband that won't be able to find you if we move."

"We'll leave a note."

"Another one? You already left him one in Aberdeen."

"Guys..." Sarah interrupts, looking out the window. "We still have to get wood in before it gets dark, and none of us are going out there alone — not anymore."

Curtis steps out of the cabin and into the pouring down rain with Larry by his side, and as they begin walking down the driveway toward the woodshed, he hears a click as Sarah locks the door behind them. He keeps his hand on the grip of his pistol, watching for any sign of Amanda lurking behind the bushes or trees that surround the property.

"You guys aren't really leaving, are you?" he asks Larry.

"Eventually I guess, I mean we can't stay here forever. This cabin is getting smaller by the day."

"We should stay together though, at least close enough to help each other out."

Larry nods in agreement as they reach the woodshed, the inside of which is already too dark to tell if they're alone or not. Curtis briefly turns on a flashlight, conscious of the fact that there's now a limited number of batteries available, then they each start loading pieces of wood into a wheelbarrow when they see that they're the only ones there.

"You're gonna need more wood before next winter," Larry comments.

"I know." Curtis looks at the dwindling stack in front of him, and the even less-impressive pile of cedar kindling next to it. "We're going through a lot more than I thought we would. A lot of this stuff was half-rotten when we got here."

He throws another piece into the wheelbarrow, then both of them stop moving when they hear a sound coming from the direction of the highway. It's the sound of someone walking through mud puddles, and not being very quiet about it either. Curtis quietly steps halfway out of the shed and peeks around the corner, and sees Amanda trudging down the deeply rutted driveway, still wearing the same dress that's so torn and worn out that he's amazed it hasn't fallen off of her by now. He hasn't seen her in months, and the time hasn't been kind to her. Her face is gaunt and sunken, and her skin is pale, with an almost a blue tint. She looks dead, or at least her appearance does — her actions though, the way she walks, look as strong as ever. He ducks back into the shed and finds a crack in the wood paneling where he can still see her, then he reaches into his pocket and pulls out his radio, speaking into it as softly as possible.

"Sarah, can you hear me?"

"Yes, I hear you. What's wrong?"

"She's coming up the driveway, keep the doors locked — and don't call me back."

He hands the radio to Larry, then waits for Amanda to pass by the walkway to the shed before aiming his gun at her.

"If you pull that trigger, we're gonna be surrounded by those fuckers — more than we can handle," Larry warns him.

"I'm well aware of that." He keeps her in his sights as he watches her walk up onto the porch and knock on the door, but she doesn't even stay long enough for an answer. Instead, she heads around to the side of the cabin, trying to look through the covered windows as she passes by them. "I don't see Beth's gun, do you?"

"No, but she could've hidden it somewhere in that coat she's wearing."

"Come on, let's get a little closer."

Everyone inside the cabin, including the two boys, are holding loaded guns as they listen to the harrowing screech of Amanda's knife as she runs it across the glass pane of the back window. Then they hear a knock again, this time coming from the back door.

"Mom, I'm scared," Ben cries, his gun shaking in his hands.

"Shh, I know sweety, she'll leave soon, I promise," she says, gently taking the pistol from him and placing it into her own pocket.

"No, she won't. She's coming in."

As the words leave his mouth, the doorknob starts to rattle. Sarah aims her gun at the door, reminding herself that what's on the other side is only a young girl, disturbed as she might be.

"Why don't we just shoot her through the door?" Matt asks.

"Because it might be your father or Larry," Sarah whispers back. "Just be patient, and only shoot if I tell you to."

A few moments later they all hear a commotion outside, followed by the agonizing screams of a girl. Sarah runs to the window and looks out through the curtain, and sees Curtis on the ground straddling Amanda, his hands wrapped tightly around her throat. As soon as Beth sees him, she unlocks the door and runs outside, hitting Curtis in the head with the butt of her rifle and knocking him down. Still dazed from the hit, Curtis tries to get up, but then finds himself face to face with the barrel of her gun.

"Beth, what the hell are you doing?" Larry screams at her.

"She's a fucking child Larry! I'm not gonna stand by and let him murder a child."

Curtis slowly and cautiously stands up, his legs still wobbly and weak. "It's too late, she's already dead." They all look at Amanda's limp body, her bloodshot eyes still wide-open and frightened. He pushes the barrel of Beth's rifle down as he passes by her. "Don't ever point that at me again, understood?" He waits for an answer, but gets nothing in return. Then as he begins to walk away, he hears a slight coughing sound, and then a desperate gasp for air. Beth kneels down next to the girl, dropping the gun on the ground in the process, then holds both of her hands, trying her best to warm them up. Curtis, seeing life returning to the girl's body, quickly picks the rifle up and walks back to the cabin, utterly disgusted by the scene. "She's not staying here."

Beth looks up at Sarah, who stares back at her disapprovingly before following her husband back into the cabin. Feeling the small, frail hands hold onto hers, she glances down and notices a number of dark-colored spots on her palms.

Larry, sitting down a few feet away on an old splitting stump, shakes his head and sighs. "What's the plan, Beth?"

"I don't have a plan." She sits down beside Amanda and inspects the marks on her neck closely, then notices the focus coming back in her eyes. "Can you hear me, Amanda?"

The girl nods, then smiles slightly.

"Even her smile gives me the creeps," Larry mutters.

"Larry, shut up."

"So what are we gonna do with her?"

"I don't know. I guess we'll have to take her someplace."

"And where would that be? We can't exactly call social services..."

"We'll have to drive her someplace."

"You mean dump her? Like a cat?"

Beth ignores his question and begins inspecting her fingernails, seeing what looks like dried blood underneath them. "We can't go north, not as messed up as Westport is — and we can't go east into Aberdeen, it's even worse. I guess we'll head south."

"How far south?"

"I really don't know, Larry, I guess as far as it takes."

Beth starts checking the pockets on Amanda's coat, pulling out candy wrappers and small pieces of jewelry. Then as she checks an inside pocket, Amanda reaches up and tries to stop her, but Beth pushes her hand away and pulls out a small photo. "Larry, look at this..."

"What is it?"

She holds it up, a family portrait of the Lockwoods, each of them with a crudely drawn circle around them. All except Curtis that is, he has a large 'X' crossed over his face.

"Beth... we need to show them that."

"No, we don't. You think it'll change the way they feel about her?"

Larry looks down at Amanda, who smiles back at him, with a warm look in her eyes that contrasts with the overall look of death on the rest of her face.

"I'm not at all comfortable with this..." Larry protests.

"With hiding the photo?"

"No, with any of it."

Amanda grabs hold of Beth's hand, who quickly jerks it away by instinct.

"I'm sorry," Amanda says softly, her voice sounding like rough sandpaper.

"That's okay, you just startled me. Do you need something?"

"Maybe a little water. My throat is sore."

Beth looks back at Larry, who nods and slowly stands up, reluctant to be a servant to a killer.

"Thanks Mr. Gossman," Amanda says, which stops Larry in his tracks.

"How did you know my last name?"

She smiles again, then sits up. "My throat is really sore, Mr. Gossman."

The wind is howling outside, and the cabin shakes every time a gust blows in from the beach. It's too dark to see anything, but Curtis can hear the constant roar of the fir trees surrounding them, and the loud cracking sound whenever one of them loses a limb — but no matter how strong the storm gets outside, the tension inside the cabin is worse, and it's still escalating.

He's sitting next to the front door, facing the two queen beds on the other side of the room, with his gun plainly visible in his grip. His sons are sleeping in the closest bed, while Larry and Beth share the other. Sarah is sitting at the small wooden table in the kitchen, watching as Amanda tries to squirm out of the ropes — the girl's eyes locked on Curtis.

"You should get some sleep," Curtis whispers to his wife.

Sarah moves her chair next to him, then notices the gun in his hand. "Will you put that in your pocket or something, you're making me nervous." Begrudgingly, he does as she asks. "And no, I'm not going to bed, Beth doesn't want you watching her alone."

"What, she's afraid I'm gonna kill her again?"

"You wouldn't?"

"Of course I would, look at her."

As much as she wants to argue with him, and as horrible as the idea of murdering somebody is, she knows that he's probably right. Amanda is cold and soaked to the bone, exhausted, her clothes are falling apart, she's bleeding from numerous injuries all over her body, and her feet are bruised and bloody from not wearing any shoes for who knows how long — and yet she's still trying her damnedest to free herself from the rope that Curtis used to bind her. She knows that the girl is never going to leave them alone, and they'll never be able to live in peace as long as she's still breathing.

"So they're leaving tomorrow morning?" Curtis asks.

"Yeah, that's what they said."

"How long are they going to be gone?"

"You mean how far away are they taking her?"

"It has to be out of the county — otherwise she'll end up back here again."

"Larry said it'll be far enough, and that they should be back in a day or two."

"Good, we really have no idea how well she knows the area."

"Ben said that she grew-up in Westport, so I'm sure she knows her way around."

Curtis stays silent for a few moments, then starts whispering — his voice so quiet that Sarah has a hard time hearing him. "You were right, we really should move."

"You mean after they get back?"

"Or after they leave. We can't risk having her back in our lives."

Sarah looks over at Beth and Larry, both of them sound asleep in their bed. "I'm sure they'll be fine, they know how to handle themselves. I just wish they weren't taking her south, which is exactly where we should be heading."

He looks back at the girl on the floor, seeing blood drip from her wrists where the rope is burning through her skin — but it still doesn't stop her from trying to break free. "What they're doing is a mistake, and it's going to end horribly."

CHAPTER 5
MENLO: DAY 3

The next morning, after finding David's crumpled body lying on the floor at the top of the stairs, George couldn't help but wonder if his friend was genuinely seeking help when he shot him, or whether it was just a poorly executed ruse to lure them into a dangerous situation downstairs. The deeply felt guilt is already beginning to take its toll on him, along with the knife wound that David left in his side. Neither he nor Christine slept during the night, fearful of what might be coming through the weakened door, or that the fires that are growing ever closer might actually ignite something on the roof — but they were relieved to discover that the barn was entirely empty, and in one piece, when the sun came up at dawn.

Once outside, George and Christine start walking west toward Willapa Bay and the town of Raymond, carrying most of David's gear as well as their own. The sun is shining brightly today, making its way through the thick smoke overhead and turning everything a strange orange color that looks more like a painting than reality. As they pass by the western barricade that was built by the ill-fated former residents, George looks up at the cemetery on the hill overlooking the valley, and sees countless gravestones with a perfectly picturesque view of the dead town below. The contrast between the two is massive — on one side of the highway is a well-organized and thoughtful way to honor the people who have died, and on the other side he sees the pastures of Menlo behind him, filled with corpses, haphazardly thrown together into piles and waiting to be burned like trash.

Just a few miles down the road they come to another cemetery, this one much smaller than the last. According to legend, (and the sign beside the highway) the grave sitting on a grassy knoll belongs to a 19-year-old man named Willie Keils. He reportedly died of malaria in 1855, only days before he and his family were to begin their journey from Missouri to the Pacific. It was decided that his body would be placed inside of a lead-lined barrel which would then be filled with alcohol, and that the family would take him out west and bury him properly wherever they settled. George had visited the site as a kid, and had driven past it numerous times on his way to the ocean, but he never really thought about what a struggle it must have been until now. It took an incredible amount of courage to make a trip like that, traveling across an untamed country by wagon, and still reeling from the death of their son. Still, he couldn't help but feel jealous. Willie's family were going someplace hopeful, a prosperous place where they could settle down and help build a community from the ground up. His situation was similar in some ways — a grieving husband taking what's left of his family to find a new home, except that in his version, hope and prosperity died months ago, along with the rest of civilization.

"It looks like the fire is to the south," Christine says, pointing toward the town of South Bend.

"Good, we're going north anyway."

"I thought we weren't heading in any particular direction..."

"We weren't, but David had this idea a while back, and I thought we might try it. We'll keep going north, looking for anything along the way that might work for us, and if we don't find it, we'll hike up into the old growth forests in the Olympics and disappear for a while.

"For a while?"

"For as long as it takes. As long as we have a dry place to sleep and food in the cupboards, we'll be just fine."

"And when we run out of food, then what? We can't just run around killing our dinner every night."

He laughs, realizing what a poor job he's done in preparing her for the dilemma they're in. "You expect us to gather canned food the rest of our lives? Those things have an expiration date, and we're gonna have to start saving them for emergencies only."

"Have you ever hunted before?"

"No, but I guess there's a first time for everything."

They largely bypass any neighborhoods as they make their way through Raymond, seeing only the occasional shadows moving around inside the houses on the outskirts of town. The streets themselves, however, are as deserted and lonely as the ones back home, littered with trash and abandoned vehicles, a few of which still have the badly decomposed bodies of their former occupants inside of them. It's not until they reach the bay itself, where there's normally not a soul in sight for miles around, that they first spot a figure on the road behind them. At first, because of the sun shining overhead, George thinks that it must be another person, a normal person, but that thought quickly vanishes when he looks through the scope of David's rifle. Their gender is still a question, but it's obvious by they way they're walking that the person is sick. He waits for a few minutes before taking a shot, but his aim isn't nearly what David's was, and the gunshot does nothing to slow them down.

They keep moving, past the marshy wastelands of the bay, and the windswept trees that line the highway along the jagged coastline of the Pacific Ocean, until they come to an area called North Cove, where the road has fallen into the sea. The erosion isn't a great surprise to George, or to anyone else that's ever spent any time on this section of the coast. The ocean currents have been taking the land in this area for decades, swallowing houses, roads, a lighthouse, and even a cemetery several years ago. The last time George was here the waves were already crashing against the pavement of the highway, only a few years after this road was moved further inland for the same problem. The setback forces them to make their way up the hill instead, through a steep overgrown forest that gives them a breathtaking view of the abandoned town below them, but also drains what little energy they have left. It's already late afternoon by the time they reach the southern edge of Grayland, and their unwelcome companion has substantially shortened the distance between them, showing no signs of slowing down.

"Dad, I can barely feel my legs."

"I know, me too. We're gonna have to find a place to sleep for tonight anyway."

She's noticed her father holding his side for a few miles now, and she can see the bloodstain leaking through his shirt and onto his jacket, but she knows better than to ask him about it — he would lie anyway. "What about him?" She points behind them, where their follower is still tracking them.

"We'll just hope they're as worthless with locked doors as the others have been."

The main street running through town isn't exactly overflowing with hiding places. The buildings are far apart, but they're also cheaply made using highly breakable materials like thin paneling and vinyl, and the relative lack of trees makes virtually every building visible from the highway. As George starts walking toward a rundown two-story commercial building, Christine grabs his arm and points to a church across the street.

"Why don't we spend the night in there? It doesn't look so dirty."

"Yeah, and the door looks flimsy as hell."

She looks closer, and sees that he's right — it looks old and fragile, and has a large glass panel right in the middle of the door. "I guess they didn't figure anyone would break into a church."

"He would." George nods behind them, where the person is standing in the middle of the road only a few hundred yards away, watching their every move. When he opens the door of the commercial building and glances back, he sees them start walking again, only toward the back of the building.

"Lock the door, I'm gonna see if I can find a rear entrance."

"Okay, I'll check upstairs."

"No, stay put. We'll both check upstairs."

After setting his bags and the rifle down beside the door, he pulls his handgun out and quickly looks over a couple of offices in the back, but finds nothing but an old metal desk and some boarded up windows. As he makes his way down the hall, however, he can hear the familiar sound of a door knob rattling at the end of the corridor. The handle is shaking violently, but the heavy steel door stays put. He aims his gun at the small window at the top, then continues forward, hoping to get a lucky shot — but just then the rattling stops, and he hears a thump from upstairs, followed by the fast steady rhythm of footsteps across the old linoleum floors.

"Did you hear that?" comes a voice from behind him.

George nearly has a heart attack before realizing that Christine is standing right next to him. "Yes, I heard it. Don't sneak up on me like that, I thought you were still in the other room."

With their guns drawn, they both approach the staircase cautiously, with George in the lead. When he steps onto the first tread he feels a sharp pain shooting from his wound up into his kidneys and back, but the feeling quickly disappears when he sees a dark figure running past the top landing.

"Hey, stop!" He pushes Christine off to the side, hiding her from sight, then crouches down and aims his gun up the stairs. "We're not going to hurt you, we just need a place to stay for the night."

"Is that the same person, or someone else?" Christine asks.

"I don't know, I think it's someone else. It looked like an older guy." There's a long few minutes of silence, and then the sound of glass breaking, followed by a painful scream. George climbs the first few steps and then stops. "Listen, I'm coming up, don't do anything stupid!" He climbs the rest of the way up, his side throbbing in agony, then motions for Christine to stay put. When he reaches the top he can see a man standing in front of a broken window, bleeding profusely from his forearm. He's dressed normally, wearing a clean-looking winter coat and blue jeans.

"Stay back!" the man screams.

George aims his gun at the floor, but still keeps it in his grip. "We're not sick, let us help you…"

"Is someone else with you?"

"My daughter, she's downstairs." He puts the gun into his pocket, then holds his hands up. "Can you let me look at that arm? You're gonna bleed out if it keeps up like that up."

The man looks skeptical, but he takes a few steps toward George, and then the door at the end of the hall downstairs begins to rattle again, and the man hurries back to the window and forces his way through it, cutting his neck and leg in the process. George runs over to see if he can save him, but he's already on the ground and hobbling his way across the highway in the direction of the church. Christine stands next to her father as they watch the man desperately try to run, but then he falls as the crack of a gunshot fills the air. Both George and Christine drop to the floor as they hear two more shots ring out.

"What is that sound?" Christine whispers.

George hears it too, a low scraping sound coming from the street. He slowly peeks up over the window sill, and sees the man being dragged across the street and into the church on the other side, his fingers hopelessly trying to grab onto the asphalt roadway to save himself. Once inside, there's another gunshot, and then the door slams shut.

"We can't stay here," George whispers.

"Dad, you need to rest..."

"As soon as the sun goes down, that guy is coming back — and there's no door that's going to stop him."

CHAPTER 6
HIGHWAY 105: DAY 3

As nerve-wracking and challenging as their boat trip to Grays Harbor was, Larry actually finds himself missing the freedom of the open waters. He was never really one for being cooped up in any one place for too long, and living in the cabin throughout this last winter was beginning to take its toll on him — especially when they were living so closely to a marina. The gathering missions that they've been on have helped, they at least got him out of the cramped conditions of the Lockwood's place — but no matter where they went, no matter how far off the beaten path they searched, they still found themselves surrounded by the infected. Although he's aware that each trip into the neighborhood is potentially dangerous, it still hasn't stopped him from steadily increasing their frequency, if for no other reason than to eliminate his own boredom.

Beth was handling the situation better than he thought she would, but he also knows that deep down she still hadn't fully come to terms with Jake's disappearance. He sometimes catches her staring down the driveway whenever she thinks that she's alone, waiting for him to come back into their lives again, and at the end of each day she becomes quiet and distant, only to wake up the next day refreshed again. It's a sad and monotonous routine that seems to be working for the time being, most likely due to Sarah's thoughtful and subtle distractions. Both of them have suffered similar traumas — being separated from a loved one, and knowing there's an excellent chance they'll never know what really happened to them. Beth's particular situation, however, is different in one important way — her husband is close-by, and has a map that leads directly back to the cabin.

He's hoping that this trip, however inconvenient that it may be, might break both of them from the mental and emotional rut that they've found themselves in — and as he maneuvers through the maze of broken down southbound cars and garbage on the highway outside of Grayland, he takes his eyes off of the road for just a second to glance over at Beth, who hasn't talked since they left the cabin.

"What are you thinking about?" he asks.

"Nothing," she replies, still staring out of her window at the ocean.

"Okay, what are you *looking* at?"

"Larry, please, can we just not talk for a while?"

He looks over at her again, and notices a tear running down her cheek. "I'm sorry, but no, we need to figure some things out — like where in the hell are we taking her?"

"Somewhere far away," she says under her breath.

"Well, we're gonna need to be a little more specific." He points toward the back of the car, and begins to whisper. "Just make sure you don't say anything too loudly, Curtis thinks it's best if she doesn't know where she is. I think he's probably right."

"I don't think she can hear us in the trunk. Besides, she doesn't have..." Cutting her sentence off abruptly, she turns around and looks behind them. "Stop the car!"

After slamming on the brakes and looking in the rear-view mirror, Larry watches the road and waits for something to appear, but he doesn't see anything. "What did you see?"

"There was a house back there... I thought I saw a woman out front."

"We've been seeing a lot of them out in the daylight lately, it's probably nothing."

"She was weeding."

"Weeding? As in gardening...?"

"I think so."

Tempted to just keep moving, Larry looks back through the trees and brush and tries to get a good look at the house with the mysterious post-apocalyptic landscaper, but he can only vaguely make out a roof line towering above the pine trees about two-hundred feet back.

"We can't just ignore it," Beth tells him. "If there's even a chance of..."

"I know," he says, cutting her off. Checking the time on his watch, he places the car in reverse and begins backing up to the pitted and worn-out gravel driveway in front of the two-story light pink house. There's nobody in the yard, weeding or otherwise, but the lawn and flowerbeds surrounding the home are in immaculate condition, complete with freshly pruned fruit trees and rose bushes.

"This is where you saw her?"

"Yeah, she was kneeling over the flowerbed next to the steps."

Larry pulls the car into the driveway, then makes his way slowly to a parking space in front of the detached garage which sits beside the house. As soon as the car stops, he can hear the subtle thumps of Amanda kicking against the lid of the trunk, a noise that he hopes doesn't cause any trouble if it's heard by somebody else.

"I'll check it out," Beth says, opening her door.

"No, we'll both do it," Larry says, as he shuts the car off and gets out. "How should we handle this?"

"Knock on the door."

"With our guns drawn?"

"Just keep it in your pocket."

Beth walks toward the front door, with Larry only two steps

behind her, both of them looking around the yard carefully. As she makes her way up the steps and onto the porch, she can see movement in the window next to the door. Larry lifts his hand to knock, but Beth grabs his hand before he gets the chance and points inside. On the other side of the house, in what appears to be a kitchen, they can see a woman walking around quickly and conversing with someone seated at the table.

"They look normal," Larry whispers, still hearing Amanda's incessant kicking.

"Yeah, they do. Go ahead and knock." He knocks a few times, but Beth doesn't see any difference in their behavior. "Do it again, but louder — I don't think they heard you." He knocks again, this time hard enough to rattle the door — but again, no reaction. The woman picks something off of the counter and places it into a wall oven, then stands at the sink.

"Come on, lets go around to the back door," Larry says, leading the way on a concrete footpath that surrounds the house. As he climbs up onto the back porch and approaches the kitchen window, he lifts up his hand to wave at the woman on the other side of the pane, but stops himself when he looks behind her. The man sitting at the table, the man that she's been having a conversation with for the past several minutes, is nothing but a dried out corpse that's been propped up in a chair and set in front of the counter. Larry looks back at the woman, who appears to be in her late-twenties or perhaps thirties, and notices that she's washing a filthy pan in the sink, going through the motions of scrubbing it with a cloth — except there's no water running, and no cloth in her hand. He freezes when she looks up at the window and gazes in his direction, but she looks right through him as if he doesn't even exist.

"Beth, let's get out of here..." he says, backing up slowly before turning around. Beth is facing the ocean, with a look of horror on her face. "Beth, what's wrong?" She points toward the beach, where around a dozen massive container ships and at least two naval vessels have run aground, one of them turned on its side directly on the beach. In the distance he can see more ships, up and down the coastline, all of them likely headed for the same doomed fate.

"It's really happening everywhere, isn't it?" Beth asks, her voice shaken.

Still nervous about the woman in the kitchen behind them, Larry walks down off of the porch and down the pathway to the top of the dunes, where they have a clear view of the scene in front of them. He takes the binoculars out of his pocket and looks at the ships one at a time, seeing no sign of any activity until he looks at one of the container ships. On the bow, he sees someone moving around, dragging their feet in an all-too-familiar gait — their body stark naked.

"Do you see anything?" asks Beth.

"No. Come on, let's keep moving."

Hearing Larry and Beth get back into the car, Amanda stops kicking and curls up onto her side instead, her feet feeling sore and cold for the first time in months. She's been experiencing the deeply buried feelings of regret that are slowly working their way to the surface with each passing day. Her mind, once clouded with confusion and tangled memories, is beginning to clear — even as the physical symptoms of the virus appear to worsen.

She's known for some time that she's been inflicted with the virus, a fact that became all too obvious when she began coughing up blood shortly before meeting Curtis. Why she didn't turn into one of the other lost souls wandering in the streets she still doesn't completely understand, but she knows that her mind is finally beginning to focus again, and as it does, she's left with the horrible reality that her actions have caused — and the mental anguish that comes with it.

Her life, from her perspective anyway, has never been easy. She was abandoned by her birth mother at a young age, and still carries a resentment with her that shields her from any real emotional attachment to friends or relatives. It became even worse when she was enrolled in school, when she quickly became an outcast in a place that had little sympathy for tortured souls, and the bullying that ensued caused an even greater rift between reality and the delusions in her mind. In time, she unconsciously learned to show people the emotions they expected from her, even if it was only a facade.

The memory of killing Diane, her step-mother, has never really bothered her, and to this day it still doesn't — but the murder of her father, and the imprisonment of her brother that led to his untimely death, haunts her thoughts every night. Their deaths triggered a chain of events that have shaped her life ever since, and in ways that she couldn't possibly have anticipated. She misses their presence, their support, and most importantly, their loyalty to her. If times were different, if the world still looked the same as it did a year ago, their deaths wouldn't weigh so heavily on her mind. Today, however, she's cold and hungry, and excruciatingly lonely. For that reason, and for no other, she regrets killing them — even if she doesn't feel the least bit of guilt for doing so.

She thought she'd found the answer in Ben, who seemed more than willing to accept her as family. Looking back on it, she feels foolish for believing that he ever cared for her, and the fact that she allowed him to escape back to his family is yet another regret that she feels compelled to do something about.

Focusing once again on her surroundings, she listens closely to Larry and Beth talk as they pull out onto the highway once again.

When the car hits a large pothole in the road, followed by a rough dip that nearly causes them to lose control, she's comforted by the fact that they haven't traveled all that far. She knows this road perfectly, and she knows they're still north of Grayland.

CHAPTER 7
COHASSETT BEACH: DAY 3

It's late in the morning, and Matt can't help but notice how empty and lonely the cabin feels without Larry and Beth there. They left early, with only a brief goodbye before they set off on their journey south with Amanda, a trip Matt was certain would end with their deaths. Ben had talked to him very little about what he'd been through, but his dad talked about Amanda as though she were the devil himself.

During the few hours that he was around her though, Matt didn't really get the impression that she was completely evil, she'd even giggled at some of his admittedly bad jokes. He had to remind himself how sweet and caring Clara Embree had been when they wandered into her home a few months back — a kindness that ended abruptly when she tried to kill both his mother and himself. His father says that both Amanda and Clara suffer from the same psychosis, and that it's brought on by the virus, a theory he's repeated on numerous occasions. Matt's own belief, however, is that there was something wrong with Amanda even before the viral outbreak occurred. She had bragged to Ben about killing her family when Westport first started to evacuate, but she also claimed that her occasional symptoms were simply allergies, a condition that she'd suffered from her entire life. If everything she said is true, that would mean she murdered her parents and brother without any influence from the illness, a detail that makes her seem even more terrifying than before — if it's true. It's hard to trust a lunatic, especially one that's trying to kill you.

With his mom and dad both outside, it's Matt's job to keep an eye on Ben, to make sure he doesn't do something foolish like wander off into the woods or wear down the batteries on the radio. So far though, all he seems to do since returning to the cabin is read comic books and old worn-out western novels that were left in the cabin from years ago.

"Did you want to do something?" Matt asks him.

"No, that's okay."

"Are you sure? I'm getting kinda bored."

"What do you wanna do?" Ben replies, putting the comic down for just a second, before shoving his nose back into it again.

"I don't know. We could play cards..."

Showing absolutely zero enthusiasm, Ben places his comic book on the bed and slumps into one of the chairs at the table, waiting wearily for his brother to get the deck of cards from the cupboard.

As he shuffles the deck and tries to decide which game to play, Matt glances up at his brother and notices that the normal twinkle in his eyes has dimmed. He looks defeated.

"Are you feeling okay?"

"Yeah, I'm just tired. Why?"

"You just don't seem the same, that's all." He starts splitting the cards into two piles, figuring that a game of 'War' is probably mindless enough for an uncomfortable moment like this. Hearing no response, he asks... "Was Amanda really scary to be with?"

"I don't really wanna talk about it."

"That's okay, you don't have to."

The two of them play for several minutes, neither of them talking, just tediously laying the cards onto the table, paying no attention to the few rules that exist. Then, suddenly, Ben stops playing.

"What's wrong?" Matt asks.

"You know how Dad said that everyone is probably dead...?"

"Yeah."

"That's not true." He looks up at his brother, who's looking back at him with a confused look on his face. "The city was full of people. Dad and I could see them across the water, doing awful things to each other."

Matt swallows hard. "All of them?"

Ben nods.

"They're all like Amanda then?"

He shakes his head, and in a frightened voice... "No, she's worse."

Overwhelmed by the events of yesterday, and her mind still reeling from the mixed emotions of it all, Sarah sits on the front porch swing and stares down the driveway, still in shock that her family is alone in the world once again. In her opinion, which nobody has cared to ask, the entire disagreement between Curtis and Beth is a gray area, and neither of them are necessarily right or wrong in their thinking. There's no doubt that Amanda is a ruthless killer, whose sole purpose in life seems to be destroying everyone that Sarah cares about, but she's also a little girl, and the idea of murdering her, even in self-defense, makes Sarah sick to her stomach. Six months ago, back in the days of social services, hospitals, therapists, and medications — the decision of what to do with her would have been made by someone trained to handle such things, and it certainly wouldn't involve her death. Those people, however, are all either dead or insane, and the burden of what happens to her now rests on the decency and morals of Beth and Larry. Curtis had brought up the idea of leaving the cabin after they left, which she was vehemently opposed to at the time — but as the night progressed, and she listened to the rambling mutterings of a young girl from the corner of the room, she finally convinced herself that protecting her family had to come before anything else.

Although she'll never admit it to anybody, part of her is relieved that the cabin isn't so crowded anymore. Living with two more people in such a small dwelling was beginning to take its toll on everybody. There was no privacy, no space to move around without bumping into each other, and definitely no intimacy. The six of them were existing, they weren't living — they were waiting around for something to happen, knowing full well that it never would. In some ways she feels guilty about abandoning Beth and Larry, especially now that they've learned to depend on each other so much — but she's also jealous of them, being able to move on in search of the unknown. She knows that Curtis won't ever move far from the area, not while their daughter, Annie, was still out there somewhere.

When Matt comes through the front door and heads toward the side of the cabin where Curtis is working, Sarah moves over to one side of the swing and makes room for him, patting the seat with her hand. "Matt, come sit with me for a minute."

Reluctantly, he does as she asks, and sits next to her. "Dad said I have to help get the wood in before dark."

"I know, but we have a little while." She wraps her arm around him, suddenly aware of how big he's getting. "How are you doing with all of this?"

He shrugs. "Okay I guess."

"And what about Ben, how is he doing?"

"He isn't talking much, he just sits around and reads those stupid comic books."

"We have to give him some time. I can't imagine what he went through when he was with her."

"Yeah, I guess." They both swing for a few minutes, neither of them talking, just listening to the peaceful sound of the trees that surround the cabin, and the ocean that can be heard a short distance away. "Mom, are we gonna have to move again?"

"Yeah, I think so, at least for a while anyway."

"Because of her?"

"You mean Amanda?"

"No, Beth."

"It has nothing to do with Beth. Why would you ask that?"

"She sided with Amanda instead of killing her. Why did she do that?"

"It's not that easy, Matt."

"If she was dead we wouldn't have to move, right?"

She doesn't really know how to respond, because simplistically, in his mind, he's correct. Without regard for what's right or wrong, it is the easiest solution. "Listen, I don't..."

Her answer is cut off when she hears a gunshot coming from down the highway, in the direction of Westport to the north. Both of them stand up and pull their own guns out, then three more shots come from the same location.

Curtis runs around the side of the cabin and stands next to Sarah, with Ben following right behind him. "Do you think that's Larry and Beth?"

"I don't think so. They were going south, toward Grayland. This is coming from the north."

Sounding even closer than the shots, they hear a woman screaming, and then after another gunshot, complete silence.

"They're getting closer, we should get inside," Sarah warns, her voice shaking.

"No, we should spend the night in the woods. The cabin is a little too obvious that someone is living here," Curtis replies, opening the door of the cabin and motioning everyone inside. "Come on, let's grab the bug-out bags."

Peering through the fog and drizzle, and leaning on an empty wooden workbench that runs the length of the wall, Curtis is watching the cabin through his binoculars for any signs of activity around their home, but the visibility is so bad that he can barely make out the silhouette of the building. The four of them are hiding in a shed on the neighboring property, one that should have been torn down years ago.

"You should try them again," Sarah says.

Still looking out the dust-covered window, Curtis takes the radio out of his pocket, then looks at his watch. It's right at 3:00pm. Larry had told him that he'd turn his radio on for a few minutes past the hour, every hour. "Larry, are you there?"

(filled with static) *"Yeah, I'm here."*

"Is everything okay?"

"Yeah, we're getting close to Grayland — why?"

"We heard some gunshots down the road earlier, and we just wanted to make sure that you weren't involved."

"Are you still at the cabin?"

"I'd rather not say over the radio."

"Right, I hear you. Do you want us to come back?"

Curtis looks at Sarah, who's nodding her head yes. "Do you still have Amanda?"

"Yeah, we do."

"Then no, we're fine. You guys should keep some distance just in case, we'll keep you updated."

"Okay, we might have to stay the night down here anyway. It's taken us longer than we thought getting through."

"People on the road?"

"No, not a soul in sight — just more cars on the highway. I'll check back in an hour."

"Sounds good."

Sarah sits down on the workbench beside him, inspecting it as a possible place to sleep for the night. "I think the kids are asleep — either that or they've gotten pretty good at pretending."

"Hopefully it'll only be for one night. I haven't heard anything else out there."

"I'm not sure we should go back, except to gather our things."

Curtis turns around and sits on the bench next to her, but keeps his gaze aimed at the cabin in the distance. "And go where?"

"I don't know, but we need to figure it out."

He finally takes his eyes off of the cabin and looks around the shed, figuring that it's too dark and wet to see anything outside anyway, and sees his two sons huddled up and lying on a bench on the other side of the room. There's almost nothing inside the building other than a few rusted garden tools and some old truck tires piled up in the middle, but it's mostly dry, and from the outside it looks entirely uninhabitable.

"There's a few old places up in the hills to the east, I guess we could check those out. I'm not sure how many supplies are up there though."

"Were they lived in before?"

"I don't know, I haven't been up there since I was a kid."

She leans in closer, whispering so the kids can't hear. "How long do you think we'll have to live like this, hiding from everybody?"

"Probably until everyone is dead."

"How many do you think are still in town?"

"I have no idea. I saw dozens when I was there looking for Ben, but I'm sure there were probably more. They all sounded sick though, including Amanda."

"I noticed that. She has a horrible cough."

"She's cold too, I noticed that when I..." He hesitates for a moment, then continues. "...when I was choking her."

"Maybe she won't last much longer — maybe none of them will."

Curtis looks out the window again, seeing the faint glow of the sun making its way through the fog and mist as it inches closer to the ocean. He can barely make out anything but the trees in front of the shed, but then he sees something flickering in the distance, a light moving alongside the road. At first he thinks it might be a car, but then he recognizes the subtle swinging motion.

It's a lantern, and it's coming closer.

CHAPTER 8
GRAYLAND: DAY 3

After a brief distance where the highway was clear of any obstacles or blockages, Larry slows the car down as they come around a corner and face complete gridlock ahead of them, stretching out as far as he can see. While the previous impediments have slowed their travel time down considerably, they were still able to get around them without too much trouble. This was different though — the vehicles here not only span the entire width of the road easement, but they also face opposite directions. The cars nearest to them are heading south toward Grayland, but most of them seem to be going north, toward Westport or Aberdeen — and unlike the other abandoned cars they've seen before, these ones appear to have been ransacked, with their doors still wide-open.

Larry rolls to a stop before reaching the blockade, looking around carefully to make sure it's not an ambush of some kind. "There's no way in hell we're getting through this..." Beth opens the passenger door and starts to get out, but stops when he grabs her arm. "Where are you going?" he asks.

"I'm gonna check it out, see what might have happened."

"I think it's pretty obvious — people were evacuating and just panicked."

"Then why is all of their shit scattered all over?"

He watches her climb out of the car and onto the pavement,

walking slowly with her gun drawn as she approaches the first car in the pileup. Already regretting it, he gets out himself and opens the back door, taking an assault rifle from the backseat and then following her along the shoulder. When they reach an area where there's barely enough room to squeeze through, he begins looking through the open doors and busted out windows next to them.

"These cars weren't just left here, it looks like someone was searching for something," he says.

"Well, it certainly wasn't food." She pulls out a bag of canned goods and boxed cereal from the passenger seat of a pickup, holding it up for Larry to see. "Huh, or guns..." She throws the groceries back into the truck and grabs a small semi-auto pistol from the floorboard, handing it to Larry. "What do you think?"

"I think this is probably out of bullets."

"How do you figure that?"

He points to the pavement under her feet, where several small shell casings are scattered. Then he takes the clip out and shows it to her. "See, empty."

She looks around at the pavement surrounding them, and then at the other cars that are nearby — but no other casings are visible, and the truck itself appears untouched other than a broken-out side window. "Are you a little creeped out by all of this?"

"I don't know if it's possible for me to get creeped out anymore. We have a twelve year old girl in the trunk of our car, remember?"

"I know, but this is strange. Where are all the people?"

"I know, it doesn't look like anyone left their vehicles voluntarily, does it?" Hearing a thumping sound coming from the trunk of their car, Larry walks beside it and bends down. "Do you need something?"

—*Muffled*— "I have to go to the bathroom."

Motioning for Beth to get in position beside him with her gun aimed at the trunk, Larry inserts the key and flips the trunk lid open, then jumps back. The girl, who's sweating profusely, grabs onto the back of the car with her tied up hands, struggling to lift herself out.

"For goodness sake, Larry, will you help her? We know she's not armed," Beth says.

Very cautiously, he reaches down and picks up her shivering body, then carefully sets her onto the blacktop facing away from him. He's alarmed at how skinny she is, and how incredibly cold her skin feels despite showing every other symptom of fever. She stands up slowly, her face grimacing with every movement, as if she's in a great deal of pain.

"Can you untie my hands so I can go?" the girl asks.

"You know I can't do that. Just walk to the edge of the road and go."

After Larry hands his gun to her, Beth watches Amanda walk to the shoulder and wait, as he takes off her coat and attempts to pull her underwear down. "Maybe I should do that..."

"What, afraid someone will call child protective services?"

"It just doesn't seem right, that's all."

He steps back several feet, then faces away from her. "Nothing about this seems right. Is she going?"

"Yeah, she's going." She notices that Amanda is looking down the road toward the cars, her eyes seemingly focused on something. "Do you see something, Amanda?"

"Are there any people in the cars?"

"No, they must have all gone on foot."

"That's not what happened."

"What do you think happened?"

Finished, the girl stands up again and manages to pull her own underwear up. "We need to get out of here, before it's too late."

"There's no sign of anybody around, we're perfectly safe," Larry says, turning toward her again. She continues staring down the road though, then takes two small steps back as her eyes grow wider.

"Amanda, what are you looking at?"

Beth turns around and takes a look for herself, but sees nothing but abandoned cars lined up down the highway.

"They're coming..." the girl says in a loud whisper, still backing away from them in the direction of the woods beside the road.

"There's nobody there, stop moving," Larry orders, following her as she steps off of the gravel and onto the grass-covered ground at the edge of the trees. "I don't wanna hurt you, but I will if you don't stop." He rushes her, grabbing onto her arm and pulling her weakened body onto the highway once again while Beth watches from a distance with her gun still in her hand. Before either of them realize what's happening, the girl spins around and kicks Larry in the back of the knee, then pushes him down to the pavement before running off into the woods.

"Are you okay?" Beth asks, helping him back to his feet.

"Shit, she's a lot stronger than she looks." Taking his gun back from Beth, he scans the densely forested woods next to them, and sees a flash of movement about thirty feet or so away. "She's right there, I can see her."

"Maybe we should just let her go here, and find someplace to stay the night down the road."

He shakes his head, looking north toward the cabin. "We're only a half days walk from Cohassett — it's not far enough." Leaving Beth behind, he pushes his way through the wet salal beside the ditch, then moves deeper into the stand of young Douglas fir. As his own shoes crunch through the thick layer of fir needles on the forest floor, he hears the crack of breaking tree branches up ahead, and then the faint sign of movement to his right as he stops and tries to pinpoint her exact location. After a brief silence, hearing only the rushing sound of ocean waves in the distance, a child's scream fills the air as the cracking sounds appear again. He runs forward, through the underbrush and rain-soaked ferns, until he finally spots Amanda lying on the ground with a bedraggled looking man standing over her, wearing ripped up clothing and dark colored paint on his face, and a framing hammer in his right hand. The man turns around and faces him, his eyes bloodshot and menacing. As Larry lifts his gun up and aims it at the guy, he hears another sound to his right, and yet another straight ahead. Backing up, he glances around the woods and sees more men closing in on him.

"Larry, you need to come back!" he hears Beth yell from back at the highway.

Still backing away, he motions for Amanda to get up and follow him, and as she runs past the man that's after her, he takes a swipe at her with his hammer, barely missing her head. "Get behind me, and don't do anything stupid."

"Untie me, I can help."

"You'll get us killed. Let's just get back to the car."

The men follow them through the woods, gaining on them a little bit with each step as they quicken their pace. When they reach the perimeter of the trees and cross over the ditch, he sees Beth aiming her gun at the other side of the road, where three more men and a woman are walking toward the car.

"Beth, get in the car!" he yells, grabbing Amanda and placing her back into the trunk, her feet trying to fight him off as he closes the lid and locks her inside. One of the men from the other side runs up behind him and stands between him and the driver's door, smiling as he points a blood-stained, rusty knife at him. Larry aims his pistol at the young man, but before he has a chance to pull the trigger, a bullet comes crashing through the side window and hits the man in the head, dropping his limp body to the ground. With more of them getting closer, Larry climbs into the car and starts the engine, slamming it into reverse as he runs over one of them.

"Where is Amanda? Is she hurt?" Beth yells loudly, still deafened by her gunshot.

"She's in the trunk, and she seems fine." He keeps driving in reverse, navigating through the few scattered vehicles still behind them, then finally turns around once he gets some distance from the people and starts driving north again. "Where the hell do we go now? It's gonna be getting dark before we know it."

Behind them, Beth watches as the crowd of people drag the two bodies into the woods, then disappear completely into the trees. "What about the beach?"

"To go south?"

"Yeah, we could take the next beach access road, then drive all the way to Grayland."

"The next access road is back up in Cohassett — it'd be well after dark before we got there."

"Stop for a minute until we figure this out," she says, grabbing a map from the backseat as he slows the car to a stop in the middle of the highway. "If my phone worked this would be a hell of lot easier."

"Are you sure that what we're doing is the humane thing?"

"You mean verses killing her? Yeah, I think this is the better option — for her anyway."

"You don't think she's gonna get killed anyway? If I wasn't there today, it's hard telling what those guys would've done to her."

She holds up the map, pointing to a number of roads along the highway that all lead toward the beach. "What about these?"

"Those aren't access roads, so the pavement doesn't actually run all the way onto the beach."

"How obstructed are they?"

"In a luxury sedan, driving over loose sand and brush? Pretty obstructed..." He takes the map from her and examines it, wishing that he'd paid more attention to the area in the past. "What we need is another vehicle, or a better road..." Handing the map back to Beth, he starts driving again, looking carefully down each driveway and private road they pass by.

"Where are we going?"

"There's a gated community at the end of the next road, I remember seeing the sign for it when we came by. If we can't make it onto the beach, we can at least find a place to stay the night."

About a quarter of a mile up the road, they turn off of the highway and onto a road that winds through some pine trees and sand dunes, before finally passing through a security gate that looks as though it's been forced open and partially torn loose from its track. The houses beyond the gate are all newer homes, each of them with multiple stories and attached garages that look out of place compared to the surrounding area. The lawns in front of them, although now severely overgrown, were obviously once carefully planned out and manicured. In its time, it was probably one of the nicer communities on the coast, but the further into it that Larry drives, the more he begins to regret ever turning down this road. On every single house, without exception, the doors and windows have been either ripped off or broken, and the contents thrown out into the weather. They can see bones here and there throughout the entire neighborhood, and complete skeletons hanging from trees in the yards, with chains and ropes still wrapped tightly around their necks.

One house in particular makes Beth divert her eyes, with it's front wall splattered with blood, and several badly decomposed corpses still tied to the porch columns — a few of them much too small to be adults. She looks across the street instead, seeing one of the only cars in the neighborhood, its tires slashed and windows broken out. Then, without warning, she feels herself being thrown forward as Larry slams on the brakes. "What're you..." She stops mid-sentence, seeing two men standing about a hundred feet ahead of them. "We need to get out of here..."

Larry puts the car in reverse, then turns his head as he starts to back up. "Keep an eye on those two." With the gate now in view, he carefully weaves around the debris in the road, then slows down to a crawl when he sees someone sliding the gate shut behind him, then securing it with a heavy chain. "Shit..."

"Can we make it through if you just floor it?"

"I guess it depends on the gate — but do you wanna risk being injured out here?"

Hearing something to her right, Beth turns her head and sees another man coming out from behind a house, then another one from inside — both of them carrying knives and wearing no shirts. Even from more than fifty feet away, she can still see the open wounds and purple bruising on their torsos and heads. "You need to do something, there's more of them coming."

After the man behind them starts throwing rocks at the back of the car, causing Amanda to scream as they pelt the trunk lid, Larry puts the car back into drive and presses the gas pedal to the floor. Not knowing whether the street actually goes down to the beach or not, he slows down some as they go around a curve, then speeds up again as they pass by the two men that were in front of them — nearly hitting both of them. When he sees a dead end up ahead, he pulls the car off of the pavement and onto a trail that wanders through the dunes. "Be ready to bail if we get stuck, this sand is pretty deep."

"Just try to stay on the grass if you can..."

Coming over the last dune, Beth glances up at the ocean ahead of them and sees a large layer of debris floating on the surface. As the car begins to slide down the other side, with both front tires spinning in the loose sand beneath them, they hear a loud crunch as the bumper crashes into the ground below. He eases it forward, feeling their weight sinking further into the sand — and then slowly, the car begins to level out as they reach the hard, wet surface of the shore.

When they get out onto the middle of the beach, where the sand is the hardest, the car turns to the right, heading north toward Cohassett again. Beth looks behind them, seeing the public access road for Grayland only a short distance away. "Where are you going?"

"Beth, we tried, but we're going back. Cohassett is only a few miles up the beach — we should have come this way to begin with."

"Larry, stop!"

"We're going back, I'm not having this discussion again..."

"No, there's something ahead of us... Stop the car."

Slowing down, it takes him a minute to figure out what's covering the beach ahead of them. "It's fucking logs," he says, slamming his fists down onto the steering wheel.

"Like tree logs?"

"There must've been a ship that dumped them," he says, as he finally stops the car and looks around.

"Can we get around?"

"Not that I can see. They're stretched all the way from the water to the dunes."

"It'll be getting dark soon. We can't spend the night in this car, not anywhere around here anyway."

He glances into the rear view mirror, and then at the sunset that's forming over the water as the night approaches from the east. "Well, it looks like we'll be spending the night in Grayland after all."

CHAPTER 9
GRAYLAND: DAY 3

Like much of the Washington coast, the industries in and around Grayland used to center around fishing and tourism, but what it was really known for was the thriving farming community that grew the one and only crop that does well in the inclement weather of the Pacific coastline — cranberries. In recent years, before the outbreak began, there were still several successful bogs in the area, and an annual festival that attracted people from all over the Pacific Northwest. The locals even had a name for the region — the 'Cranberry Coast', which stretched all the way down to North Cove in the south.

Aside from the cranberry bogs, Grayland was similar to Westport in virtually every other way — in fact, if you weren't from around the area you might not realize when you've crossed over from one town to the next. Short, twisted up pine trees are scattered throughout the region, their branches permanently disfigured from the constant wind, and thick patches of Scotch broom that have invaded the area cover much of the ground around the trees. The houses, mobile homes and commercial buildings are more spread out than in most towns, with no one single area that you might consider 'downtown'. It gives the impression of privacy and seclusion when traveling through, but in reality, there was very little that happened along highway 105 that wasn't well known by the other locals — rumors and gossip are simply a way of life along the coast.

Over an hour has passed since they watched their stalker drag another man into the church across the street, and every minute that goes by George is more convinced that his injuries are likely too severe for him to move on, especially if they're being pursued. Seeing the worried look on Christine's face, he knows that she's aware of it as well.

They have maybe two or three days worth of food and water, and after that it would be up to her to venture out and gather more supplies, which is something that she's never done on her own before.

"It'll be dark soon," Christine says, carefully peeking out of the window.

Still lying on the floor, he looks up at her standing beside the window, and sees the orange glow of a sunset against her pale skin. "You shouldn't be there, he might see you."

"He'd have to be a hell of a shot from all the way over there."

"Yeah, well, we don't know who he is. Maybe he's a sniper."

"He's one of the others, one of the strong ones — otherwise he wouldn't be out walking in the daylight."

"He might not even be sick."

"Healthy people don't act like that. He's sick, just the dangerous kind of sick."

Letting out a gasp, she drops to the floor and lies down, unconsciously holding her breath as she slides next to her father. Fighting through the pain, he sits up slightly and faces her.

"What's wrong?"

"There's a car coming down the road, I saw its headlights."

"From which direction?"

"North."

Careful not to make any noise for the effort, he struggles to get to his knees and looks out the window to see for himself. Just as she said, there's a car weaving its way through the debris on the road. When it reaches the church it slows down, then stops just past it, the engine sounding as if it's about to die. Christine kneels down next to George, and they watch as the car just sits in the middle of the road, then slowly turns into the parking lot across the street.

"We should warn them shouldn't we?" Christine asks.

"They'll see the blood on the steps, and on the door knob."

Both the driver and the passenger doors open, and a man and woman step out onto the gravel and make their way around to the trunk. The man reaches in, then jumps back quickly as if he's scared of whatever is inside. Then he tries it again, using his jacket to wrap around whatever it is, then pulls out a young girl who appears to be tied up with ropes and bungee cords.

"Oh my god, do you see that?" Christine whispers, in shock at what she's witnessing.

"Shh..., I see it."

The man carries the girl in his arms as she struggles to get away, while the woman carries their bags to the side entrance of the building — and then they disappear inside.

"Dad, we have to help her..."

George sits down again, his legs finally giving out on him. "I can't do anything, and you're not going to either."

"But you saw..."

He cuts her off abruptly. "I know, and there's nothing we can do."

Christine looks back at the church, and sees the woman come back out to the car and lift two rifles off of the backseat before heading back inside. Her mind, already in tatters over the idea that her dad might be gravely injured, begins conjuring up every horrible scenario possible for what the girl has already been through, and what her captors have planned for her next.

"Did you find anything?" Beth asks, as she lays the rifles down on one of the pews.

Larry walks in from the back, then sits down across the aisle from her, groaning in relief. "Not down here, the place looks cleaned out. I haven't checked upstairs yet."

"We need to find another car and get out of here."

"Our car is fine, I think it's just out of gas."

"Then let's siphon some out of another car and get back on the road — I don't really wanna spend the night in town."

"It took us all damn day to make it a few miles down the highway with all the shit on the road. If we're gonna have to stay the night somewhere — it might as well be here."

"Do you think this is far enough to dump her?"

"No, I'm sure she knows where we're at. It wouldn't take her long to figure it out even if she doesn't."

"Where did you put her?"

"In the kitchen, in some sort of pantry in the corner. I think she's falling asleep."

"She must be getting hungry by now."

"I offered, again." He stands up and looks across the street, at the fading sunset and pine trees that cover the sand dunes. He never thought that any place could be as eerie as Aberdeen was, half of the city burned to the ground and the other half crawling with savages and lunatics. Hell, Aberdeen wasn't exactly the land of prosperity even before the outbreak — but while Grayland didn't have people wandering the roads, or ash falling from the sky like some apocalyptic scene from the bible, there's still something about it that doesn't seem right. It's too quiet, with no sign of life anywhere.

"What do you think those gunshots up there were all about?" Beth asks, breaking the silence.

"One of them probably got hold of a gun, ended up shooting themselves." In the faint light still left, he can see her rearranging the same bag for at least the third time. "Do you want to go back?"

"No, but I do feel guilty about leaving them. It feels like we have something there."

He stands up and switches on a flashlight. "Yeah, but on the bright side, you've gained a daughter."

"Ha ha," she replies, unamused.

"I'm gonna go check upstairs. You should figure out where we're gonna sleep tonight."

She pats her hand on the hard wooden pew, sending loud echoes throughout the building. "Already found it."

"Lovely, sounds restful." He walks back to the kitchen, looking in on Amanda to make sure she's still there and breathing, and he hears her softly crying with her head buried in her hands.

"Amanda, are you okay?" he asks, leaning down to try to see her face, but still keeping his distance.

She lowers her hands, exposing a look of heartbreak on her face. "I hurt."

"What hurts?"

"My throat."

"I'll see if I can find something that'll make it better, okay?"

She nods and lies back down, watching as he proceeds toward a doorway marked 'Steeple Staircase'. He doesn't see the intense look of hatred on her face as soon as he turns away from her.

Before opening the door, he notices a speck of red on the doorknob, still wet — then he sees a small puddle right below it on the floor. He glances back at Amanda, who's now sitting up and staring at him with an innocent look in her eyes. With the gun still in its holster on his hip, he slowly opens the door and shines the light up the staircase, which has a bright red streak of blood all the way to the top. When the beam reaches the top landing, he sees a man looking back at him, his clothes and face soaked in blood, and his chest heaving with every breath drawn. Larry immediately shuts the door again, then locks it with the small rusted chain beside it. He looks around the room for something else to secure it, then spots a tall cabinet in the corner that's roughly the same height as the space between the door and the opposing wall. He struggles with the cabinet, sliding it across the tiled floor while also hearing footsteps coming down the stairs, then he pushes it over with a loud crash, and wedges it in front of the door.

"What the hell is going on?" Beth yells as she enters the room.

Right after she speaks, the man begins pounding and scratching at the door, screaming at the top of his lungs.

"We're not alone," Larry replies, pointing at the rattling door.

"Is that yours?" she asks, pointing toward the counter beside the door.

Larry turns around and sees a revolver, covered in mud and blood. "No, it's not." Grabbing a dish towel off of the counter, he wraps it around the gun and then walks back toward the nave. "I'll be back in a minute, I'm gonna sanitize this thing before handling it."

The man's screaming quiets down, then stops altogether, but he's still beating and clawing on the door as Beth kneels down in front of Amanda with a bottle of water held out. "You have to drink something, sweety — you'll get sick if you don't." She has to be careful not to get too close, since the girl already tried biting Larry right after they tied her up the night before, but when Amanda lifts her head to take a small sip, Beth can see red and purple streaks underneath the skin on her chest and down both arms. She's seen something like this once before, when Larry's wife died of the disease.

Larry walks back in, wiping down the revolver with a sanitizing wipe. "It still has one round in it, the others are empty shells."

"I think Amanda is really sick. Did you notice these lines on her skin?"

"Yeah, I saw them earlier."

"She needs antibiotics, and something to warm her up before she catches pneumonia."

Larry sits down on the cabinet blocking the steeple door, feeling the sharp impacts every time the man throws himself against it. "What she needs, what we all need, is a place without someone trying to kill us, but there isn't much we can do about that right now."

"We have antibiotics out in the car."

"Beth, she's dying, pills aren't going to save her. She's barely strong enough to sit up." He shines the flashlight on Amanda, seeing her chest rise and fall dramatically as her breathing becomes more strenuous. He noticed the markings on her skin when he carried her in, but he can see now that they're more pronounced than before, and the skin itself looks almost transparent. "Try to get some sleep, sis, I'll take the first watch."

"What about tomorrow? Are we moving on?"

"I don't know, but whatever is behind this door is gonna wake up the entire neighborhood."

CHAPTER 10
COHASSETT BEACH: DAY 4

Lying on the ground, wishing that he had better eyesight than he does, Curtis impatiently watches his son, Matt, as he spies on the cabin in the distance with binoculars. It's still early in the morning, and he can feel the cold dampness of the wet fir needles as they soak through his coat from the rain the night before. The sun is shining to the east of them though, filtering light through the trees and giving them a reasonable amount of visibility.

"What do you see?"

"Nothing, everything looks normal."

"Do any of the windows look like they've been broken?"

"The ones on this side look fine."

"Come on, let's see if we can spot anything on the highway."

They walk, crouched down along a narrow ridge that winds its way through the trees, paralleling the property that the cabin sits on, until they come to a bend that gives them a view of the highway below, and the sand dunes beyond. Curtis takes the binoculars from Matt and looks down on the road, seeing the same abandoned cars that normally litter the asphalt.

"When you were in Aberdeen, did you see any other people?" Matt asks.

"I wasn't actually in the city, I was on the other side of the river."

"But you could see it, right?"

"Sort of."

"So did you see any other people?"

"You mean like us?"

"Yeah."

"No, I didn't."

"Did you see any that weren't like us?"

"I did."

"How many were there?"

Curtis would really prefer not having this discussion, especially not right now — he hasn't even told Sarah the full extent of what he saw across the water. Knowing that Matt won't be satisfied with no answer at all, he puts the binoculars down and looks at the dunes with his naked eyes, searching for any signs of movement in the grass and shrubs. He can hear the crashing of the waves on the other side, and the seagulls hollering overhead, but the fog is still too thick to see the water itself. "There were a lot of them, more than I thought there would be."

"Hundreds?"

"No, probably more than that."

"Do you think they'll come here?"

"I don't really know, Matt." He looks at his son, and sees the uneasiness in his eyes, the fear. That obviously wasn't the answer he was looking for. "I don't think it's always going to be like this. I think someday all of those people are probably gonna end up dead from the virus, or from each other, but until then we have to be extremely careful."

"And if they all die, then what?"

"That's the big question, isn't it? I guess we'll have to figure that out when it comes. It depends on how many others are out there, like the four of us."

"And Larry and Beth..."

"Yeah, and Larry and Beth."

Matt takes the binoculars from Curtis, and then looks intently in the direction of a house across the highway.

"What are you looking at?"

Matt hands the binoculars back, then points toward the house. "Over there, on the front lawn next to the path."

It takes Curtis a moment to get his bearings, and then he sees what his son spotted. Sprawled out in front of the house is a naked body, lying face down and covered in blood. He looks around the neighboring houses, and sees two more bodies, all of which are in the same condition, and all of them stripped of their clothes. Another one is on the pavement in front of a pickup on the highway, but is still fully clothed with no blood visible. He keeps an eye on it for a minute, trying to gauge whether the person is actually dead, or just playing dead — but he quickly looks away when he notices a long-handled ax that's embedded into the back of their head. Whatever happened here, it certainly doesn't look like self-defense, not with the bodies spread out as far as they are.

"Do you think those were the gunshots?"

"I'm sure they probably were." Curtis hadn't been in those houses in months, not since they emptied them of their belongings, but the idea that there were infected people squatting this close to them is a little unnerving. What's even more unnerving is the fact that somebody seems to have slaughtered all of them, and might still be somewhere in the area. He looks back at the cabin, where he can now see the front door, and it's still in one piece. The other houses on the street all have their doors kicked in.

"So are we going back home?"

"Yeah, but not for long, we'll just grab some things and move on."

"We still haven't figured out where we're going," Sarah whispers, following closely behind Curtis as the four of them walk quietly through the woods toward their cabin. All of them are armed, but Curtis is the only one with his gun already in his hand.

"We can't go north, the road is blocked, so we'll have to head south and then into the hills."

"Maybe we can meet up with Larry and Beth..."

"We'll find someplace isolated, away from everything — maybe near a creek or a lake."

Annoyed at him for ignoring her suggestion, she decides to let it go, and instead focuses on the cabin in front of them. From the outside it looks perfectly normal, exactly the way they left it the day before. As they come around to the front, however, Sarah notices that something looks off about their pickup. The tires, all of them nearly new when the outbreak occurred, are all completely flat. "Curtis, look at the tires..."

He takes a close look around the place, fearing that someone might be watching them — but he doesn't see anything suspicious. "You guys stay out here, I'll check the cabin."

"How are we gonna go anywhere like that?"

"We can drive on flat tires, far enough to get away from here anyway."

Unlocking the door, he slips inside and makes a quick scan of both rooms, thankful that the building is so incredibly small, then brings his wife and kids inside with him. "Pack the food, medicine and guns first. I'll load the truck, I don't want any of you going outside, understand?"

"Yes, I understand, but I think we should radio Larry first. We could really use their help."

"They're probably a couple of hours south of us by now, and out of range. I don't want to waste time trying to reach him."

"Fine." Angry, she hands him a box that's already taped up. "This one is first."

"What's in it?"

"Pictures."

"Sarah..."

"I'm not leaving without that box. Take it."

Hearing the tone of her voice, threatening and angry, he takes the box and packs it into the bed of the pickup. For the next thirty minutes, the four of them work feverishly to fill the truck to its limit, and by the time it's done they're dismayed at how little they managed to fit compared to what was stored inside the cabin.

Sarah looks around, surrounded by the memories of the last several months, both good and bad, and finds herself already missing the place. "We can always come back later and get the rest I guess."

"Sure, after everything settles down. We could probably..." Curtis is cut off by the sudden knocking on the front door. He motions for Sarah and the boys to go out the back, but he only sees her and Matt. "Where is Ben?" he whispers.

"He's in the bathroom," Matt answers.

The knocking continues, then a male voice is heard. *"I know you're in there, and I don't mean any harm, I'm just looking for someone."*

"Who are you looking for?"

"Beth Wilson, my wife."

Curtis and Sarah look at each other, both of them shocked. "And what's your name?"

"Jake Wilson."

Curtis stares at the door for a moment while Sarah watches him, baffled at why he doesn't open it.

"Hello? Are you still there?" the voice asks.

"Why aren't you answering him?" whispers Sarah.

He reaches down and unsnaps his holster, resting the palm of his hand on the gun's grip. "Why did he slash our tires?"

CHAPTER 11
GRAYLAND: DAY 4

Hearing the sound of a dog barking in the distance, which is something that she hasn't heard for quite some time, and seeing the bright flickering rays of sunshine coming through the side windows of the nave, Beth wakes up feeling refreshed for the first time since this entire ordeal started. At first she even wondered whether all of it was just a horrible nightmare, but that thought was fleeting, lasting only until the moment she realized where she'd been sleeping. The pew benches were barely tolerable to sit on, let alone sleep on, but she barely remembers even closing her eyes before falling asleep.

Wondering why Larry never woke her up to take watch, she stands up and stretches her sore back and neck, then walks into the other room where she sees Amanda standing in the doorway of the closet. She still looks as though she died the week before, but today she looks stronger somehow, and the skin on her face looks a little more flushed and normal looking. She glances at Beth, then continues staring across the room toward the kitchen, with a look of concern on her face.

"Amanda, what are you looking at?" Beth asks as she enters the kitchen, seeing Larry still sitting on the overturned cabinet. His face is looking tired and defeated, and when he sees Beth he just shrugs.

"I couldn't do it," he says.

"Do what?"

"Kill whoever the hell is behind this door." He lowers his head, slowly shaking it from side to side, clearly disgusted with himself. "I tried, I got myself all worked up, but I just can't bring myself to do it."

"You're exhausted, that's all."

"How am I supposed to make it out here, protecting us, when I can't kill this asshole?"

"I'll kill him." Both Larry and Beth turn toward the voice, the words sounding strange coming from the mouth of a young girl.

Beth backs up closer to her brother, feeling weirdly disturbed by the deadly tone in Amanda's voice. Ever since that day in the abandoned house, her voice has sounded so pure and innocent, that Beth had started to think of her as nothing more than a gravely ill child that needed help.

"Give me back my knife, and I'll do it."

"Sweety, Curtis threw your knife away."

The girl's voice turns to an even harder tone, more commanding than before. "Then find another one, there must be one in here somewhere."

"Forget it, kid. The last thing we need is you running around free," Larry responds.

"Then open the door yourself, and *you* do it."

"Why don't we just leave and forget about it?" Beth asks.

Larry is looking at Amanda, at the taunting, judging look in her eyes, aimed squarely at him. She has zero respect for him, which could prove to be dangerous down the road. "The minute I get off of this cabinet, he's going to push right past it."

"Then open the door, I'll shoot him," Beth answers back.

Still looking at Amanda, Larry tightens the grip on his gun, then stands up off of the cabinet. "No, I'll do it." He starts pushing the cabinet away from the door, then stands back and aims his gun. "Open the door, then stand clear."

Beth turns the handle slowly, then swings it open quickly, but Larry doesn't do anything, he just stands there with a blank look on his face. She aims her own gun at the steeple door, and then circles around to get her own look. The staircase is empty, aside from bloodstains on the wooden steps, and the obvious fingernail marks on the inside of the door itself.

"Shit, he's upstairs," Beth says, as she moves through the doorway and onto the first step.

"No, he's gone."

"He's not gone, he's just up there resting somewhere."

"Beth, look at the window."

He points to an open window at the top of the stairwell, and Beth notices the cold air moving across her legs and feet. When she turns around and starts to shut the door, something catches her eye, and after looking more closely she discovers that there's not only fingernail marks on the surface, but actual fingernails as well, embedded into the wood.

"Do you hear that?" Larry asks, listening closely for the noise to come back. It only takes a few seconds before he hears it again, the sound of breaking glass. "There it is again..."

Without answering, Beth slams the attic door shut, then runs back into the nave and looks out at their car, which has had every window busted out of it. The doors are also wide-open, and all of their belongings are scattered across the parking lot — bullets and all. Even the jars of canned peaches they found a month ago have been smashed on the pavement. Larry also notices the hood slightly open, and the battery lying on the sidewalk in front of the car, its contents spilling out onto the concrete.

"What are we gonna do? Should we go out there?"

"We have no idea where he is, he could be waiting for us." Larry looks around the parking lot, and at the trees and overgrown brush surrounding it. "We need to get away from the windows, he could still be armed."

They both back away, toward the kitchen, when they hear a loud thump from somewhere in the building. Beth sees Amanda still standing in the same place, looking curiously at the other end of the room.

"There's no way he's that fast... There must be two of them."

They hear another thump, this time clearly coming from above them, followed quickly by the sound of footsteps racing down the stairs. Beth runs into the kitchen, with Larry right behind her, then braces herself against the door — dropping her gun in the process. As she bends down to pick it up, the deafening explosion of a gunshot echoes throughout the building, and she looks up to see a bullet hole in the door right above her. Larry grabs her arm and pulls her away just as another shot rings out.

"Come on, let's get the hell out of here!" Larry screams.

"Grab Amanda, we can't leave her!"

Larry picks up a blanket from the floor and wraps it around Amanda, then picks her up and follows Beth through the church and into the parking lot. He only gives the car a quick glance before looking around at the rest of the town, seeing only a few close places that three people can hide — and then he hears the sound of approaching footsteps from the church behind him.

"Behind that dumpster over there, quick..." Larry whispers to Beth.

"What about our supplies still in the church?"

"We'll get them later, come on..."

Avoiding the boxes of spilled ammunition on the ground, both of them make it to the dumpster on the other side of the parking lot, out of sight from the side door of the church. Larry gently lays Amanda down on the pavement, unwrapping the blanket from around her.

"Don't try anything stupid, understand?" he whispers. She simply nods in reply as he takes off the rope restraints from around her ankles, leaving the ones around her wrists still in place.

Larry pulls his pistol out just as he hears the church door open, then he leans out far enough to get a good look at the church, and sees the man standing just outside the door, looking around the neighborhood. He carefully aims his gun at the man's head, feeling his body tense up as he places his finger on the trigger. Curtis had warned him months ago that killing someone wasn't as easy as it looks, even if the person was trying to kill you. He thought he understood what Curtis was trying to tell him, but as he feels his hand squeezing the pistol, he realizes that until you're in that situation, you can't possibly know what it feels like.

"Wait..." Beth whispers, pointing toward the front of the building.

Larry takes a quick look in that direction and sees two more men coming from around the corner, both of them walking in broad daylight and looking completely unaffected by it, and yet even from a hundred feet away he can tell that both of them are clearly infected. Their skin has a gray, almost waxy look to it, like a corpse that's been dead for awhile. Leaving the church door open, their pursuer walks toward the road, a pistol dangling loosely from his left hand, then he moves right past the two men that are still standing on the sidewalk. A few seconds after he turns and heads north on the highway, toward Westport, the other two follow him.

"We need to find someplace to hide, now..." Beth whispers.

"Your radio light is on, Mr. Gossman" Amanda says, her voice sweet and childlike once again.

Forgetting that he turned the volume off, Larry grabs the handheld radio and turns it on as he surveys the nearby buildings once again. The only one of any decent size that's close to them is the commercial building across the street.

"*Beth, Larry, are you there?*" Sarah says over the radio.

"Make it quick, we have a bit of a problem here."

"*You guys need to come back, as quickly as possible.*"

"Why, what happened?"

The radio stays silent for a few seconds, then Sarah comes back on, her voice sounding upset. "*Tell Beth that Jake is here, and that he needs her.*"

With a look of shock on her face, Beth quickly grabs the radio from Larry. "Sarah, is he okay?"

The radio crackles, and then a few intelligible words come through. "*...he's doing here... you need to be careful...*"

She waits for something further, but everything goes quiet. "Sarah, do you read me? Are you there?"

"Come on, we have to go..." Larry says, as he stands up and carefully looks down the highway in the direction the men went.

"I think the battery might be dead," Beth says, as she grabs Amanda's hand and follows Larry toward the road.

"We can deal with it later, right now we have to get out of sight."

When they reach the center of the road, Beth can see the three men about a half-block to the north, moving in their direction once again. "Larry..."

"I see them, just keep moving."

"Dad, I think they're coming here. What should we do?"

Christine is watching out the window at the scene in the street below her, hoping that neither side actually fires their gun and attracts every soul from a one mile radius. She can hear the man and woman kicking at the front door downstairs, and she knows it's only a matter of time before they get in. After that they'll only have the flimsy hollow-core door at the top of the stairs to get through.

"Is the door locked?" George mumbles, his voice growing weaker by the hour.

"Yes, they both are." She crouches down, then slides her hand under his chin, lifting it up until she can see his face. "Dad, what should I do?"

"Do they look sick?"

"I can't tell."

"If they are, kill them."

She can feel her body shaking as she hears the door downstairs begin to break apart. After a few tense minutes of yelling and commotion, the building suddenly becomes quiet.

"Are they gone?" George asks.

"No, I can still hear them down there. They're climbing the stairs..." She points her gun at the door, her hand trembling violently. She nearly screams when they begin kicking the door at the top of the stairs. "Stop, or I'll shoot!" she manages to blurt out, not certain if she sounded tough or frightened.

"Open the door, they're almost in!" screams a man on the other side.

"Let the girl go, and back off!"

"I can't do that, she's dangerous."

"Is she sick?"

"No, we're not sick."

Christine looks back at her father, who nods his head. Reluctantly, she reaches out and unlocks the door, then steps back and stands next to George. When the door opens, and she watches the three intruders enter the room, she can tell right away that the young girl is obviously sick. Her skin is paler than it should be, her body jerks slightly whenever she stands still for very long, and her eyes look darkened and dead, like there's no soul inside. Christine has seen enough of the infected to recognize the benign from the dangerous, and this girl is

99

anything but benign.

CHAPTER 12
COHASSETT BEACH: DAY 4

"It's getting kinda cold out here..."

The voice sounds calm and relaxed, and for a moment Curtis actually considers opening the door and inviting Jake inside — but then he remembers the carnage they saw along the road, and the slashed tires on their pickup, which was done before he even knew that Beth was gone. Instead, he motions for Sarah to close the curtains on the other side of the room, enveloping the cabin in almost complete darkness.

"Jake, I don't mean to be rude, but we've learned the hard way that you can't trust anybody these days. You understand that, right?" He checks to make sure his semi-auto pistol is loaded, then watches as Sarah does the same with her revolver. "Jake, did you hear me?"

"Yes, I heard you," he finally replies, in a voice still filled with a smug sarcasm.

"There's a house right around the corner with a wood stove and some food. It's nothing fancy, but it's warm and dry."

"Thanks, but I think I'll pass."

Sarah steps back away from the door, then motions for Curtis to follow her. "Is it me, or is he acting strange?" she whispers.

"It's not you, there's definitely something odd about him. Why don't you try to get Beth on the radio again..."

"I already did, she's not answering."

101

"I can hear you guys whispering in there!" Jake says loudly. *"Are you sure that you got through to Beth?"*

"Yes, we talked to both of them, and they'll be here as soon as they can," Curtis responds in a friendly voice, trying his best to conceal his growing annoyance.

"You wouldn't mind passing that radio to me, would you? I'd like to talk to her myself."

Curtis looks up at Sarah, who's nodding her head in agreement. "I'm sorry, Jake, but you're gonna have to trust us." Seeing the look of disapproval on his wife's face, he leans in closely and whispers quietly in her ear. "We can't open the door for this guy."

"We could leave it on the back porch," she whispers back.

"No, there's something not right about this. Go sit with the boys, and don't make any sound."

"What are you gonna do, shoot him?"

"No, it probably wouldn't do any good, he's probably wearing Kevlar or something."

"Listen..." they hear from the other side of the door. *"...you can't stay in there forever, you don't even have any food. Why don't you open the door and invite me in, then let me talk to my wife?"*

Curtis can hear the calmness disappearing from Jake's voice, and from his comment it seems clear that he's been watching them for a while. His family had just finished packing all of their food and supplies into the pickup when Jake knocked on their door, and now all that's left are a few stale crackers and a half empty bottle of water. Worse yet is the fact that Jake has access not only to their food, but also the guns and ammunition they'd managed to collect from the nearby houses. Waiting for Sarah to move out of the way, he aims his gun at the door, unsure if Jake is standing directly behind it. "If you're trying to intimidate me, it's not working."

He hears laughing from the other side of the door. *"If I were trying to intimidate you, you'd know it. There's nothing more I can do to convince you?"*

"After we're gone, you can have the entire place to yourself — we'll even leave the radio here." He can hear someone leaning or pushing against the door, and for a brief moment he considers firing a shot through it to end the tension — but he's also afraid of making too much noise with all of the people they've seen recently in the daylight.

"Alright, so be it, I'll be down the road a ways. Are you headed north or south?"

"Why?"

"I wouldn't head north, there's a good sized group of daywalkers coming this way from the harbor."

"Daywalkers?"

"Whatever the hell you call them — those fuckers that move around during the day."

"How many are there?"

"Several dozen, maybe a hundred. They're probably a day away. Good luck."

"Yeah, you too."

Curtis listens for the sound of footsteps on the porch before peering out through the curtains, and when he does he only catches a brief glimpse of Jake's face before he turns and begins walking down the driveway. He has an assault rifle slung over his shoulder, and at least one pistol holstered on his hip, but his clothes are filthy and covered with what Curtis can only assume is blood.

"Is he gone?" Sarah asks.

"Yeah, for now."

"He sounded okay there at the end, even helpful."

"He did, yeah, but he has blood all over him." Curtis turns around and grabs a box that's been sitting on the table. "We need to finish packing and get the hell out of here before it gets dark — or he comes back."

"We're not waiting for Larry and Beth?"

"No, we need to leave now before it's too late."

Curtis opens the front door and looks down the winding driveway, seeing nothing but the salal bushes swaying in the wind. He hands the small box to Sarah, and then picks up the last remaining plastic tote off of the floor and carries it to the pickup outside.

"Matt, why don't you two get the gun in the woodshed." Hearing no footsteps or movement behind him, Curtis looks and sees both boys on the porch, frozen with fear. "It's okay, your mother and I will be right here."

Stepping off of the porch and onto the gravel below, Matt's legs feel weak and wobbly, and he gets halfway across the driveway before realizing that Ben isn't with him. When he finally looks back toward the cabin he sees him standing on the porch, staring down the driveway toward the road. To distract him, Matt reaches down and takes his hand, feeling the fear-induced tremors in his hand.

"Come on, this is almost over."

"No, it isn't."

"It is, you have to trust me. Dad will figure something out."

"He's one of them."

Matt can see the pure terror in his brother's eyes as they begin to walk across the driveway toward the woodshed. "What do you mean he's one of them?"

"That guy, he's like Amanda. He's crazy."

"Don't worry, there's four of us and only one of him."

Holding onto Ben's hand, Matt looks up at the woodshed and sees something lying on the ground right in front of it. As they get closer, he can see that it's someone's feet sticking out from the doorway of the shed, their skin wrinkled and white. Ben immediately lets go of

Matt's hand and starts to back up.

"Just wait here, I'll get the gun..." Matt tells him. "Don't move, okay?"

Waiting for Ben's nod of agreement, Matt approaches the shed carefully, hoping that whoever is lying there is already dead, and not leading him into some sort of a trap. When he rounds the corner and looks inside, he sees the naked body of an older woman who is very clearly deceased, her face beaten and bloodied beyond recognition — but Matt recognizes her anyway. Her messed up hair, pure white and full of tangles, gives her away. The family has seen her wandering the neighborhood to the north several times over the last month or so. She always kept her distance no matter what, making them question whether she was sick like all the others, or simply afraid of people and what they were capable of — and she always wore clothing, the same bluejeans and light jacket.

Beside her, he can see drag marks leading from the body to the woods behind the shed — and in that same direction, only fifty feet away or so, he sees a glimpse of more pale skin sticking up from the ground.

"Is that another one?"

Startled, Matt turns his head and finds Ben standing next to him. "Ben, you should have waited like I told you."

"How many do you think there are?"

"I don't know." He looks around for the gun, a .22 rifle that his father placed there just in case they needed it — but after thoroughly searching the small building, he finally gives up and walks back outside. Taking a quick look at the driveway where his parents are still arraigning things in the pickup, Matt turns and starts to walk into the woods, with Ben pulling on his shirt as he walks by him.

"Matt, we need to get back, we shouldn't wander off."

"It'll just take a minute...."

Looking back at the cabin, making sure that his position is hidden from view by the shed and trees, Matt's shoes crunch loudly over the needle-filled mulch of the forest floor. He can hear the sound of crows overhead, and the constant buzz of flies somewhere ahead of him. As he climbs a small incline in the ground, he realizes that the body part that he's looking at is actually a bare foot, and it's resting on the edge of a ravine that drops about twenty feet below. A small creek winds its way toward the ocean at the bottom, moving through a dense thicket of huckleberry and salal bushes. As beautiful as it could be, the place is also littered with bodies, haphazardly thrown into the gully like trash. He can't tell how many there are, but he guesses at least a dozen, and probably more.

"Do you think Jake did this?" Ben quietly asks behind him.

"Dammit Ben, can't you stay where I tell you?"

"Do you think it was him?"

"Who else would've done it?"

"It could've been Amanda."

Matt looks back into the ravine, wondering how long the bodies have been there. Some of them look fresh, but others have obviously been there a while. It wasn't Amanda that moved the body into the woodshed, that much he knows for sure, but it might have been her that killed them. Whoever it was, they've clearly been in the area for quite some time.

"Somebody wanted us to find this," Ben says.

"I know," responds Matt, who starts walking back to the shed.

"If it's Jake, we're gonna have to kill him."

"I think we're gonna have to kill him whether he did it or not."

When they reach the shed again, Curtis is standing beside the truck, motioning for them to come back.

"What took you so long?"

"The gun is gone, but we found something that..." Matt stops when he realizes that Curtis isn't listening, but is staring toward the highway instead, where a man carrying a rifle is walking up the driveway.

"Sarah, boys, get back in the cabin..." Curtis says, his voice stern.

As Jake approaches them, Sarah places herself between him and the boys, then motions for them to back up. She notices that Curtis' gun is in his hand and aimed at the ground, and suddenly remembers that she placed her own gun on the passenger seat of the truck while she was busy packing.

When Jake gets to within about twenty feet of Curtis, he holds out a hand and smiles. "Hey, I think we got off on the wrong foot..."

"I don't think you really underst..." Curtis begins to say, then Jake takes his rifle from off of his shoulder and swings it hard into the side of Curtis' head, knocking him out instantly.

CHAPTER 13
GRAYLAND: DAY 4

"Are you hungry?" asks Beth, holding out a package of saltine crackers for Christine to take from her.

Wrapped up in a blanket and huddled up next to her father, Christine shakes her head and looks back across the room at Larry, who is standing guard in front of the staircase door. She feels overwhelmed by everything — the concern over her dad's health, her distrust of these two strangers that have invaded their hideout, and most of all, the clearly infected girl that they've stashed somewhere around the corner in the hallway behind Larry. She wants to believe they're trustworthy and honest, just two decent people trying to survive in this new world — but her ability to trust is quickly diminishing, and with every person they come across, she becomes all the more convinced that her father is the only one she can truly count on.

"How long have you two been staying here?" Beth asks, still trying to break the ice.

"We just got here," Christine replies curtly, gripping her gun tightly underneath the blanket. She can still hear the two men on the staircase, scratching at the lightweight wooden door.

"Where from?"

"Adna, near Chehalis."

"I like it down there. We're from Hoodsport, do you know where that is?"

"Yeah, I guess," Christine says, suddenly distracted. She looks over at her father as he coughs slightly, hearing a rattling from deep down in his chest.

"How long has he been sick, Christine?"

"He isn't sick, he was stabbed a couple of days ago."

"Do you want me to look at him?"

"No — thanks though." She jumps as the men on the stairs start pounding on the door, sending vibrations across the floor. Larry stands to the side and points his gun at it, as if the door is coming apart from the thrashing. "Are they coming through?" Christine asks him, her voice frightened.

"No, I don't think so. I'm pretty sure one of them still has a gun though."

"Don't worry, we'll take of them if they do come through," Beth tells Christine calmly.

Christine looks at her, seeing a kind face and warm eyes, and finds herself feeling safe for the first time in a long while. "I have a gun — I just thought you should know."

"I figured as much. That's okay, so do I."

Christine looks at her, and counts at least three visible pistols. "Yeah, I kinda figured that out." She slips the blanket off of her and wraps it tightly around her father, then sits down next to him again. "You walked all the way from Hoodsport?"

"No, we had a boat. It went down in the harbor."

"Have you heard anything..." She trails off, not sure how to end the question.

"From the outside world?"

"Yeah."

"No, we haven't. What about you?"

She shakes her head. "My aunt lived in Seattle, and my dad talked to her just before the phones went dead — she said everyone was leaving."

"I have a feeling they didn't get very far."

They hear the front door open again, and another set of footsteps begin climbing the staircase. Christine straightens up and cocks her pistol, then looks over at Beth, who still looks calm.

"Have you noticed that people are walking around more in the daytime lately?" Beth asks.

"Yeah, we've noticed that too. It used to be only on cloudy days."

Beth stands up and looks out the window, at a church parking lot that's only dimly illuminated by the last remnants of dusk. She sees two more people rummaging through their stuff that's been scattered around what's left of their car. "So was Chehalis bad?"

"Bad enough to get out."

"Did you see anything directly to the south?"

"There's a big fire down there, I wouldn't go that way if I were you."

"Well, we were planning on heading that way after we get my husband."

"You won't get very far, not in a car anyway — the road is washed out just a few miles from here."

"Thanks for the heads up." Beth looks down the highway in both directions, barely able to make out the buildings down the street.

She's still curious as to why the town seems so empty. Besides the few people they've seen, there's no sign of any activity in the area, recent or otherwise. In the other towns they've seen, the roads and sidewalks would've been swarming with activity by now.

"Have you seen any other towns this empty?" Beth asks.

"One — have you heard of a town called Pe Ell?"

"Yeah, were there any cars?"

"No, it looked like everyone left in a hurry."

"That's the odd thing about this town — none of the cars seem to be missing."

Christine stands up, careful not to wake George up, then turns on a flashlight from her pocket and quietly walks across the floor until she can see Amanda, who's sitting huddled up against a corner only a few feet from Larry. "What's the story with the girl?"

"What do you mean?"

"She's sick."

"She's a little..."

Christine cuts her off. "She's sick, we both know she is. Is she your daughter?"

"No, she isn't my daughter — and yes, we think she might be sick."

"Then why do you have her?"

"It's complicated. We didn't know what else to do with her."

"You have her tied up — is she dangerous?"

"Yes, very."

The men on the staircase, at least three of them from Beth's count, all start shouting and hitting the door, rattling the hinges and forcing Larry to back up further away from the hallway and into the room with Beth and Christine.

"You should bring Amanda in here with us," Beth tells him.

He switches on his flashlight, then aims the beam at Amanda. "I can see her from here, she's not going anywhere."

The screaming gets even more intense as the assault on the door becomes more aggressive, and as Larry notices the top hinge begin to pull out from the wall, he places his gun in his holster, then barricades the door with his body. Beth moves in behind him, quickly glancing down at a frightened Amanda before aiming her own gun at the door.

"Don't shoot unless you have to," Christine says, whispering to Beth as she stands next to her. "You'll just draw attention to us."

Beth notices that the young teen has a flashlight in her hand instead of a gun, but she doesn't say anything to her — considering how much her hands are already shaking, the last thing she needs is a gun. The room is almost pitch black now except for the artificial lights coming from Larry and Christine, and the air fills with dust each time they slam their bodies against the door. She sees the doorknob shaking violently, and a hand suddenly appears from underneath, stretched out and reaching inside. Larry steps on it as hard as he can, nearly losing his balance in the process, but it has no effect — the hand, now partially caved in at the knuckles, continues to search desperately for something to grab hold of.

Then it all stops, all but the screaming.

The hand disappears, and the door stops shaking — then the sound of loud thumps can be heard as something falls down the stairs, and the building suddenly falls into an eerie silence.

"What happened?" Christine whispers.

"Shh, I hear something," Beth responds.

They all listen closely, and hear the faint footsteps of someone walking slowly down the staircase, followed by the closing of the front door.

Larry steps back and stands with his gun aimed at the door. "Christine, move back around the corner for a minute."

"What're you doing?" asks Beth.

"Open the door, then stand back out of the way."

Beth watches as Christine sits down next to George, who's now wide-awake, then she grabs the doorknob and takes a deep breath before unlocking the door and opening it all the way — ignoring his order to stand completely out of the way. At first she sees nothing but darkness, but as Larry's light shines further down the stairs, she sees a trail of blood leading to three crumpled bodies scattered across the staircase. Immediately she looks to her side, where Amanda was sitting just moments ago, but now she sees nothing but a blanket on the floor, and the loose bindings of rope that were tied around her hands.

"How did she kill them?" George asks, his voice weak but clear.

"A knife — I'm not sure where she got one," Larry answers, trying to keep his voice low enough for Beth and Christine to get some sleep.

"But how...? There were several of them, right?"

Larry is watching out the window, hoping that the faint moonlight will reveal just how many people are out wandering the streets, but he still doesn't see anybody. Aside from a single coyote and a couple of owls, he hasn't seen any signs of life in Grayland all night. "To be honest, I'm not really sure. Maybe it's because she looks unsuspecting, or maybe she's quicker than she looks, I really don't know. I'm not even sure how the hell she came around so fast."

"You saw where she got out?"

"Yeah, there's an open window down the hallway."

"I've seen a few other people like her, and they won't stop until you kill them."

"Yeah, we've seen a few of them as well."

"If she's like the ones I've seen, she'll come right for you eventually — and you'll have to be ready when she does."

Looking out the window to the south, Larry can see an orange glow to the horizon that he assumed was the last remnants of a sunset earlier in the night — but it's obviously too late for that now. "You mentioned a fire to the south, right?"

"Yeah, down toward South Bend."

"Any idea how big it is?"

"It has to be huge, we started seeing it several days ago. The smoke is pretty bad to the east."

Across the field on the other side of the church parking lot, Larry sees something moving toward them, a dark shadow that's too large to be a cat or dog. It disappears into the trees for a moment, but when it comes out the other side, on the edge of the lot, he can clearly tell that it's a person carrying something.

"There's someone out there," he tells George.

"Are they coming here?"

"No, now they're just standing in the parking lot, facing this way. I think they're looking at me."

The person approaches their car, then begins pouring something onto the hood and down the sides. As the flames begin consuming the car, Larry can't tell whether it's Amanda or not, but they're now staring directly at him, holding something long and narrow in their hands, like a pipe or baseball bat.

"What's going on?" asks George.

"Someone just torched our car."

"If it's her, you're gonna have to kill her."

"I know, but it won't be tonight. Don't worry though, she'll follow us north tomorrow."

"Why don't you stay here for a day or two? You can figure out a plan."

"No, we have to get back. We have someone waiting for us."

George looks down at Christine, who's finally fallen asleep. "You need to take Christine with you..."

"What about you?"

"I'm dying, I wouldn't even make it down the stairs."

"You think she'll leave without you?"

"No, she won't."

"So you want us to hang around until you die?"

George points across the room. "See my backpack over there? There's a small plastic bag inside."

Taking a quick glance outside again, where the person is still watching him, Larry then walks across the room and fishes through the backpack, finding a small bag with a dozen or so pills inside.

"What are they?"

"Can you get me a drink of water, please?"

"First tell me what they are..."

"I think you already know what they are."

Larry contemplates it for a minute, trying to come to terms with what he's doing.

"Christine had to watch her mother die a horrible death — I'm not going to force her to do the same with me."

Thinking of his own wife, Jennifer, and the agonizing final days watching her slip away from him, Larry hands the bag to George, then gives him a bottle of water. After chewing and swallowing every pill, he offers the bottle back to Larry.

"That's all right, keep it."

"You'll take her then?"

"Yeah, we'll look out for her." He looks back out the window, and sees the first glow of morning light appear in the east. The person, however, is nowhere to be seen — and the engulfed car is now mostly just a smoking skeleton of blackened steel. He takes a closer look at the town, noticing for the first time that there's no broken windows or kicked in doors, and no bones scattered in the streets and sidewalks like the other places he's seen and heard about. Aside from the young girl they've introduced to it, the town is exactly what they've been looking for.

"Do you believe in God?" George asks, his voice slurring and sleepy.

"I used to, before all of this. I think I still do."

"A little hard to have faith now, isn't it?"

"Well, it definitely raises a few questions, that's for sure." Larry looks down at George, whose eyes are filled with tears as he holds his sleeping daughter close to him. "I do believe though, as hard as that might be right now."

"And what about Amanda?"

"What about her?"

"Are you gonna find her?"

"I don't think I'll need to — she'll find us."

CHAPTER 14
COHASSETT BEACH: DAY 5

Curtis wakes up, startled by the sound of a slamming door, his head pounding from a splitting headache that becomes even worse when he opens his eyes. When he tries to reach for the back of his head where the pain seems to be originating from, he realizes that both of his hands are tied tightly to his side somehow.

"Sarah...?"

"She's not here, Dad."

Curtis recognizes the voice as Matt's, but he sounds hoarse. He opens his eyes slowly and looks around the room, seeing both of his sons huddled closely together on a bed, but only Matt has tears streaming down his face — Ben looks strangely calm in comparison. "Where is she?"

"She went to the campground to get Jake's bag."

"And where is Jake?"

"I don't know, he just left."

Curtis looks down and sees that his hands and feet are tied to the kitchen chair with rope, so tightly that he's already beginning to lose feeling in his left hand. "Matt, where did he go?"

Matt looks nervously out the window, as if he's watching somebody.

"Is he out there? Do you see him?" Curtis asks, still waiting for a reply.

"No, I can't see him."

"Matt, listen to me carefully... You need to get me out of these ropes — right now, okay?"

Matt begins to breakdown and cry, his entire body trembling with fear, then he backs further onto the bed and away from his father. Curtis wants more than anything to scream at him out of frustration, to demand that he stand up and act like a man instead of cowering in the corner like a child — but instead he takes a deep breath and calms down, trying his best to remember that Matt is only barely thirteen, and under a tremendous amount of pressure for any age. He looks at Ben, hoping that he can get more of a reaction out of him, but Ben's attention seems to be elsewhere, staring at the same window beside the door that Matt was a moment ago.

"Ben, what are you looking at?"

He simply points toward the window, saying nothing at all. Curtis turns his head around and can only catch a glimpse of what's outside — a flickering orange light that's dancing across the glass pane.

"What is that? Is that a fire?"

"He set the truck on fire when he left," Ben says, his voice remarkably unaffected by the events.

With his heart suddenly racing, Curtis desperately struggles to turn the chair around, then watches helplessly as the pickup and all of their possessions go up in flames right in front of him.

"Ben, you need to get me free..." He glances behind him and sees Ben still staring at the truck. "Ben, do you hear me?"

The boy points at the window again, this time looking genuinely concerned. "I think the fire is spreading..."

Curtis looks outside again, seeing the same intense flames shooting up from the pickup as he saw before. Then something catches his eye — a few small sparks of embers floating down from the porch roof and onto the wooden deck below. He realizes that the fire has spread to the roof, and the sound of crackling wood can be heard overhead as the flames race across the needle-covered cedar shakes.

"Ben, help me get out of this, now!"

Sarah looks back at the cabin, which is only partially visible through the thick fog lingering in the air — and realizes that she doesn't actually fear leaving the property, although she has every reason to. What terrifies her is leaving her sons in the care of a madman, and the fact that Curtis was still unconscious and possibly clinging to life when she left. Jake really gave her no other choice though — it was either this, or he promised to brutally murder her husband and boys while she was forced to watch, and from everything she's witnessed so far, she has no reason to believe that he's bluffing.

Beth had told Sarah very little about Jake during their times together, since the pain of losing him still ran too deep to discuss — but what she did manage to share made him sound reasonable and thoughtful, she even called him the kindest person she'd ever met. The man still holding her family hostage, however, the man that forced himself into their lives and then threatened to destroy everything in it — that man seems anything but kind.

The highway in front of her looks different from the one she'd walked on months before — this time the leaves on the maple trees are just starting to bud out, and the pavement is covered in thick pollen and dead fir needles that came down during the harsh winter storms. Her destination is to the north of here, between Cohassett and Westport — a campground that was once owned by Joseph Embree, the same mysterious man that built the Regency Hotel in Westport.

While the campground never had the same rumors and controversy as the hotel, it did have its share of scandal in the months leading up to the Regency's last closure. Sarah remembers hearing stories when she was a kid about the disappearance and presumed death of a young girl that was staying in one of the cabins, and the fact that the girl's father was accused of the crime. Sarah remembers actually staying there with her family when she was young, and seeing the infamous cabin on the far south side of the grounds still boarded up after all those years — a futile attempt to keep the public from taking souvenirs of the crime scene.

Making her way north, past the empty houses that her family has scoured in recent months, she can see the decaying human remains that Curtis warned her about, scattered on the front lawns and alongside the road. With the appearance of Jake in the neighborhood, and the bodies that Matt and Ben found in the ravine, it's not much of a mystery as to how they ended up there. The real mystery is how long Jake has been in the area, and why it took him so long to finally make contact.

It's not until she reaches the outskirts of Cohassett nearly a mile away that she sees the first sign of human life — a middle-aged man wandering aimlessly through the woods to her right, talking to himself loudly as he crashes through the brush and wetlands. When he sees Sarah he stops talking and stands motionless in a bog halfway to his knees, watching her intently as she continues walking. She glances back at him a few times, worried that he might begin following her, but she can see him struggling against the mud as he tries hopelessly to move again.

Shivering against the cold wind coming off of the water, she wonders why Jake was so insistent that she make the journey with only a thin shirt on. She knows from walking this route before that it could take her most of the afternoon to make it to the campground and back, and that's if everything goes perfectly smooth with no distractions — something that seems increasingly unlikely the further down the road she travels. In late-October of last year, they saw absolutely no sign of people until they spent the night in Westport, and even then the people were skulking from one shadow to the next, afraid of even the dimmest of moonlight. This time, however, she's startled by the number of people walking in broad daylight as she approaches the residential area of Cohassett. They're clumsy, filthy, and slow — but they're also persistent when it comes to pursuing whatever they find interesting. By the time she reaches the entrance to the campground she can count at least six people stalking her, the closest being about two-hundred feet away. She considers trying to lose them somewhere among the two-dozen cabins spread across the property, but she can already see the sun finding its peak in the sky above, and she knows that she's quickly running out of time.

Jake was excruciatingly vague when it came to what she was looking for, but there was one thing he made abundantly clear — she had until sundown to make it back to the cabin. Any later than that, and her family would be killed slowly and painfully. His demand was to find a nondescript bag that he'd left at one of the cabins, which was filled with something vitally important to him — but exactly what it is seems to be a guarded mystery.

Seeing the worn-out faded sign along the highway, she turns and starts making her way down the driveway of the campground. It looks different than what she remembered, with knee-high grass surrounding each of the campsites and wild vines growing over the front gate. Looking down the row of cabins, all of them lined up with views of the sand dunes and not much else, she decides to search the one nearest to the driveway in hopes that Jake chose the most convenient one to stay at.

She walks up onto the covered porch and reaches out to open the door, her hands shaking so much from the cold that she has a hard time actually gripping the knob — but then she thinks twice about simply barging in. Afraid she might be walking straight into a trap, she peers through the window first and spots something lying on the bed — a large white duffel bag with a logo on the side that says "Washington Start Department of Corrections". Figuring that it must be Jake's bag, and seeing nobody else inside, she reaches for the door handle again, concentrating on steadying her grip long enough to turn the knob and push on the door, but it doesn't move. Not wanting to attract too much attention from the people on the road, she gives the door a firm shove, but it still doesn't budge. As panic begins to set in, she begins hitting the door harder and harder, ignoring the attention that the noise is likely making. When it finally does give way, after repeated kicks, a loud crack echos through the campground as the thin wooden door splits in two and partially falls apart onto the floor just inside the entry. Suddenly aware of just how vulnerable her situation is, she spins around and looks toward the road again, and this time sees at least two dozen people walking toward her from multiple directions.

Carefully stepping over the broken slab of wood on the floor, Sarah rushes to the bed and tries to tear the duffel bag open, but then notices that it has a small padlock that's sealing it shut. She also detects the strong odor of chemicals coming from inside, and a wet spot underneath it where something has leaked out. When she attempts to lift it off of the bed, however, she nearly falls over from the weight of it, and is left with no other choice but to drag it to the doorway. As she tries to pull the bag over the remains of the door, she catches the handle on a piece of splintered wood sticking up from the floor. Feeling the strain on her legs and arms, she begins yanking on the handle, seeing the fabric ripping apart with every pull — and then she hears the sound of someone stepping onto the porch behind her.

She gives the bag one last tug before finally giving up on it, escaping into the single bedroom of the cabin instead.

Once inside the dimly lit bedroom, where dark, filthy curtains cover the only window in the room, she locks the hollow-cored door and presses all of her weight against it. At first all she can hear is the sound of heavy rain beating down on the metal roofing overhead, but then she hears the unmistakable sound of clumsy footsteps on the other side of the door, and the heavy, labored breathing that always seems to accompany them.

"Open the door..." comes the frail, crackling voice of a man, which catches Sarah off-guard.

"You can speak?" she answers back.

"Open... the door..." the voice answers back, the words slurring horribly.

"If you can understand me, please let me go... I need to be somewhere else..."

"Open!" they respond again, this time more forceful and angry.

"I'm sorry, I can't," she cries. Not hearing any sign of them trying to break in, Sarah steps back and grabs a jacket hanging from a hook on the backside of the door. After putting it on over her wet shirt, she opens up the curtains on the window and sees a rusted set of metal bars covering the outside — and a small crowd of people walking across the tall grass in front of the cabin. After one of them makes eye contact with her, she closes the curtains again and backs up against the far wall, noticing another door right next to her — its handle smeared with what looks like dried blood. Still worried about possible contamination, she picks up a t-shirt from the floor and uses it to open the door. Inside what used to be a bathroom, she can barely make out the outline of someone sitting on the toilet, but she can also tell from the smell that they've been dead for quite some time. As her eyes adjust to the darkness, she sees what looks like a flashlight sitting on the corner of the vanity, and a small revolver sitting next to it. Surprisingly, the flashlight still turns on, and when it floods the room with the sickly yellow light, she can see the dried up blood splattered on the wall behind them, and the shotgun lying on the floor that apparently ended their life. Sarah reaches down and picks the shotgun up, trying not to touch any of the parts that have human remains on them, but to her dismay, the gun is completely empty, aside from the empty shell casing still inside of it. She turns around and checks the revolver too, and finds two bullets still loaded.

Turning around and facing the bathtub and shower, she sees a handwritten note lying on the floor in front of the body, the contents of which are barely decipherable through the blood. She takes both the revolver and the note back into the bedroom and searches the closet and nightstand for any other ammunition, but comes up with nothing. Exhausted, both physically and mentally, she finally sits down on the bed and listens to the person still breathing loudly on the other side of the door. She can hear others coming into the room behind them, stumbling over the numerous objects lying in the middle of the floor. Fighting the urge to sleep, she opens the note and starts reading it by the light of the flashlight.

To whom it may concern,

Everyone is dead, including my sweet Mary. I thought I had it too for a while, but my cough went away, and now I'm left with nothing. I want to be clear that I don't blame her for what she became, and I hope she doesn't blame me for what I did to her. Some things can never be forgiven though. We leave behind two children and six grandchildren, and I can only pray that they've found a safer place than we did.

If anyone reads this, please be careful out there. This sickness changes people somehow, it certainly did to my Mary. None of them can be trusted. Stay away from people, any of them — and whatever you do, don't go anywhere near Westport.

I'm tired. And I'm sorry.

Samuel Ross

Sarah sits on the bed for a moment and stares at the blood-stained note, her mind momentarily distracted from the terrible position that she's been placed in. For these past few months her family has been so focused on avoiding encounters with outsiders that they've somehow lost track of what the rest of the world must have gone through after the outbreak. Whoever this man was, and whatever the reason that he chose this ending, he obviously had a family and a life before the virus struck. All that's left of him today though, is the small amount of information that he left in the note. The rest of his story, of who he is and what he did, has been lost forever.

Still contemplating the thought, she shuts the flashlight off and stares at the door to the living room for a moment, trying to focus again on how to get past the people on the other side of it and back to her family. Just as she starts to stand, determined not to give up, she hears a scraping noise coming from somewhere close. When she takes a step toward the locked door, she realizes that the noise isn't coming from outside the room, but from inside the bathroom. She reaches for the flashlight that she left on the bed and turns it on again, shining it inside the cramped, bloody room once again, and seeing exactly the same gruesome scene as before. Then she hears the noise again, this time much more clearly, and she notices that the shower curtain is moving ever-so-slightly.

"Is someone in there?" she asks, gripping the revolver in her other hand.

She watches as the curtain slowly slides out of the way, at first revealing nothing but darkness — but then a hand appears on the edge of the tub, pulling itself into Sarah's view. When she shines the light on them, she screams and nearly drops it, horrified at the sight. As they struggle to get out, Sarah drops the light onto the floor and quickly shuts the door again, wishing that it had a lock on this side. She sits down on the bed again, hearing the scratching sounds of fingernails against both doors and the window. She wants to break down and cry, or scream at the top of her lungs — but she knows that it won't do her any good. She reaches over the side of the bed and picks up the flashlight from the floor, then switches it on and takes another close look around the room. The light is noticeably dimmer than before, no doubt from the batteries becoming weak, but on the second sweep of the room she notices something underneath a small dresser in the corner of the room — an area where the floorboards look different somehow.

Turning off the light once again, she pushes the dresser out of the way and begins to pull the carpet back from the wall — and then she hears the bathroom door start to creak loudly as it slowly opens up. She stands up again, aiming the revolver at the doorway, dreading what she knows is about to happen.

CHAPTER 15
GRAYLAND: DAY 5

Looking down at the staircase, which is covered with the remains of Amanda's victims, Beth sits and waits impatiently as Larry tries to console Christine after the death of her father. She wants to comfort her as well, and part of her feels guilty for not doing so, but the only thing that stands in the way of her being reunited with Jake is the young girl's heartbreak — and no matter how hard she tries to feel sorry for Christine, there's an overwhelming temptation to simply leave her behind and forget that she ever existed.

"She wants to bury him," Larry says quietly, squatting down beside Beth.

"Larry, we don't have time..."

"It's her father, Beth. We can't just leave him like this..."

She shakes her head and glances over at Christine, who is still sitting next to George. "How long will it take?"

"We'll bury him in the dunes, it shouldn't take very long."

"It's none of our business," she responds coldly, staring down the steps once again.

Larry leans in closer to his sister, his mouth right next to her ear, his low whisper full of anger. "Listen, I never argued with you when you made the decision to leave the cabin, to save *Amanda* of all people, who is a fucking murderer in case you've forgotten. The only reason we're here instead of back in Cohassett is because of you, don't forget that."

"You don't have to remind me, I'm well aware of that," Beth responds, her eyes welling up with tears as her frustration builds.

Larry sits down next to her, disgusted at the scene in front of them. He knew Amanda had killed the men, but he had no idea how brutal their deaths were until this moment. Although it seemed to happen in a flash, the girl still managed to slice into each of them multiple times, leaving blood on almost every square inch of the wooden steps. "I don't know if we can make it to the cabin in one day without a car, not if we get such a late start."

"Maybe we should keep looking for a car. There has to be something in town that runs."

"I don't think it's worth it — somebody spent a lot of time and effort to make sure that nobody left town."

Beth looks up at Larry and sees the concern on his face. "Well, I'm sure we'll find somewhere to stay along the way if it gets dark. Besides, with the highway as messed up as it is we'll probably make better time on foot anyway."

"Amanda will follow us, you know she will..."

"I know."

"...and she's gonna try to kill us."

"I know, Larry."

Through the gentle mist of showers slowly soaking the area, Larry looks out at the beach in front of him, and notices how peaceful and undisturbed everything here looks. There's no unusual debris washed up on the sand, and no infected people wandering around the dunes like they do up north — in fact they haven't seen a single sign of anybody all morning. The other towns they've been to in the past have seemed deserted as well when they first arrive, but they've learned the hard way not to trust any first impressions.

Grayland, however, is different.

The other towns didn't really seem empty, they appeared dead. Littered with trash and scattered bones, they looked like a wasteland even before you realized the buildings were actually full of madmen and murderers. Grayland, however, doesn't look like that at all. It looks as though everyone simply walked away and left it, even leaving their cars behind.

He looks down at Christine, who is sitting next to George's newly covered grave, and places his hand gently on her head. "Are you ready?"

Christine stands up, still looking at the loose sand over her father. "Won't this wash away when the first storm comes in?"

"No, it'll be fine," Larry says, hoping the girl isn't aware that he's lying. He checks his watch and sees that it's a little past noon, then he turns and faces Beth, who's remained quiet but respectful through the makeshift ceremony. "Did you still want to head north? We could always stay another night."

"No, I don't wanna stay here another night. They'll be looking for us if we stay much longer."

"Maybe we could wait until the rain stops," Christine suggests, drawing a look of contempt from Beth.

"Come on," Larry says to her softly after Beth walks away. "We're on the coast. If we wait until the rain stops we'll never get there."

Having already gathered the bags of important supplies in the church, the three of them begin walking toward the highway, past the burning remains of their car and the rest of their belongings. Christine looks back at the beach, taking note of a large spruce tree that's growing near her father's final resting place — then she sees a brief glimpse of movement behind it.

"I think there's something back there."

"Where?" Larry asks.

"Where we just came from."

"Some*thing* or some*one*?"

"I just saw a shadow moving. Do you think it's the girl that got away?"

"Probably." Larry answers, not bothering to look back.

"Are you gonna try to get her back?"

"No, we're not."

"What if she wants back?"

"We kill her," Beth answers, surprising Larry.

Christine opens her mouth to respond, but when she feels the obvious tension in the air between her two new companions, she decides to keep quiet instead. Looking back again, she sees a faint shadow moving through the dunes, then sees it appear on the road behind them.

About a half-mile further, where the highway turns inland slightly and away from the ocean, they come across an older mobile home park that looks as though it was well-maintained at one time. Windswept pine trees tower overhead, shading much of the community from what little sunlight exists on the coast — and dead branches from one of the winter windstorms cover parts of the asphalt drive and rooftops. The parking spaces appear to be mostly full, the same as the rest of Grayland. The driveway, like everything else in the area, is covered in a thick layer of sand — and right behind the park is a large bog that Larry says looks like an overgrown cranberry field. He spots a piece of paper attached to nearly every door, then stops walking right in the middle of the road.

"What is it?" asks Beth.

"Those look like notices."

"Probably something from before the virus."

"They would've blown off by now, wouldn't you think?"

"Larry, it's already getting late…"

"I know, but it'll just take a minute."

He turns and walks down the driveway, heading to the first door in the park. Stapled beside the entrance is a letter-sized, laminated piece of paper that looks weathered and slightly crumpled, but otherwise seems to be in one piece.

"What does it say?" Beth asks, watching Larry rip the paper from the wall.

Larry reads it to himself for a minute, then begins reading.

> *Attention, residents of Grayland, the town has hereby been ordered to evacuate by the Sheriff's Department and the city council.*
>
> *All residents are urged to proceed to South Bend, where a shelter has been setup to provide housing and food. Any belongings you wish to leave behind can be left at the fire station on the north end of town next to the Gentle Breeze Estates, where they'll be safely locked up and guarded throughout the event.*
>
> *Violators of the evacuation will be arrested and dealt with accordingly.*
>
> *Sheriff Nelson Daniels*

"What's with all the cars then?" Beth asks. "And where the hell is Gentle Breeze Estates?"

"I think we're looking at it," Larry says, handing the piece of paper to Beth.

Beth looks around at the two-dozen or so decrepit trailers, then sees a block building on the north side of the property. "Estates, huh?

Even as messed up as everything is right now, this place still doesn't look like an estate."

"South Bend is gone," Christine says softly.

"Gone? Your dad said it was on fire..." says Larry.

"We saw it from across the bay. It wasn't just on fire, it was destroyed."

"The entire town?" Beth asks doubtfully.

"It looked like it. We walked through a few days of smoke before we saw it."

"We still don't know whether anybody made it there," Larry says.

"If they did leave, this could be the first town that we've come across that really is empty..." Beth says, looking at Larry.

Larry walks back up onto the porch of the trailer and looks inside, seeing items scattered around the floor and half-empty closets, as if someone had left in a hurry. "Well, it wasn't empty yesterday. Those men that Amanda killed came from somewhere, and only one of them followed George and Christine into town."

"Okay, maybe it's not completely empty, but it's probably as close as we're going to get."

"You wanna stay here after we get Jake?"

"Do you have a better idea?"

Larry steps off of the porch again and takes a look around the area. Some of the houses are surrounded by gardens and fruit trees, and the beach is only minutes away, full of clams, mussels, and fish. They've seen dozens of towns along the shores of Hood Canal and the Strait, and none of them looked as isolated and promising as this one. "It's probably not the worst spot, I'll give you that."

"And we won't be too far from the Lockwoods. We could even start clearing the highway between here and there."

Larry begins to walk again, but instead of heading back to the highway, he heads straight north toward the block building.

"Larry, we need to get to the cabin before the sun goes down."

"It'll only take a minute, and it's on our way."

As they approach the building, which turns out to be the fire station, with its dark windows and mostly empty parking lot, Larry looks through the clear garage doors and sees nothing but some buckets and a few cardboard boxes stacked in one corner. The building itself looks almost new, with white concrete block walls and a red-colored metal roof with solar panels attached to it. On the north side of the building, facing the highway, the main entrance door can be seen propped open.

"Isn't it odd that the notice doesn't have a date on it?" Beth asks, still holding the evacuation order in her hand.

"Yeah, maybe. I'm sure there were other things on his mind at the time."

Larry walks up to the edge of the doorway and sticks his head in to look around, careful not to cross the threshold. Although the lobby of the department is dark, he can clearly see a scene of chaos inside, with blood smeared all over the walls and what looks like human bones spread across the tiled floor.

"This doesn't exactly look promising..." Larry says as he carefully steps inside, his shoes almost slipping on the thin layer of sand blown in through the open door.

Beth steps through next, followed by an obviously reluctant Christine. Beth walks over to one of the walls and looks carefully at the blood, relieved to see that it looks old and dried up. "This place reminds me of that police station in Dungeness."

Spotting some crumpled up clothes in the corner of the room, Larry picks up a pair of pants out of the mess and discovers that they still have a gun and holster attached to the belt. The rest of the pants are ripped and tattered.

"Did people do that?" Christine asks, standing just inside the entrance.

"It was probably animals — maybe coyotes or raccoons."

"Is that what killed them?"

"No, I'm sure they were already dead."

"From what?"

Larry looks around at the blood-stained hand prints on the wall, then down at the floor, where the faint imprints of bare feet can be seen in the sand. "I don't know, but I think someone has been here recently."

"There's another note on the door over there." Beth says, as she carefully avoids stepping on any bones or blood stains as she crosses the room and takes the note off of the door on the far side of the lobby.

"What does it say?"

"It says to leave town before it's too late."

"Another notice from the Sheriff?"

"No, I don't think so. This one is hand written."

Beth glances behind the desk and sees another large cluster of bones piled up, but then her eyes spot something else on the floor — a drag mark in the dust and sand that's just barely visible, leading from behind the desk to underneath the same door that the note was attached to. "Larry, you might want to see this..."

Christine sits down in a chair just inside the front door, as Larry joins Beth behind the desk. Not at all interested in what's happening, she turns around and watches the trees across the street bending hard from a sudden wind that seemingly came out of nowhere. She can also see a thick bank of dark clouds rolling in from the ocean in the distance.

"Guys, there's a really nasty looking storm headed this way," Christine says, pointing out the window.

Larry, ignoring Christine for the moment, looks behind the desk and studies the marks for himself — then places his hand on the doorknob and slowly turns it, filling the room with a loud creaking sound from the rusty hinges as the door opens and reveals a long, dark hallway on the other side.

"Do you see anything?" Beth asks from behind him.

"That's an awful lot of bones behind the desk, don't you think?"

"It kinda seems like it's..." She stops talking mid-sentence and listens to a tapping sound coming from down the hallway. She watches from behind Larry as he takes his flashlight out and shines it down the corridor. There's more bones lining both sides, hundreds of them, leaving only a narrow pathway down the middle, and even that's stained with filth. A vile, putrid stench hits both of them at the same time, and before Larry can manage to close the door again, he sees a dark silhouette on the other end of the hall, moving in their direction.

"Christine, get out!" Beth yells, as she backs away from the door with her gun drawn. Her and Larry are only about halfway to the entrance when they hear Christine exit the building behind them, and then they hear the hallway door slowly open again, but they can't see anything but darkness on the other side. Then a long, pale, emaciated arm appears in the dim light of the lobby, grabs the handle of the door, and slams it shut.

Both of them stop for a moment, then Beth continues moving backward toward the front entrance. "What the hell was that?"

"I don't know, but I think we need to get the hell out of town."

CHAPTER 16
COHASSETT BEACH: DAY 5

A year ago, before the virus struck, and before her life had turned into a never-ending series of hardships and heartbreak, Sarah used to purposely ignore any of the stories that involved violence in the news. She knew that it took place, and that it was becoming far more common in the suburbs of Portland where she lived — but she still preferred to keep her head buried firmly in the sand, especially when it concerned children. She simply hated the idea of aggression.

As the winter months passed by though, she found her own thoughts shifting toward a more violent course whenever the topic of the infected came up. The fact that she'd personally killed Clara Embree with her own bare hands, an act that would've horrified her in more peaceful times, has now forced her weakening conscience to view the infected as something less than human. Any sympathy that she felt for them at one time has since grown into a deep hatred for their very existence — and the more isolated her family finds themselves, the more intense the feelings become.

In recent weeks, the only time she doesn't think of them as something to eradicate is when she hears about the young children among them, which seems to be a rarity. Beth had mentioned seeing a few of them wandering around the streets of Sequim while they were there, and Curtis saw one in Westport mixed into the crowd as well — but other than Amanda, Sarah hadn't seen an infected child until this very moment. The boy, maybe a year or two older than Amanda, is still sitting on the bathroom floor after climbing out of the bathtub and opening the door. For a moment the two of them stare at one another, but his eyes appear lifeless and glazed over, making Sarah wonder if he was perhaps blind — but as she raises her arm in the air, making no sound at all, he follows her every movement and then struggles to get to his feet.

"Stay back, don't come any closer!" Sarah yells, as she holds back tears and aims the gun at him. Backing up against the wall next to the window, she places the bed between her and the boy. Instead of walking around it he tries reaching over it, grabbing desperately at the blanket and pillows until he finally climbs on top of the mattress and begins crawling closer to her. She moves away from him toward the foot of the bed, then slips the gun into her pants pocket as she bends over to take a drawer out of the small dresser. When she turns around he's still moving in her direction, and in the subdued light she can see in greater detail just how frail and sick the kid looks. She waits for him to get a bit closer, and then she lifts the drawer up and smashes it into the side of his head as hard as she can, instantly knocking him out. For a moment she just stands there, listening closely to whether or not he's still breathing, and hearing nothing but the scratching at the window and the commotion in the next room — and then she sees the boy start to move again. She was hoping that she'd killed him, or at least injured him badly enough to give her time to escape — but when he opens his eyes and looks straight at her, she lets out a deep sigh and fights back tears, then she places a pillow tightly over his head. Almost immediately, she can feel him struggling against her, and when his hand reaches out and grabs her arm, she finally pulls out the revolver and fires a single shot into his head.

For a brief time after the gunshot, the room goes completely silent, with no activity outside the window or in the front room — but it doesn't last for long. Soon she hears the return of footsteps outside the door, but they seem to be moving further away, before disappearing altogether. After throwing a blanket over the kid's body, Sarah watches him for a few seconds to make sure he's actually dead, then walks to the door and quietly unlocks it. She takes a couple of deep breaths before slowly opening the door, revealing a chaotic mess in the next room — but no people in sight. Aiming the nearly empty gun at the front door, she moves cautiously across the floor and looks out the window at the entrance to the campgrounds, expecting to see crowds of people waiting for her — but instead sees only one person out by the road, staring back in her direction. As she starts to step through the open doorway though, an older man suddenly appears in her way, causing her to fall back onto the floor inside the cabin. He follows her inside just as she finds her way back onto her feet, then he lunges at her with both arms and trips on the crumpled up rug in front of the door. She hurries to get around him, keeping her back against the wall to maintain some distance, but he still manages to grab her leg as she passes by him. Firing her last remaining bullet into his chest, she finally breaks free from his grip — but then she hears something on the porch outside, dragging and stumbling across the old wooden planks.

She aims the revolver at the door, hoping that the now-useless weapon might scare one of them into backing off, but it doesn't work. As more of them move into the room, she steps back inside the bedroom and counts at least five people enter the cabin before she closes and locks the door once again — knowing that the only thing that protects her now is the flimsy piece of veneer in front of her.

Standing with her back against the door, she feels the pounding fists and shoving from the people on the other side of it, then she remembers the odd floorboards that she spotted beneath the dresser earlier, and when she pushes it away with her foot, she sees a crudely made hatch door cut into the floor. Fearing that the bedroom door won't hold together for much longer, she pushes the bed against it, then wedges the dresser between the bed and the far wall, hoping that it'll keep the door in one piece long enough to get out.

Hearing the wood cracking from around the door jam, she stands over the hatchway and pulls on the metal handle in the middle — but it won't budge. Thinking that it's probably just that the boards are swelled up, she puts all of her strength into it, and manages to tear the handle away from the wooden planks. She stands up straight again, trying to think of another way out — and then she hears something behind her break loose. Turning around, she sees that the door is now ripped halfway off of the hinges — and the people behind it are now trying to reach through the narrow opening and into the bedroom.

Knowing that nightfall is quickly approaching, along with the fatal deadline that Jake gave her back at her family's cabin, she collapses onto the floor in tears, too weak and distraught to fight any longer.

CHAPTER 17
GRAYLAND: DAY 5

Larry follows Beth and Christine out of the fire station, then ties a half-shredded shirt from the pavement around the two handles of the double doors — a mostly worthless attempt at securing the entry, but he figures that it's better than nothing at all. A strong gust of wind is blowing in from the beach, pelting the group with heavy rain and flying debris that was scattered across the parking lot and street out front. Not wanting to go back inside, the three of them look around for a moment, and then Larry begins walking back toward the trailer park.

"Where are you going?" Beth asks him, yelling over the wind and falling rain.

"We can't stay out in this, we need to find shelter for a while. I'm gonna check out those trailers we saw earlier."

In the few minutes that it takes them to get across the parking lot, both their clothing and the bags they're carrying are completely soaked. Larry climbs up onto the nearest covered porch and opens the sliding glass door, surprised to find it unlocked — then he takes a step back and peers through the glass to see if there's anybody inside. Seeing nothing of interest, he opens the door further and steps inside, smelling the usual musty odor and dampness that virtually all of the houses have these days.

"Nobody has been in here," Beth says behind him, dropping her two bags on the wooden deck.

"What do you mean?"

"I meant nobody has ransacked the place — it looks untouched."

Still standing outside, Christine looks around closely before placing her foot over the threshold. Glancing to her left, she looks out to the north at the fire station and sees two shadows exit the front door and run around behind the building, and then several more that run across the street toward the sand dunes.

"Larry, I just saw a bunch of people leave the fire house..."

Beth and Larry hurry back from the house and stand next to Christine, but by the time they do the rain is falling hard enough to obscure the visibility in the distance.

Beth does manage to catch a glimpse of one of them as they pass between a couple of neighboring trailers in the park, running faster than any of the infected she's seen up until now. "I just saw one of them."

"We should get inside," Larry says, stepping back into the moldy living room. After Beth comes in behind him, he looks out at Christine and finds her still standing in the same spot, looking around in every direction. "Christine! Come inside, it's not safe out there!" When she doesn't respond, he grabs her by the arm and pulls her in, sitting her down on a dusty couch on the other side of the room. He kneels down in front of her and expects to see tears in her eyes, but there aren't any. Instead, he sees a look of pure terror on her face as she stares straight ahead, like she's in some sort of a trance. "Beth, close all the blinds, we don't need anybody watching us."

"Is she okay?"

"She'll be fine, she just got shook up." As Beth closes the blinds, enveloping the room into near darkness, Larry sits down beside Christine and puts his arm around her. "Christine, are you still with us?"

"There were so many of them..."

Suddenly nervous, Larry glances up at Beth and sees the same expression of worry on her face. "How many did you see?"

"I don't know, there were too many," she answers, as she suddenly breaks down in tears.

As Beth peeks out through the blinds, Larry lets go of Christine and grabs one of their bags in front of him.

"What are you looking for?" Beth asks.

"I'm seeing how much ammo we have."

"We should have plenty, there's at least a couple hundred rounds in each bag."

Seeing several boxes inside, he closes the bag again and leans back into the couch. "Do you see anything out there?"

"No, just rain."

"There was a town like this when we came over the hills..." Christine says, completely out of the blue.

"What do you mean, like this?" Larry asks.

"Like nobody left, except no one was around either."

"Do you remember the name of the town?"

"No. My dad didn't like the looks of it — I guess it gave him the creeps, so we never looked around very much."

He sees Beth holding up two fingers, which he figures must be a signal that she's spotted two people outside. Hoping Christine didn't see it, he nudges her leg with his to get her attention. "Hey, you've never really talked about Chehalis very much... What was it like when you left?" he asks, trying to distract her from falling apart completely.

She shrugs. "Same as most places I guess. Lots of the infected walking around at night, and a few of them during the day."

"Did you ever see anybody that wasn't infected?"

She stays silent for a moment. "Just our neighbor, David, and an older couple across the street from us that looked okay."

"And what happened to them?"

"David came with us when we left, and was killed along the way."

"And what about the people across the street? Are they still alive?"

"No, one of the daywalkers killed them."

"Daywalker?"

"That's what David called them — he said it was from a book or something. He said the ones that walked in the daylight were the most dangerous — they aren't as dumb."

"How many of them have you seen?"

"Seven."

"You counted them?" Beth asks.

"You don't really forget them."

"Yeah, I guess that's probably true."

"Can I ask you a question?" Christine asks Beth.

"Of course."

"Why were you trying to save one of them?"

"You mean Amanda?" Seeing both Larry and Christine staring at her, Beth sits down in a chair next to the window and listens to the rain hitting the metal roof overhead, trying to come up with an answer that even she believes. "She's a little girl, and I figured that it doesn't matter how fucked up the world is, killing someone that age can never be the right thing to do."

"She's not a little girl anymore."

"She's twelve, and she's sick."

"Somewhere out there, right now, she's figuring out how to kill you, to kill all of us. Little girls don't do that."

Instead of answering, Beth opens the blinds far enough to see through them again, and this time sees three people coming up the driveway from the road.

"Larry, there's three people coming this way — they all have bags."

He gets up from the couch and leans over next to his sister, and sees what looks like two men and a woman jogging up the driveway. They head straight toward the closest place to the highway, a house just a few doors down from their position, and then they disappear inside.

"They didn't look like they're from the fire station..." Beth says.

"No, they don't even look sick, but they also have no idea how much danger they're in."

"Larry, are you still up?" Beth whispers.

"Yeah, what's wrong?"

"Nothing, I just wanted to talk. We haven't really had a chance since we left the cabin."

Larry quietly gets up and makes sure that Christine is still asleep on the couch, but it's impossible to tell whether she's faking it or not. He figures that Beth wants to talk to him without Christine overhearing them, and given the circumstances, it's probably not a bad idea. Although she's already proven herself to be mentally and emotionally stronger than he was after his wife's passing, he also knows that every person has their breaking point, and hers can't be too far off. Beyond the stress of living in a post-apocalyptic world, she's also the last living member of her family. Larry still has his sister, Beth has not only him, but also apparently her husband, and the Lockwood family still have each other. Even Amanda, as lonely as her existence seems, was given the choice of having her family beside her as they struggled to live in this new world. Christine was never given that choice — her family and friends were taken from her one by one, and now all that's left is her father's naive promise of a better life, somewhere down the road.

He stands next to Beth, who's tightly clutching a pistol in her right hand as she stares out the window, and he listens as the rain still falls steadily onto the cheap tin roof overhead, filling the room with so much noise that it's difficult to have a quiet conversation. Every couple of minutes the trailer shakes and groans from a gust of wind out of the west, and the constant, rhythmic sound of dripping water can be heard from a leak in the roof somewhere over them. Through the window, shrouded in the darkness, he can barely make out shadows moving around the dimly moonlit trailer park. At first he thinks they might be branches and debris flying across the parking lot from the wooded property across the street, but after watching them for a minute it becomes apparent that the shadows are actually people — and their numbers are growing.

"How many do you think are out there?" Larry asks her.

"I don't know, there could be dozens — but that's not what I wanted to talk to you about..."

"Okay, what is it?"

"We've always assumed that these infected assholes are dying, right?"

"I guess so, yeah."

"And what if they're not?"

The same thought had occurred to Larry, in fact he'd already discussed it with Curtis shortly after they saw the first group of people walking in broad daylight. "Then we're in more trouble than we thought."

"They're getting stronger, Larry — and faster."

"All the more reason to get away from everything."

He looks out the window again, then slumps down in his chair after seeing a man standing on the bottom step of the porch, facing away from the trailer. Afraid to even breathe, they watch as the man slowly turns around and looks straight into the window, his face obscured with some sort of dark paint or dirt as he gets closer to the window and peers inside. When he places his hands onto the glass in order to see better, they can both see the deep scars and blood stains on his forearms, and the markings on his bare chest that look like fingernail scratches — all of which look filthy and unwashed. After looking around inside, his eyes never focusing on either Larry or Beth, he backs off and walks down the steps again, then disappears from view completely.

"What the hell was on his face?" Beth whispers.

"The hell if I know... He didn't look sick, did he?"

"He was awfully skinny for a healthy person."

Larry looks more closely at the others as they pass by, but most of them are too far away to see any detail in their appearance. Then another man comes to within twenty feet or so, and from the side Larry can make out the same strange substance on his face, and the same lack of clothing on his upper body.

"We need to wait until morning, and then get the hell out of here."

"What if they're still here in the morning?"

"Then I guess we'll shoot our way out and hope for the best. I don't see any weapons on any of them."

"And after that? I'm fine with no longterm plans for now, but we need an immediate plan."

"We'll go back to the cabin."

"Somehow I don't think they'll welcome us with open arms when they find out that Amanda is still on the loose."

"Then we'll find someplace else, somewhere safe. Besides, Amanda might be halfway back to the cabin already."

Beth glances out the window again, and sees four people standing in the driveway, all of them looking directly at her.

"Larry..."

As the words leave her mouth, she hears the sound of a door opening in the back of the trailer — and then the sound of creaking

146

floorboards can be heard as the smell of fresh air enters the room from down the hallway.

"Beth, wake up Christine."

"I'm already awake," Christine answers quietly from the other side of the room. "Larry, I can see someone at the other end of the hallway..."

CHAPTER 18
COHASSETT BEACH: DAY 5

Curtis has never been a violent person — to people, animals, or even the bullies who tormented him throughout his later years in school. In fact, it was one of the traits that Sarah found so attractive in the beginning, asking him out despite the protests of her more popular circle of friends. His gut instinct has always been to either talk things out, or ignore them altogether and hope that things just work their way out. Most of the time they did — until a few months ago anyway. Since meeting Amanda Williams, and the other residents of Westport, his views on violence have changed dramatically, so much so that his new perspective has become a bit worrisome. Never in a million years did he ever think that murder would be his first and only inclination when seeing a young girl — and yet that's exactly what happened when he spotted her walking down his driveway. Although he still doesn't regret trying to kill her, part of him is troubled that the thought occurred to him at all.

As he sits in the middle of the room, staring up at the old, cracked cedar planks on the ceiling of the cabin, he tries to ignore the anger and frustration building inside of him. Somewhere outside of these walls is a man he's never even met, who for whatever reason has decided to terrorize his family and destroy every possession they own — and instead of being able to do something about it, he's forced to sit quietly, tied to an uncomfortable wooden chair, pretending to be calm and reassuring while a fire spreads across the cabin roof and down the walls only a few feet away.

While Matt sits against the headboard, scared to move for fear of what Jake might do, Ben is moving slowly toward the edge of the bed near Curtis. He can see the anxiety building in his son's eyes as his feet finally hit the floor, and then he disappears behind him as he tries to loosen the ropes.

"Ben, we have to stay on the bed!" Matt cries out.

"Is that what he told you?" Curtis asks, struggling to free himself from the ropes as Ben tries helplessly to loosen them.

"He said he would kill all of us if we didn't stay put..."

"Matt, he's going to kill us anyway if we don't get out of here — if that fire doesn't kill us first."

Still reluctant, Matt looks out the window and sees the orange glow of flames growing brighter, and then realizes that he can feel the heat coming through the single-pane of glass that's halfway across the room from him.

"Dad, what about the propane tank?"

Curtis glares at him in disbelief, biting his tongue so that he doesn't scare Ben.

Knowing that the old, rusty propane tank sits right next to the window beside the back door, and that the fire is sending burning embers down from the rooftop past the same window, Matt finally works up the courage to climb from the bed. Reaching behind the nightstand, he grabs a small hunting knife and then sits at Curtis' feet, trying to cut through the ropes that bind his legs.

"Careful, don't cut me..."

Curtis can hear the roar of the fire outside getting worse as each minute passes, and he sees the faint hint of smoke starting to drift through the crude wooden planks in the ceiling.

"Boys, I don't think we have much time — are you getting

anywhere?"

"This one knot is really big, I'm trying to cut it," Matt says.

"Okay, open the other door, then drag me outside. You can finish cutting it out there."

Curtis spins himself around so that his back is facing the rear door while the boys open the door, and then they each grab the back of the chair and start pulling it across the old spruce floorboards, until at last they feel the cold, wet droplets of water falling on them from the clouds above. As they pull the chair into the mud and water outside, Matt looks over in horror as he sees the fire burning the siding behind the propane tank. The entire roof is engulfed, and he can hear the cracking and splintering of wood from inside the cabin as the structure begins to collapse. Unfortunately, the rain is nothing more than a light drizzle at the moment, and is obviously having little to no effect on the flames.

They continue to drag Curtis until they nearly collapse, and end up stopping behind some bushes in the backyard.

"See if you can find something in the shed to cut me loose, we need to get back further," Curtis tells them. He begins looking around the rest of the property for any signs of movement, aware once again that Jake could still be somewhere close.

It takes a few minutes for the boys to free his hands, a job made even more difficult by the rain and darkness — but once he's completely free, they begin circling around the property, behind the woodshed and toward the driveway.

"What's that noise?" Ben asks, as they stop next to the shed and look around the property.

""You mean the roaring sound?" Curtis replies.

"Yeah."

"I think it's the wind to the south, it's probably gonna be here in a few minutes. There must be another storm moving in."

They start walking again, crouching down as they make their way into the trees — then Curtis stops and motions for the boys to stay quiet.

"Somebody is walking up the driveway..." Curtis whispers.

At first, all he can hear over the wind is the faint sound of footsteps in the mud, and then a dark figure comes into view, and it doesn't take him long to figure out who it is. Jake is holding what looks like Curtis' pistol in one hand, and a rifle in another, whistling as he walks down the drive. He stops when the cabin comes into view, and Curtis can hear him laughing as the roof finally caves in and collapses completely. He's standing only about thirty feet away when he holsters the pistol and takes out a flashlight instead, aiming it at the ground in front of him. As he walks further down the driveway, shining his light back and forth across the muddy gravel, Curtis realizes that they crossed that part of the driveway only a few minutes before, and their footprints are undoubtedly still visible in the mud.

"Come on, we need to get out of here, quietly..." he whispers to Matt and Ben.

Trying to keep their feet on solid ground, the three of them wind their way through the trees that lead to the highway, praying that they don't come face to face with somebody from town. When they finally reach the downhill slope of land next to the road, Curtis looks back and sees Jake squatting down, looking closely at something on the ground.

He found the footprints.

Standing up again, he shines the light toward the forest where they just came from. After a few seconds, he begins moving the light around in the same general direction, forcing Curtis to drop to the ground with the boys to avoid being seen. As Jake starts to move in their direction, Curtis sees a bright flash of light, and then hears, and feels, a loud explosion that causes the ground under them to rumble.

When he looks up, he sees a fireball rising into the sky, illuminating the trees surrounding the cabin, and filling the entire area in a fiery glow that extends all the way to the highway. He raises his head a little higher, and sees Jake staring back at him, his rifle aimed a little to his left. Curtis looks over and sees Ben standing up, and just as he pulls the boy back down to the ground, he hears a gunshot go off, and a bullet ripping through the brush right next to them.

"Everyone stay down!"

He listens closely, expecting to hear another shot, or maybe the sound of Jake getting closer to them. Instead, all he hears is the steady drops of rain around them, and the flames that are now starting to finally settle down. Almost as quickly as it appeared, the intense glow of light fades away, replaced with the cold darkness of night once again.

"Matt, do you still have that knife?"

"Yeah."

"Give it to me."

Feeling the knife in his hand, he unfolds it and looks at the small blade, which looks pathetic knowing what he's up against.

Then he hears something — footsteps.

He grips the knife tightly in his hand, bracing for a fight — but then he realizes that the footsteps aren't coming from the same direction as Jake, they're coming from the driveway near the road. Staying as low to the ground as possible, he slowly begins to back up, crawling across the damp ground and away from the driveway, motioning for his sons to do the same.

"Wait..." whispers Matt.

Curtis stops, looking back at the boy. "What is it?"

"Look at the road..."

Curtis turns his head around and looks at the highway, which is filled with a dozen or more moving shadows, all of them moving toward the burning cabin — most of them heading straight up the driveway, but a few are taking a shortcut through the woods, in their direction.

"Whatever happens, just stay quiet and low — understand?"

The boys both nod their heads, hiding their faces behind the brush. Curtis does the same, but keeps both of them in his field of vision. It doesn't take long before he can hear the cracks and rustling of breaking branches and leaves behind them, and as the mindless local residents pass by only a body length away, he holds his breath as he hears the sound of breathing and groans coming from at least three people close to them. One of them, an older man that's covered in filth and wearing ripped up clothing, stops on the other side of Ben, then glances around quickly and sniffs the air — but he never bothers to look down. As he starts to move again, dragging his feet through the short brush and debris, he suddenly changes direction and walks right into Ben, falling to the ground right in front of Curtis. The man stays still for a moment, with his legs still draped over Ben — and then he begins reaching out in front of him, placing his hand on Matt's shoulder as he struggles to get back to his feet again. Curtis glances back toward the cabin, seeing no sign of Jake, but a crowd of townsfolk gathering in the same general area — and then he very slowly and deliberately grabs the back of the man's head and holds it firmly into the dirt, while the other hand drives the small hunting knife into the back of the man's head. Hearing more noise coming from behind him, he looks up and sees two more men walking by only twenty feet away or so away, but they seem far more interested in what's happening in front of them. After a few moments of holding the man down to control his convulsions, Curtis finally pulls the knife out and releases him, making sure that his movements have settled down to only light twitches that won't attract too much attention. The stench of human waste and infected tissue is permeating the air, and

Curtis motions for the boys to follow him back down the hill and into the damp, clean air that's coming in from the beach.

"Where are we going?" Ben asks.

"We're going to find your mom, before Jake does," Curtis replies, relieved to see the road clear once again.

As the three finally reach the pavement, they hear several quick gunshots coming from the hill above the cabin. Then another burst several seconds later.

"Do you think they killed him?" Ben asks, climbing onto the asphalt highway.

Curtis, seeing the blood on the knife from the dim moonlight overhead, wipes the blade off on his pants as he begins walking north. "No, I think he's just picking them off. Come on, it won't take him long to catch up."

"What if he runs out of bullets?"

"He won't, he's been at this for too long." Curtis looks behind them, wondering whatever happened to Larry and Beth, and what they'll think when they finally reach what's left of the cabin — if they ever do. Hearing yet another gunshot, this time closer than before, he forces himself to walk through the pain in his injured legs and into the darkness ahead. The moonlight, what little there was, has quickly disappeared, enveloping the three of them into the obscurity of night. Even the side of the road fades from sight, leaving them blind to what's only an arm length away.

"Dad, I can't see anything."

"I know, but try to keep your eyes and ears open, there's bound to be more of those things out here."

Feeling a few drops of rainwater hit his face, Curtis can hear the wind suddenly picking up in the trees overhead. As the wind becomes even stronger, Curtis isn't surprised when a downpour of heavy rain begins falling, quickly drenching their light clothes and leaving the roadway slippery and their footsteps loud. After a brief flash of light shows up in the pavement ahead of them, Curtis assumes for a moment that it must be lightning, but when it happens again he grabs the boys and pulls them off to the side of the road and behind a thicket of blackberry vines — unsure of whether it provides enough protection or not.

"What is it?" Matt whispers.

"Shh, stay quiet."

When he sees the light again, he realizes that it's coming from a good distance down the road. A single flashlight beam, searching the roadway through the dense blanket of fog and rain, is moving steadily toward them. Then suddenly, it disappears, leaving everything black again.

"Did he stop?" asks Matt.

"No, he's still moving. I can hear him in the mud puddles." Curtis stands up, seeing the faint glow of firelight still emanating from the cabin on the hill above them. Then he turns around and holds onto the hands of his sons, and begins walking west toward the beach.

"Where are we going?" Ben asks him quietly, his small voice shivering in the cold.

"We can't stay on the highway, and there's an old road through the dunes that runs right next to the campground. I doubt Jake knows anything about it."

"What if we run into somebody?"

"Then we keep moving. Most of them don't seem to move very fast."

"And what if mom is already on her way back?"

That thought had already crossed Curtis' mind, but he really didn't know how to respond. "Don't worry, I'm sure she'll stay out of his way." Hoping that his empty words of encouragement lifts their spirits, the three of them continue to trudge through the wet, sticky sand of the roadway, hearing the massive waves of the ocean crash against the dunes not far from where they're walking. As they climb over a fallen pine tree, it's aromatic scent still thick in the air, he spots a glint of light shining off of a post up ahead. Recognizing it as the chain link fence that surrounds three sides of the campground, he begins running through the tall grass and brush between the road and the property. He remembers the controversy when they installed the fence several years back, when residents in the area complained that it might interfere with the designated tsunami evacuation route from the beach — but the owners placed it here in an attempt to stop homeless groups from occupying the empty cabins during the slow winter months. As they get closer, Curtis can hear the rattle of metal wire, and unsteady sound of staggered footsteps in the wet grass on the other side of the fence. They're soon face to face with a few dozen people, all of them trying to make their way through the wire in a pathetic attempt to escape.

"Is that where mom went?" Matt asks.

Curtis tries to look around the rest of the grounds, but he can't really see much of anything. "Come on, there must be another way in..."

CHAPTER 19
COHASSETT BEACH: DAY 5

Behind her, Sarah can hear someone's hands scraping against the cheap hollow door, and the deep, rattling groans of the people still trying to force their way into the room. Somehow, miraculously, her desperate barricade of furniture and bedding seems to be holding — helped by the one remaining hinge that's still attached to solid wood. The room had been nearly pitch black only a few minutes ago, with a hard downpour of rain coming down on the roof — but standing in front of the window she can see the pale blue light from the moon making its way once again through the clouds and onto the cabins that are scattered around the grounds.

She vaguely remembers staying here as a kid once. In the middle of the property, surrounded by every cabin on the place, was where the adult campers all used to get together to light campfires and roast hot dogs and marshmallows, while the kids ran around in the dark corners of the grounds, away from the watchful eyes and boring stories of their parents. In her memories, it always seems like a magical time, feeling the warm ocean breeze of summer move through the air as they ran through the sand dunes and pine trees after dusk. It was also the same summer that she developed her first crush, an infatuation that lasted only a day and a half as it turned out, but she still remembers it like it was yesterday. Her family had been here the entire week, and his arrived on Friday evening, bringing with them an arsenal of food, fireworks and alcohol — a combination which seems rather irresponsible in retrospect, but nobody seemed to think anything of it at the time. Before leaving, their parents all exchanged phone numbers and addresses, promising to keep in touch — but as the months passed by, life got busy again, and none of them were ever heard from or talked about again. As enamored as she was with their oldest boy, she doesn't even remember mentioning him to any of her friends back home, and to this day even his first name escapes her. Not that it makes any difference today anyway — she knows that he's probably dead, along with his younger siblings and his parents, and her own parents for that matter. She's most likely the only survivor of that camping trip, and considering her current circumstances, she's not completely certain that's a good thing.

She's suddenly startled by a loud crash in the next room, tearing her away from the memories of her youth, and back into the harsh reality surrounding her today. After briefly glancing back through a crack in the door, she sees two women fighting in the middle of the living room, throwing punches and wrestling to the ground. She watches for a minute, then turns her attention back to the window. The grounds outside are filled with moving silhouettes, walking in and out of the cabins with no apparent purpose, aimlessly wandering in the same patterns again and again.

Except for the cabin on the far left side of the property.

One person has been standing and facing her on the porch for a while now, occasionally shifting their position when someone blocks their view. Although she can't be certain it's not Jake, her gut tells her that it's probably one of the 'watchers', as Beth calls them. She said they first noticed them in Sequim — people that didn't act like the others, and mostly just stood back and observed everything around them. They also follow you, staying hidden in the shadows, waiting for an opportunity to strike when your guard is down. The man that grabbed Ben off of the wall was apparently one them, according to Beth anyway.

Looking around at the rest of the grounds, she notices that something has piqued the interest of the people toward the entrance of the property. After looking in that direction for a few moments, a couple of them start walking that way, followed closely by a few others. When she hears someone step outside of the living room and onto the front porch, she takes another look through the crack in the door and sees three more people in the middle of the room, all of them watching whatever is outside. She considers making a run for it, hoping that everyone is distracted enough to let her slip away without being noticed — but that thought quickly disappears when she hears a gunshot somewhere nearby. She hurries back to the window, almost tripping over a box of clothes lying on the floor, and then carefully scans the area in front of her.

The campground seems silent somehow, even deserted — and it takes her a moment to recognize that anyone is still out there. The man watching her from the porch is gone, and so are the dozen or so people that were walking between her cabin and the next one over. The lone person still out there, who looks small enough to be a child, is slowly walking toward the road near the gravel parking lot — and then they suddenly stop in their tracks and start to turn around, scrabbling to get away from whatever is out there. Sarah sees the bright light from the muzzle flash behind them like it's in slow-motion, and sees the person fall to the ground immediately afterward, but it's not until the second and third shots that she hears the cracking of the gunfire that follows. Her first instinct is to drop to the floor, but she raises her head just high enough over the window sill to see whether it might be Jake or Curtis — or possibly somebody else. The first thing that she recognizes is the long trench coat that Curtis bought only a few weeks before they moved here — but as they get closer, she can see that they're heading straight toward her cabin, not even looking at the others, and Curtis wouldn't know which one it was.

"Sarah! Are you still in there?"

This time she drops completely to the floor, recognizing Jake's voice immediately. She hears another gunshot, and then another, and can feel the thud as two bodies hit the floor in the living room. She crawls to the hatch in the floor, trying desperately to pry it open — and then she hears the sound of footsteps on the porch, and another gunshot that sounds like it came from inside the cabin. Her fingers are sore and bleeding, which makes it that much more difficult to get a good grip on the makeshift opening, but she can feel the wood starting to give way, and the cold rush of air from the crawlspace below as it cracks open on one side.

"Sarah, you can come on out, I cleared the room," Jake says, his voice calm and reassuring, and still sounding as if he's outside.

When the hatch finally opens, it makes a loud popping sound, and Sarah sees a beam of light appear on the wall behind the headboard almost immediately after. She considers climbing through the opening before he spots her, but instead decides to back herself against the wall underneath the window. She can see the beam search the entire room, and then stop on the open hatch.

"Shit..." she hears Jake grumbling through the window.

Hearing him step off of the porch and onto the gravel path, she stays put and doesn't move, afraid of making any sound that might give away that she's still in the room. A minute later the faint sound of another door opening can be heard, and a glow of light comes up through the open hatch in the floor. Knowing that she doesn't have much time, she jumps up and pushes the dresser away from the bedroom door, and then rushes through the doorway, nearly slipping on a puddle of blood coming from one of the women lying dead on the floor.

Once she's outside, she gives the campground another quick scan, and after seeing no sign of anybody around she steps from the noisy gravel and onto the rain-soaked grass beside the pathway. She knows there's no point in running toward the highway, since everything in that direction is in the open where she'll be easily spotted, so she decides instead to run north, where there's more pine and fir trees shading the ground below them. When she reaches the next cabin over, she runs around the corner and waits there for a moment to catch her breath, then peeks around to see if she's in the clear. She sees Jake walking up onto the porch, shining the flashlight into the living room, and then around the rest of the campground — a pistol clearly visible in his other hand. She watches him for a moment, waiting to see what he does next — but he doesn't move, he just stands there carefully surveying the area.

With the wind still howling in the trees overhead, and the light sprinkles of rain starting once again from the storm, Sarah doesn't hear the heavy breathing coming from behind her at first. It's not until she hears the cracking of a fallen branch on the ground that she glances behind, and by then it's too late. Whoever it is grabs her around the waist, and places their hand over her mouth to stop her from screaming. Their hand smells horrible, like human filth — pulling her deeper into the shadows of the brush behind the cabin.

CHAPTER 20
GRAYLAND: DAY 5

Beth can hear the floor in the hallway softly creaking as the person gets closer, followed by a door slamming shut as another gust of wind hits the trailer. Larry stands up and moves to the middle of the room, aiming his gun in their direction. "Larry, don't shoot unless you have to..." she whispers.

"There's no need to whisper, I'm pretty sure they already know we're in here," he replies in a normal volume. "Keep an eye on those people outside..."

Beth looks out the window again, but the entire trailer park seems to be empty. "They're gone, I don't see anyone." She stands up alongside Larry and carefully inches her way to the right, until she has a clear view of the hallway and bedroom at the end. She can only see the silhouette of a man standing halfway down the corridor, but he looks massive — tall and overweight, and carrying something in his right hand that looks like a large machete.

Larry motions for Christine to get off of the couch and to stand behind them, but when she does the person takes a couple of steps forward, then stops again.

"Can you talk?" Larry asks, but he doesn't get a reply. They just stand there, breathing heavily and making small shaking motions with the blade they're carrying. "If you take one step further, I'll shoot you — do you understand?"

"I don't see anyone outside, do you want to make a run for it?" Christine asks as she grabs her bags.

"I think we might have to," Larry responds. "Any ideas as to where we could go?"

"That house up front, the one with the family in it," Beth says. "We can't go running down the highway in the middle of the night, especially with the weather like this. There's no way we could hear anybody coming."

"Okay, Beth, set my bags next to me, then grab yours. We'll go around to the backside of the house, maybe scope it out a little before we approach them — but we have to stick together, no matter what."

"What if they won't let us in?"

"I guess we'll figure it out." He sees Beth put her gun away, and then she moves his bags right next to him. As she turns around to pick up her own bags, the person down the hallway steps forward a few steps, very slowly. Larry begins to open his mouth to order the trespasser back, but then he notices two more people moving in behind them. All three are moving slowly down the hall, and all three appear to be armed with similar machetes. "Christine, go — now!" He fires a shot at the person's chest, and for a moment they stop moving and actually block the passage, but then they regain their posture again and continue forward. He can clearly see now that it's a man, probably in his late thirties or forties. Larry fires two more shots, this time at his head, and the second bullet lands squarely in the middle of his forehead, dropping him backward into the other two.

"Larry, come on!" Beth yells from outside the door.

Watching the two people scramble from beneath the man, Larry fires another two shots before holstering his gun and grabbing the two bags next to his feet. Once they're all outside, with no way to lock the closed door behind them, they quickly make their way down the stairs and onto the sidewalk, all three of them running for the house as they hear the front door of the trailer opening behind them.

The small house they're trying to get to, which is the only stick-built structure on the grounds, is close to the entrance of the park, on the west end near the highway. With the wind and rain blowing directly at them, and the moon almost completely obscured from sight, it's impossible for them to see more than about ten feet in any direction — but they can hear people laughing and howling throughout the small town, some of them sounding alarmingly close.

"Larry, I think there's somebody in front of the bushes over there..." Beth says, pointing to their left at a clump of rhododendrons.

He glances over and sees the person that she's talking about, a middle-aged woman that looks healthier than most of the infected survivors they've seen — but then again, most of the people do in this town. She's getting closer and walking at an angle, as if she's herding them in the same direction they're already going — and when he looks over his back, he sees a small group of people doing exactly the same thing. "Just keep moving, ignore them."

Finally reaching the house, they find a screened-in, covered deck attached to the backside of it — and no signs of lights or activity visible on the inside. When Larry turns the handle and finds that it's unlocked, he stops for a moment, fearful that they might be walking into a trap.

"What are you waiting for?" Beth asks.

Larry looks around, and not only sees the same people following them as before, but more out by the highway as well — all walking slowly in their direction, with several of them carrying blades or pipes in their hands. Still feeling uneasy about trapping themselves in an enclosed space, Larry steps inside of the shelter and then motions for Beth and Christine to do the same once he takes a quick look around. He sets his bag down on a table, and then starts laying handguns down in a line across a bench, making sure they're all loaded.

"What are you doing?" Beth asks him.

"They're up to something, and I'm not waiting around to find out what it is."

"So you're gonna kill all of them?"

"That's pretty much the plan, yeah."

"Larry?" Christine says, her voice frightened.

"What is it?"

"You'd better look at this..."

Peering out into the darkness, barely able to see the road through the heavy rain, Larry spots a man dragging something up the driveway behind him. It looks like another person, or possibly a corpse — it's hard to tell for sure. As he drags it past the people lined up along the driveway, each one takes turns beating on it or kicking it as he passes.

"I wouldn't worry about them too much, I'm sure they're already dead."

"I'm not talking about the dead guy, I'm talking about the people down the road."

Larry hears Beth gasp right before he sees what she's talking about — a line of men and women, all armed with some sort of primitive weapon, stretching into the darkness as far as he can see, and they're still coming. There must be at least thirty of them already in sight.

"Do you have that many bullets?" Christine asks.

Larry turns back to the table, then begins placing the guns back into the bags. He has more than enough bullets, that's not a concern, but there's no way they'll be able to hold back a crowd that large with only a limited amount of cover.

"Are you armed?" comes a frail voice, barely audible.

Larry looks up and sees a woman standing in the doorway to the house, wearing a heavy winter coat with bright reflective colors covering it. "Yes, we're armed."

"Are you from around here?"

"No, we're from Hoodsport, we just got here yesterday. Are you alone, ma'am?"

"No, my husband is in here too, and our son."

Seeing some movement in the window next to the door, Larry can see the outline of a man standing next to her, with a rifle aimed in their direction. "I don't think it's safe out here, do you think we can come inside?"

The woman looks to her right, then opens the door all of the way and motions them inside. Locking the flimsy door on the screened wall first, Larry follows Beth and Christine up the stairs and into the home, where a bolt-action rifle is aimed right at his head. Walking further inside, into an area lit with several burning candles, he hears the woman lock the door behind them, and he sets his two bags down in the middle of the living room floor, then sits down on one of the couches — exhausted and out of breath.

"I'd feel better if you'd hand over your guns," the man says, still aiming the gun at Larry, his hand trembling with fear. He's tall and skinny, with thick eyeglasses that look slightly tinted. He also has a full beard and long hair, but nearly every man they've come across does.

"That probably isn't a good idea. Have you seen what's outside?"

"Yes we have," the woman replies, before turning to the man. "Bill, they're obviously not sick, put the gun away."

Beth and Christine set their bags down next to Larry's, then join him on the couch — as Bill eases the rifle down to his side.

"My name is Rachel, and this is my husband, Bill. Our son, Travis, is sleeping in the bedroom."

"I'm Larry, and this is my sister Beth, and our friend, Christine. You might wanna wake your son up, there's a pretty good-sized crowd headed in this direction, and it looks like it could get ugly."

Rachel leaves the room, headed for the back of the place, while Bill sits down across from them, his gun still resting across his lap.

"Where did you say you're from again, Hoodsport?" Bill asks.

"Yeah, up on Hood Canal," Beth answers. "Are you from around here?"

"Not really, we came from Olympia."

Beth can't help but notice how fidgety he is, like he's having a nervous breakdown. "Did you come through Aberdeen?"

"What's left of it, yeah. It's mostly just smoke and ashes."

"You didn't run across a man named Jake by any chance did you?"

"No, I think you're the first healthy people we've come across since we left Olympia."

Rachel walks in, with a teenage boy around Christine's age behind her. He looks healthy enough, but tired. They both sit down at the kitchen table, which is on the edge of the living room. Beth turns around and peeks out through the venetian blinds, and sees two silhouettes standing in the parking lot in front of the house.

"Are they doing anything?" Larry asks her.

"No, they're just standing there, watching us."

"Have you been south of here?" Bill asks.

"Christine has."

"You didn't find anything?" Bill asks her.

"No."

He waits for her to say something more, then turns to Beth. "She doesn't say much, huh?"

"She does once she knows you better. I take it Olympia was bad?"

"It's empty, everyone is dead."

"Dead, or sick?"

"Dead," Rachel replies. "We didn't see people walking around until we got to McCleary, and it took us a while to figure out there was something wrong with 'em. Do you have any idea what the hell is going on here?"

"I was gonna ask you the same thing."

"Are they sick or what?"

"I'm pretty sure they're sick, but they're not like any of the ones we've ever seen. We found hundreds of bones in the fire station next door."

"Hundreds? Who are they from?"

"The former residents of Grayland would be my guess."

"Where are you headed?" Bill asks Larry.

"We have a place up by Westport, although I'm not sure we're staying there for long. After that, I'm not really sure. How about you guys?"

"We're not really headed any place in particular, we're just trying to find someplace better."

"Olympia sounds better than this," Christine says softly.

"Like I said, everyone there is dead," Rachel responds.

"Dead is better than this, trust me."

Nearly an hour has passed, and although they've seen some movement in the gathering crowd outside, so far none of the infected have made any attempt at entering the house. Despite their curiosity of what other people have witnessed or learned, both groups have fallen into silence — mostly due to sleep deprivation. Travis seems to be the only one capable of getting any meaningful sleep, and he's also the only one that hasn't talked the entire time they've been together.

"So I take it the cars don't work in Olympia either?" Larry asks, finally breaking the silence.

"Some do, but the roads are all blocked just outside of town, so driving was kind of out of the question," Bill responds.

"Yeah, we haven't found many that run around here either, it's weird."

"Well, I think that was kind of the point."

"The point of what?"

"The EMP…"

Seeing the confused looks on Larry and Beth's faces, Rachel chimes in. "You guys didn't hear about the detonation?"

"No…" Beth answers.. "You mean like a nuclear detonation?"

"No, hundreds of nuclear detonations, spread across the country," Bill says excitedly, searching his backpack and pulling out a piece of paper, which he then hands to Beth. It's a hand-written note, mostly filled with illegible scribblings.

"I'm sorry, what is this?" Beth asks.

"It's a loose translation of their message."

"Whose message?"

"They sent it out on TV and radio right before everything went dark — it was on every station."

Beth looks at Larry, who looks as lost as she is. They listened to the radio quite a bit in those early days, but there were periods of time when they turned everything off to hide from Sean, who was still looking for them in the waters of the straights.

"They said that they were setting off a series of high-altitude explosions that were designed to cripple the power grid," Bill continues. "They were hoping to slow down the advance of the virus by limiting transportation, or something like that."

"That worked out well, didn't it?" Larry adds sarcastically.

"We saw the flashes from our house," Rachel says. "It lit the sky up that entire night."

"We saw them too…" Christine says. "…David and my dad and me. The sky looked like it was on fire for hours — it was kind of pretty in a way."

"And that's when the power went out?"

169

"Ours went out a couple of days before, but that's when the radios went dead."

Larry stands up and stretches, then looks out the window behind the couch. "Is there a working bathroom in here?"

"We've been using the bathtub," Bill answers.

"That'll work I guess."

After watching Larry head down the hall, Beth turns to Bill, who is still gripping his rifle with both hands. "How are you guys set for ammunition?"

"It's fully loaded, thirty rounds I think."

"How much else do you have?"

He glances at Rachel, then back at Beth. "Just the thirty rounds, and the one gun. We haven't really needed anything more."

"Oh." Beth is stunned, and a little speechless. "Well, I guess we have plenty to spare."

Larry walks back into the room with a strange look on his face, then he sits down next to Beth again.

"What's wrong?" Beth asks him.

"I saw her," he says quietly.

"You saw Amanda? Where?"

"Under the carport next door."

"What was she doing?"

"Just standing there, looking this way."

"Wait, who is Amanda?" Bill asks.

Beth stands up, then motions for Christine to do the same. "I'll let Larry explain, Christine and I are gonna use the bathroom, before any of those people decide to make a move." Walking down the hallway, Beth turns on a small flashlight once they're away from the candles, but holds it down low to the floor where it doesn't attract too much attention outside. She can tell the first door on the left is the bathroom right away, not only because of the bright white linoleum

170

on the floor, but also because of the horrific smell coming from it. After hesitating at first, she enters the room while Christine stands outside and waits her turn.

"Those people out there might kill Amanda, right?" Christine asks.

"They could, yeah."

"But you don't think they will..."

"Honestly, no, I don't think so. She survived in Westport for months, and I'm not sure it was much better than this." She drops her pants and squats down over the edge of the tub, not even daring to look inside. "That boy out there is kind of cute..." she says, trying to lighten the mood.

"I'm not interested."

"In boys, or in general?"

"In general."

"Why? There's not exactly a lot of boys to choose from at the moment..."

Christine looks down the hallway at the living room, where the family with no apparent last name is sitting. "He'll be dead soon, like everyone else."

CHAPTER 21
COHASSETT BEACH: DAY 5

Sarah stiffens up as she feels the cold hands hold onto her tightly from behind. She wants to scream, or fight back — but she knows that Jake is on the other side of the building, and he'll kill both of them if she makes a sound. When they start to drag her feet backward and into the darkness, she lets out a small moan.

"Shh, it's Curtis..."

Sarah feels the hand covering her mouth slowly move away, as she's pulled into a covered lean-to attached to the cabin — an area almost overflowing with stacked plastic chairs and tables. Wedging themselves between the cluttered mess and the wall, still partially exposed to the alleyway between the cabins, they watch as Jake's flashlight beam continues to search the area.

"Where are the kids?" she whispers quietly.

"They're locked in an old car down the perimeter road. They're safe."

They can hear Jake's footsteps as he walks slowly through the soaked grass, the steps becoming louder as he closes in on them. He turns the corner and stops, then shines his light down the alley near their location, just past their hiding spot. It takes a minute for them to realize what he's looking at, and then they spot someone in his beam, the same man that was watching Sarah so intently earlier that night. The man walks closer to Jake with his arms folded neatly behind his back, with a slight smile on his face as he stares straight ahead. Then he stops and looks right at Sarah, his smile suddenly disappearing. As he looks back toward Jake again, they hear a loud gunshot, and the man stumbles to the ground, gripping his chest where the bullet hit. The light stays on the man for a few more moments, waiting for the last signs of life to slip away from him — and then it fades away again, along with the sound of the footsteps.

"We have to get out of here," Curtis says, as he peers around the corner, seeing nothing but darkness down the alley. Taking Sarah's hand, he steps over the man's body and moves into the pouring rain. He leads her north, staying close to the dark shadows surrounding the cabins and other outbuildings, and away from Jake's continuing search. Eventually they find a hole in the chain link fence, next to a dead body that looks freshly killed. On the other side of the fence there's a pathway that winds through the dunes toward Westport. When they reach the top of one of the dunes, Sarah's leg finally gives out, and Curtis has to hold her up to keep her from falling.

"Sit down for a minute, take a breather," Curtis says.

"How much further is it?"

"It's not too far, but you need to rest..."

Curtis eases her down to the wet, sandy ground, then sits down next to her. The rain has lessened to a light mist again, but the wind is still howling through the trees behind them. Off in the distance, they can still see Jake's light searching the campgrounds, going frantically from one cabin to the next.

"He'll find our footprints in the sand eventually..." Sarah comments.

"We'll be long gone by then. Besides, he's not thinking straight anyway, he's sick."

"I feel terrible for Beth — she must be so excited."

"It might not make any difference."

"Why would you say that?"

"They should have made it back already, and Grayland isn't that far away. I think something happened." He looks back to the southeast, where their home used to be, but there's nothing but darkness there now. "The cabin is gone — Jake burned it to the ground, along with the truck." He looks at her face, trying to see her reaction, and questioning whether he should have told her so soon — but she just keeps looking at the campground, looking just as tired and defeated as before.

"We should go, I don't want the boys alone," she says, standing up and continuing on the path. Further down the trail she can see the beach in the distance, the water invisible in this weather aside from the occasional whitecap reflecting in the faint moonlight. A year ago you would've seen lights from the fishing boats offshore, moving up and down in the swells as they worked through the night — but tonight there's nothing but the shadowy movements of people on the shoreline, looking through the remnants of shipwrecks on the beach.

"I didn't think there'd be this many people still around," Curtis says, glancing back at the campground, where the flashlight beam has now disappeared.

"Is that the car?" Sarah asks, pointing to an old 1971 Buick Estate station wagon that's sitting just off the pathway next to a rundown single-wide mobile home.

"Yeah, that's it."

When they get closer, Sarah can see the outline of two heads looking out through the rear windshield at them — one of them holding a massive pistol in his hands.

Off of the pathway and back onto the perimeter road, the

174

Lockwoods walk down the middle of the road toward town, looking every house over closely to find one suitable for the night.

"We need to find one with the doors closed," Curtis says, stopping in front of an old craftsman house that looks pretty much like all of the others on the street. "Maybe we can find one that hasn't been torn to pieces."

"It just needs to be someplace dry for the night, other than that I don't care what it looks like," Sarah replies.

Curtis looks down at Matt, who's still carrying the pistol he found in the car. The .50 caliber semi-automatic looks ridiculous in his small hands. "Matt, let me see the gun for a bit."

His hands are shaking as he holds it out for his father to take. "Why? It's out of ammo, like you said."

"I know, but nobody else knows that." After taking the gun, Curtis leads them up the sidewalk and past an open garage door, with no sign of any car inside. "They must've left with everyone else." He climbs the steps and onto the porch, then looks through the yellow textured glass next to the door, seeing a cluttered mess of junk on the inside. Somehow though, he gets the impression that it's always looked that way. He tries the doorknob, but it's locked — then he looks around for a hidden spare, and finds two of them under the mat. "You gotta love small towns."

Sarah stays outside with the boys, as Curtis searches the house room by room. After finding no people inside, they all huddle together in the dark in the master bedroom, protected by two securely locked doors and insulated curtains on the window.

Curtis sits on the edge of the bed with the others, then sets a plastic bag down beside Ben. "I found them in the pantry, they're soda crackers I think." He hears a rustling sound as the boys tear the bag open. "They're probably stale as hell, but they're edible."

"They're stale, but they're okay," Ben says.

175

"I smell bleach," Sarah says, covering her nose and mouth to mask the strong scent.

"Yeah, I thought that I'd wash up in a mud puddle out back, and I found a bottle of bleach by the back door — sorry."

"Well, I guess you smell better than you did before." She gets up and limps to the other side of the room, then sits down in a chair next to the window.

"Is your leg still bothering you?"

"Yeah, I did too much walking on it today. I don't think it's ever gonna be the same after that crazy bitch stabbed me."

"Her name was Clara Embree," Matt informs her.

"I really didn't need to know that Matt. I'd rather forget that she ever existed."

"So, any idea what we do next?" Curtis asks her.

"As soon as the sun comes up we need to search this place for anything useful, especially clothes and food."

"And weapons..."

"Right — preferably one with ammunition though."

Curtis joins Sarah by the window, parting the curtains slightly to see out onto the dimly lit highway. "We can't move north, we know what's in Westport — and we can't go east into Aberdeen, it's even worse than Westport."

"It might not be a bad idea to stay low for a while, at least until Jake stops looking for us. If we can find enough food to keep us over a few weeks we should be okay."

"There's a school down the street."

"Somehow I don't think we'll find much for guns and food there," she says.

"No, but we can take whatever we find there, and it does have heavy doors that lock securely." He looks up at her, as she stares at something out the window. "What are you looking at?"

"There's a guy across the street."

Curtis looks closely, but doesn't see anything but garbage strewn across the neighboring lawn. Despite the close proximity to the ocean, this neighborhood wasn't exactly neat and tidy before the outbreak, and now it's also covered with debris that's blown in from the beach — mostly wreckage from a couple of nearby container ships that ran aground a month earlier. "Where? I don't see anybody."

"They just went back in the house on the right, the dark one."

He watches the front door, which is partway open already, and sees someone coming out again, except this time they're backing up through the doorway. When they emerge into the moonlight, he can see that they're dragging a body down the sidewalk and onto the driveway — then they sit down next to it, slumped over as if they're exhausted. "Do you think he's infected, or one of us?"

"I think he's infected. He was stumbling around when I saw him go inside."

Curtis sees the man moving again, this time slumping further onto the body. At first he thinks the guy might have passed out, but then it becomes obvious what he's doing. Curtis looks at Sarah, feeling guilty somehow for watching it, but he's surprised to see her continuing to stare. "You realize what he's doing, right?"

"Larry and Beth told us that they saw cannibalism on the peninsula, I figured they were probably doing the same thing here."

Looking back at the scene, Curtis sees two more people approaching. When they get close to the body, however, the man already there stands up and swings his fists at them, driving them away.

"We can't let the kids grow up seeing this," Sarah says. "These aren't even people anymore, they're just animals."

"We'll find someplace safe, somewhere normal."

Sarah laughs, more from being tired than amused. "Curtis, there's no place normal anymore. That stuff in the truck was the last trace of our normal lives, and now it's all gone."

He can hear her start to cry, and then she pulls the curtains together, closing the outside world from their existence once again.

"Every picture we had of Annie was in that truck..."

"I know, I'm sorry." He stands up, then pulls Sarah to her feet. "Come on, let's get some sleep. Tomorrow is gonna be a long day."

With all four of them huddled together on the old, musty queen-sized mattress, Curtis lies awake and stares at the ceiling, unable to stop his mind from racing. Only a few days ago, it seemed like everything was coming together. They had plenty of food and clean water, extra people to help with gathering supplies and defending their home — and most importantly, hope that things could actually be better someday. Tonight though, as he listens to the savagery outside, and the rumbling stomachs of his wife and kids next to him, none of that hope seems to exist anymore.

CHAPTER 22
GRAYLAND: DAY 5

Christine wakes up to a crashing sound, then calls out for her father as soon as she recognizes it as someone hitting the doors and windows of the house.

"Shh, it's okay Christine, but we need to get out of here," Beth whispers into her ear.

Sitting up on the couch, she turns around and hears someone slamming their fists against the window behind her, screaming obscenities at them as the blows become harder and harder.

"How many are there?"

"We don't know, but they're at every opening."

"They're not at the back door," Bill corrects her.

"You don't think it's strange that they've covered every door and window with a crowd of people, and they just happened to forget the back door? It's a trap, they want us to go through there."

They hear glass breaking in the back bedroom, and then vibrations in the floor as someone crashes around behind the door. Bill aims his gun down the hallway, his hands shaking so badly that Larry can hear the rifle rattling — then he notices that Bill's finger isn't even on the trigger.

"Beth, see if you can find an opening into the attic."

She shines her flashlight around on the ceiling, searching the kitchen and living room first, and then she spots a small two-foot-wide opening in the hallway — just outside of the bedroom door where all the commotion is coming from. "Larry, it's right there."

Aiming his pistol at the door, he starts inching closer to the hallway. "Bill, drop your gun, I don't want you shooting me by mistake." After hesitating for a moment, Bill finally lowers his rifle, and Larry steps into the hallway and reaches up to grab the loop hanging from the door. When he does though, the floor creaks a little under his weight, and the person in the bedroom starts pounding against the door, then rattling the unlocked knob. Just as Larry grabs the handle to keep it from turning, he hears a gunshot from behind him, and then nothing but a loud ringing in his ears as he realizes that Bill fired his gun through the door.

"What the hell are you doing?" Larry screams at him.

"They're gonna get out!"

"You could've killed me!" Holding onto the door knob with one hand, he reaches up and grabs the loop on the ceiling, then pulls it down to lower the stairs that lead to the attic. "Beth, can you help with the stairs?"

"Are you sure you can hold the door closed?" she asks, as she unfolds the staircase and feels the cold draft coming from the attic space above.

"They're barely twisting it," he tells her quietly. "It's more noise than anything." He loosens his grip on the knob, and then lets go of it briefly to see if they're actually trying to open the door — but as he suspected, they're barely turning the handle, and simply trying to make as much noise as possible. "Beth, Christine, take a couple of guns out of the bags and put 'em in your pockets, then load the bags into the attic. We might have to make a run for it."

After taking two extra revolvers out of the bag, and a few boxes of ammo, Beth carries one of the bags into the attic, and when she turns around to grab another one from Christine, she sees Bill grabbing one of them and then backing up toward the back door. "Bill, what're you doing?"

"I'm not going up there. I'm not walking past that door..."

"You can't go out that back door... Like Larry said, it's a trap."

"Come on baby, let's go," Bill says, pulling on Rachel's arm.

Beth hands the bag in her hands back to Christine, then aims her gun at Bill. She can see the fear and indecisiveness in Rachel's eyes, but Travis only looks tired, like he has all night — in fact, he still hasn't said a single word the entire time they've been together. "Bill, drop the bag, you're not stealing our shit!"

"Let him have it, we won't be able to carry it on the run anyway," Larry tells her.

"Thank you, we won't forget it," Rachel says, backing up toward the back door with Bill.

"You're gonna die out there, Rachel — all three of you," Beth says.

Bill points his gun at Beth for only a second, his body full of nervous twitches, then he opens the back door and looks around quickly before pulling Rachel out the door with him. Travis follows, not bothering to close the door behind him.

"Come on, we have to go!" Larry yells, watching Christine hand another bag to Beth. When she turns around to pick another one up, Larry sees a middle-aged man standing in the open doorway, holding an iron pipe in one hand, and a coil of heavy rope in the other. "Christine, forget the other bags, get into the attic, now!"

Beth, who was already halfway up the ladder, pulls herself all the way up, then reaches down and helps Christine. Larry lets go of the door knob and grabs a third bag before climbing the stairs himself, and sees the bedroom door open just as he makes it to the top. The person who comes out, a boy who's probably only barely a teenager, starts crawling up the stairs at a frantic pace, losing his footing repeatedly as he slips on the dusty steps. Larry sits down on the ceiling joist to steady himself, then takes his gun out of the holster and shoots the boy in the head — dropping his lifeless body onto the carpeted floor below. He carefully climbs down a few steps, looking down into the room for the other man, but he doesn't see any sign of him. Holstering the gun again, he reaches down and folds the stairs back up, then carries the cord back up to the top and pulls the entire mechanism into place again — filling the attic space with near complete darkness.

"Okay, now what?" Beth asks.

"We need to get to the outside access panel — or wait until morning, whichever doesn't get us killed I guess." He turns on a flashlight, then uses his pocketknife to cut the pull cord from the stairs to prevent anyone below from opening the hatch. "Watch your step up here, we need to move a quietly as possible."

Over most of the attic, the only place that you can safely place any weight is on the ceiling joists, which have insulation installed between them. Running from the stairs to the far wall on the east side of the house, however, is a thin line of plywood that leads to what looks like another doorway in the wall. Beth is leading the way, crawling across the cold, dusty boards, and dragging a bag that's filled with guns, food and medical supplies. When she reaches the doorway, she can hear screams coming from outside, and a voice that sounds like someone pleading for help. She turns around and looks at Larry, who shakes his head and shrugs.

"We have to keep moving, sis, they were warned."

She opens the door, which sits about twelve feet off the ground with no way to get down, then spots a group of people walking away from the house below her. "These people don't move like the others." she whispers. "They're not uncoordinated at all, or stupid by the looks of it."

"Is it clear under you?"

Beth leans over and stares down at the gravel parking area below, seeing nobody in any direction. "It looks okay, yeah. I think they're off chasing Bill and his family."

"Well, at least he's useful for something." Larry picks up his bag, which is filled with the same general assortment of supplies as the others, then swings it over for Beth to take. When he does though, he hits the corner of the bag against one of the trusses and sends dust flying through the air. Worse yet, several bats take flight and start fluttering around the attic, one of them landing on Christine's jacket sleeve. Panicking, she begins slapping at the rodent, and ends up falling backward onto the insulation.

"Don't move..." Larry tells her calmly. "Just reach out and take my hand, okay?"

She slowly reaches out for him, but she's still too far away. As she leans forward to get closer, she hears a dull cracking sound, and the next thing she knows she's sitting in the middle of the kitchen floor, facing an open back door and a group of people staring at her from across the parking area.

"Christine, just stay put, I'll come get you," Larry says from above.

She stands up and reaches for her gun, but it's not there — neither of them are.

"Larry, is my gun up there?"

"I don't see it anywhere. Here, take mine..."

"No, it must be down here somewhere." She looks around the room at the broken pieces of drywall and insulation, then she hears the sound of crunching gravel coming from outside. Turning to the door again, she sees a crowd of men and women moving closer — one of them carrying a rifle that looks suspiciously similar to Bill's.

"Over here..." comes a whisper from behind her.

Christine back away from the door, then turns her head, seeing a shadow standing in the front door. "Beth?"

"Follow me, they're getting closer."

With the people getting closer, she runs out the door and into the rain without hesitating, then looks around for Beth. After seeing movement around the front corner of the house, she follows and ends up running to the trailer next door, hiding behind a car that's sitting under the carport. She looks around again, peering out into the trailer park for any sign of Beth or Larry, and then she hears breathing coming from behind her.

"Don't go out there, they'll see you."

Christine recognizes the voice, and it's not Beth. She slowly squats down and looks back, and sees Amanda sitting behind her, calmly watching the scene in front of them.

"We can't stay here for long," Amanda tells her. "They're hunting you."

"They're hunting you too."

"They don't even know I'm here."

Something about the girl sends a chill up Christine's spine, and she wonders for a moment whether she's safer here or out there with the hunters.

"Where should we go?"

"There's a big barn on the other side of the cranberry bogs. I used to come here with my mother when they'd harvest the crop."

"Is it safe?"

"It's safer than here."

Christine can see several of the hunters coming out of the front door of the house, then spreading out in different directions. One of them, a young woman wearing filthy, torn clothes and no shoes, is paying close attention to the ground, and it suddenly occurs to Christine that she must be looking for footprints. She noticed that Amanda was running on the gravel and concrete sidewalks when they made their way here, but in her panicked state she accidentally ran across the sparsely green lawn.

"Stay still, and don't make a sound," Amanda whispers.

The woman kneels down and looks closely at what's undoubtedly a footprint in the mud, then lifts her head up and stares at the carport, as if she's looking directly at Christine. Feeling her whole body shaking, she reaches into her pocket and takes out the knife that her dad gave her the day they left home, then unfolds the three-inch blade and holds it at her side. She turns her head to see if Amanda has armed herself with anything, but to her surprise, there's nobody there. Her heart starts to race as she looks around frantically for her, but there's no sign of her anywhere — and the woman looking for them is starting to move closer. Through the rain and darkness, she spots two people running toward the highway, staying low and each carrying a bag. She knows immediately that it's Larry and Beth, but she's afraid to scream for help, not knowing how many other people are nearby, or whether they could actually hear her through the storm anyway. As they disappear from sight, she stands up and faces the woman in front of her. From the expression on her face, Christine is certain that the woman sees her, there's an evil grin plastered on it as she holds her arms straight out.

It's not until she gets to within about twenty feet that she can hear the woman wheezing, which is the first indication they've seen that these people are actually infected like all of the others. The woman laughs when Christine points her knife at her, and then her expression turns serious, even painful — and a second later she slowly slumps to the ground, and Amanda appears standing behind her, holding a bloody hunting knife in her hand. Christine looks at her own knife, which is shaking violently in her hands, then carefully folds it back up and puts it in her pocket.

"Come on, the others are following Larry and Beth," Amanda says.

Still crippled with fear, Christine forces herself to move, following

Amanda across the trailer park to a pathway that heads east toward the bogs. When they reach a thicket of underbrush beside them, Amanda pulls her inside of it, snagging her skin with blackberry thorns and stinging nettles. She reaches down to free her coat from one of the vines, and Amanda holds her arm still — pointing at a small wooden bridge down the path that crosses over the cranberry bog to a farm on the other side. At first she thinks that Amanda must be pointing out the barn that they're trying to reach, which she can see on the other side of the bridge — but then she spots two men heading toward them on their side of the bog, both of them dragging a body through the mud. When they reach the edge of the water, they both drop the body on the ground and then begin removing the person's clothes.

"They're still alive, I can see them moving," Christine whispers.

"It's one of the scourge."

"The scourge?"

"It's what my dad called the people dying from the virus — he said they were the scourge of humanity."

After one of the men walks away, leaving the other to finish undressing the person, they return in only a few minutes carrying an ax. Christine looks away as he raises the ax over his head, but she can still hear the blunt sound of it hitting something, and the scream that follows. She looks up at Amanda, who's still staring at them, her mood seemingly unaffected by the brutality of the scene. Finally, after the third swing, the cries suddenly stop, leaving only the sound of the blade and subtle splashing of water — and then nothing.

"Come on, they're leaving," Amanda says, pulling Christine's hand as they emerge from the brush and back into the open.

Still heading toward the barn, Christine stares straight ahead as they cross over the bridge and past the spot where the person was butchered. Even then, however, something still catches her attention further out in the water. A bright yellow shirt is floating on the surface, surrounded by every color imaginable. She stops halfway across the bridge, looking over the side at the flooded cranberry bog below, and sees countless articles of clothing beneath the surface, stretching out as far as she can see in the darkness of night.

"Hurry up..."

Christine sees Amanda motioning for her to follow, then watches as the young girl runs to the front of the barn and pulls the massive sliding door open, then disappears inside. As she steps off of the bridge and heads to the barn herself, she hears the sound of screaming coming from her right, near a cluster of smaller buildings. The instant she hears it, she knows exactly what it is, and exactly who it's coming from, but she also knows there's nothing she can do for Bill. As she waits and listens for any sign of Rachel or Travis, Amanda suddenly yanks her arm and pulls her inside the barn, then closes the door behind her.

"Amanda?" she whispers quietly, seeing nothing but darkness around her.

"I'm right next to you — don't move."

She hears the strike of a match, and then sees a small candle burning, illuminating Amanda's pale, gaunt face as she moves through a maze of farm equipment that's been stored in the wide main aisle in front of them. Trying to keep up and close to the faint light of the candle, Christine follows her up a steep and narrow staircase that leads to the hayloft. She has a feeling that Amanda has been here before, and much more recently than she's letting on.

"Do you know where you're going?" she asks the girl, who sits down in front of a small opening in the side of the loft. It looks out over most of the town, although you can't see much of anything in the darkness. "How did you find this place?"

"There's about thirty of them I think, maybe more."

"Who? Those people?"

"The hunters."

Christine sits down close to Amanda, trying not to make her uncomfortable by looking directly at her. She's still mindful that she has a a rather large knife in her hand, and that she clearly knows how to use it. From this high up she can see the tops of the dunes in the distance, lit up by the bright sand in the partially obscured moonlight, and a few people walking around on the highway and side streets throughout the town — but most of them that are visible are gathered around one place, a metal building that's only a stone's throw from the barn they're hiding in, the same building that Bill's screams are coming from. Every now and then, one of them enters the building, and she can hear the horrible cries for help even more distinctly than before. None of them, however, ever come out.

"Have you ever seen anything like these people?" she asks Amanda.

"There were a few hunters in Westport for a while, but they didn't last long."

"What happened to them?"

"I killed one of them, Curtis killed another, and the other killed himself."

"He committed suicide?"

"He poured gasoline all over himself, then set it on fire. He was a nice man before the virus."

"You knew him? That must've been difficult."

"He ran the cafe down the street from our house — we used to go there every Sunday after church."

Feeling cold again now that they're not running, Christine covers her head with the hood of her coat, trying to protect her ears from the bitter cold air in the loft. She has no idea what time it is, but she knows that sunrise can't be that far off — a glow is already showing in the sky to the east. For some reason, whether it's a severe lack of sleep,

or a strange sense of security from her new traveling companion —
she suddenly feels more at ease around Amanda. She looks at her
closely, studying her face and hands, which are the only parts of her
that are actually visible, and sees almost no signs of sickness other
than being a little pale and emaciated. She looks hungry, and cold, but
she doesn't look like the other infected people that she's seen. "You
look better than when I saw you last — healthier somehow."

"I'm feeling a little better, I'm not as sore as I was."

"So did you really only have allergies, or was that just a story?"

She looks up at Christine with a deranged, homicidal stare — then
places the tip of her knife against Christine's side. "You ask a lot of
questions."

"I know, I'm sorry." Frozen with fear, she can feel the blade
piercing into her skin. "Please, don't hurt me. I didn't mean anything
by it."

Easing up on the knife, Amanda places it on the rough-cut
floorboards once again, but still keeps it in her grip. "You should get
some sleep before the sun comes up — we have a long walk
tomorrow."

"Where are we going?"

"Back to Westport, to find Ben." She grabs Christine's hand,
squeezing it with an amazing amount of strength, then gently runs
the blade across the top of it, watching as a small, thin line of blood
falls onto the floorboards below. "Don't even think about leaving. If
you try, I'll kill you — slowly."

After her hand is released, Christine manages to climb to her feet
again, then finds some loose, moldy hay in the corner of the loft. She
lies down on it, trying to place as much pressure onto her new wound
as possible, and begins watching Amanda from the safety of darkness.
Whether she's feeling physically stronger or not, the girl is
deteriorating, both emotionally and mentally. She closes her eyes,

trying her best to block out the painful cries coming from the next building over, and the painful throbbing from her own hand — and then she hears Amanda's voice, speaking so softly part of the time that it's hard to understand what she's saying. Still not able to comprehend all of what's she's talking about, she does manage to hear her ask Ben a question, and the soft voice replies with an answer. The girl is speaking as both of them, with Ben's voice comforting and encouraging her. Christine opens her eyes just a little, wondering if she should just pretend to be asleep, or make a run for it while Amanda's back is turned to her. As her eyes adjust to the darkness again, however, she sees her still sitting in the same spot, only now she's facing Christine, still speaking in the same soft, soothing voice.

CHAPTER 23
GRAYLAND: DAY 6

In the last few days before his wife died, Larry could feel his own will to live growing weaker as Jennifer slowly slipped away from him. Sitting at her bedside day after day was like torture, listening to her struggle for every breath as the sickness quickly took over her body. In the darkest hours of his despair, he seriously considered committing suicide after she was gone — he even hoped that he would catch the virus from her, saving himself from having to live without her.

When they were first married, back when their future plans seemed more like a reality than a dream, time seemed to pass by effortlessly, without any of the worries or anxiety that normally only plague the older generations. They knew that they had time to make mistakes and shirk responsibilities, youth had given them that opportunity — but as the years passed by, with none of those ambitious dreams coming true, that same carefree spirit and exuberance for life had begun to resemble laziness, which is something that Larry learned to embrace with an almost passionate enthusiasm. Whether any of this ever bothered Jennifer or not, Larry will never know, since she never pestered him or complained the entire time they were married — even during the months when their income was non-existent. As he cared for her in those final days, there was a part of him, buried beneath the grief and heartache, that felt guilty for missing out on the experiences that were now an impossibility, for both her and himself — the world just wasn't going to be the same without her. As deep as his depression was, which seemed insurmountable at the time, he told himself that he couldn't leave this world until Beth was safe. Looking back on it though, he knows there was a more selfish reason why he didn't follow through with killing himself — he simply didn't want to die.

After seeing so much death and violence over the last six months, and the anxiety of being hunted by Sean for days on end, Larry thought he knew what true fear was — but he was wrong. The scene that Beth and himself are watching through the windows of the local elementary school are beyond horrific, so much so that Beth is now facing the empty chalk board on the wall behind them instead. The people, whether native to Grayland or not, have taken over the town, and are now hunting anything and everything that moves. An unorganized horde of individuals is now scattered across the area, capturing the few infected people still around, but also dogs, cats, and even a wild rabbit that was unlucky enough to be caught by one of them. The smaller prey are usually eaten or mutilated immediately, but the people are always dragged alive toward the bogs, which is gratefully out of sight from the school.

"I don't know how you can keep watching that," Beth says, lying down on a table in the corner of the classroom, out of sight from the windows.

"I know, I don't know why I'm watching either."

"Yes you do, you're hoping to see Christine out there. I think it's great, I just don't know how you can handle seeing that stuff."

"I can't imagine that she's still alive — not after tonight."

"Whether she is or not, you're not gonna be able to do anything about it, even if you do spot her. It's just too dangerous." She can barely see the outline of his body in the other corner of the room,

192

sitting in the shadows next to a wall of windows that face the town. "The sun is gonna be up soon — you should get some rest before daylight."

"I'm fine."

"You can't be, you've been up for two days. Do it for me, okay?" She sees him stand up and move to the hardwood floor, groaning as he eases down on the hard surface. Relieved that he listened to her, she closes her eyes and starts to drift off, then hears the sound of several gunshots somewhere outside. Seeing Larry already standing up again, she jumps off of the table and joins him. "Do you see where it's coming from?"

"Over there, the house we just came from," he says, pointing to the house in the trailer park, which is only a short distance away. A man and woman are exiting the home, each with pistols in their hands. The man is firing his, apparently at random targets around the town, but the woman is simply walking behind him. "Those are our guns, from the bags that we left in there."

When both of the man's guns are finally out of ammunition, he turns around and tries to grab one from the woman, but instead of giving in, she backs up and takes a swing at him.

"Give me the fucking gun!" they can hear the man screaming as he dodges her attacks.

Larry and Beth look at each other, surprised to hear him actually speaking coherently. The woman says something back, which is too quiet to understand, and then tries to duck as the man picks up something from the ground and hits her with it. She falls to the ground instantly, and he climbs on top of her and continues to pummel her with whatever the object is, then takes one of the guns from her hand and aims it directly at her head. Beth looks away before the sound of the gunshot is heard, and then makes her way back to the table as the shots continue — stopping only when the gun

193

is obviously empty.

"He's done, he's dragging her back to..."

"I don't want to know," Beth interrupts. "I can't take it anymore."

Larry pulls a chair out from one of the desks and sits down, laying his head down on the hard surface of the desk. "These are even more uncomfortable than I remember." Lifting his head up again, he starts going through the two bags they managed to take with them, laying everything out to take inventory. "We have to decide what to do next."

"I thought that was pretty obvious. We wait until the sun comes up, then get the hell out of here — back to the cabin."

"What about Christine?"

She lets out a long sigh, but it sounds more like a groan. "I have a husband to get back to, and the longer we stay in this town, the more likely we're going to die here. Besides, she already knows where the cabin is, if she's still alive she'll find us."

In some cold, inhumane corner of Larry's brain, he knows that she's right, but the thought of leaving a grieving teenager alone in this town makes him sick to his stomach. He knows deep down that it's something that will haunt him for the rest of his life.

"Do you agree?" Beth asks.

"No, I don't... but I guess that doesn't matter, does it?"

"No, I guess it doesn't."

Larry looks at the inventory in front of him, dismayed at what little they have left. Counting what they already have on their person, they now have six guns between them, one rifle and five pistols. The real problem is ammunition and food, since most of it was apparently in the other bags. Despite their intention of splitting everything equally between the bags, preparing for an occasion just like this one, somehow in the chaos and confusion their supplies ended up concentrated — leaving them with a few dozen extra rounds for two of the guns, and barely enough food for another day.

"We need more food," he tells her.

"I can make it to Cohassett without food — we don't need anymore than what we have."

"What we have is an energy bar and some crackers, it's not enough." He waits a moment for a reaction, but she just lies there, staring at the ceiling. "I'm gonna find the cafeteria — it might still have some food, or something else we can use."

"Like what, bullets?" She watches him pack everything back into the bags, then turn around and walk away, toward the door to the main hallway. "Hey, you can't just leave me alone..."

"I guess you'd better hurry up then. Don't forget your bag."

Turning on a flashlight, Larry aims it down the trash-filled hallway, where piles of debris are shoved up against the lockers that line the corridor. The debris itself is a strange mixture of things — from household items like small furniture and kitchen utensils, to clothing, car parts, and even an old recliner sitting upside down next to the water fountains. It's all filthy, with old, rotten leaves and dirt mixed into the mess.

"We could probably use some batteries for the flashlights too," Larry says, noticing that the beam is becoming weaker.

"This place might not be as secure as we thought. They've obviously been in here, look at all this garbage..."

Larry stops and shines his light at the floor, then uses his foot to clear away some of the trash.

"I see a sign that says the cafeteria is two doors down," Beth says.

"Look at this..." He reaches into a pile of clothing and pulls out a shotgun, then checks to see if it's loaded. The barrel is covered in something that looks like dried blood.

"Anything in it?"

He closes it back up, examining the markings on the side. "No, it's empty. It's a twelve gauge, semi-auto though, it could come in handy."

"It looks like someone was beat to death with it, the barrel might not even be straight."

Ignoring her, he holds onto the gun and continues down the hallway, stopping in front of the double doors of the cafeteria. He looks through the windows of the door first as she steps back and takes her gun out, then he quietly pushes one of the doors open and just stands there.

"Why aren't you going in?" Beth asks him.

"It smells in there."

"Smells like what?"

"Death." Holding his hand over his nose, he enters the room slowly, carefully looking everything over with the light. There's bones everywhere, along with more piles of clothing and other personal belongings. The floor under his feet is sticky and stained red from the blood covering it, some of it rather recent by the looks of it. There's flies too, lots of them, creating a loud buzzing sound toward the other side of the room — and a constant dripping sound coming from the area in the back.

"Man, you weren't kidding about the smell..."

He looks behind and sees Beth tiptoeing across the floor, still holding her gun in her hand.

"Just watch where you point that thing, I really don't wanna get shot again," Larry says.

"Maybe we should use my flashlight for a while, we really shouldn't run either of them completely down."

"Yeah, that's probably a good idea."

He pulls out his pistol after she turns her light on, watching as her light fills the room with a bright glow, illuminating everything in a crisp white color that seems to only accentuate the darkened blood and filth throughout the space. Along the walls, stacked at least six feet in the air, are over a dozen piles of human bodies, all of them in various stages of decomposition — from bones to freshly killed. She shines the light onto the floor and sees a stream of blood running from several of the piles to a drain in the middle of the floor, and more corpses spread out on the cafeteria counter on the opposite wall.

"We need to get out of here, Larry..." Beth says, backing up toward the open door that they just came through.

"Shh..." Larry hushes her, grabbing her by the wrist that's holding the flashlight and aiming it down to the floor.

Beth listens closely to the silence, then shuts the light off. "Did you hear something?" she whispers.

"I thought I heard a..." He stops mid-sentence, hearing the sound of creaking hinges from a door somewhere in the kitchen ahead. They both crouch to the floor when another door opens and floods the room with daylight — and they watch from the shadows as two men come through the doorway, dragging something behind them. When they pick it up and set it down onto the counter, Larry and Beth can both see that it's the naked body of a woman. Larry's heart starts beating rapidly at the thought that it might be Christine, but when they flip her over and expose her face, he can plainly see that the woman is much older. Feeling a tap on his shoulder, he looks behind and sees Beth backing out of the room, careful not to touch the floor with anything but her shoes. He does the same, but realizes once he starts moving that he accidentally set his bag down in the grime when he dropped to the floor. As he exits the room and follows Beth back down the hallway toward the classroom, he can hear the sound of crashing and yelling coming from the kitchen — and then footsteps. He stops and drops the bag, getting both his gun and his flashlight ready as he peers into the darkness. The footsteps, slow and heavy, get louder as they approach the door, and then it suddenly slams shut. Larry turns his head, and can just make out Beth's silhouette facing him about ten feet away — when he hears the door slowly opening again, and a low, raspy laugh as someone steps into the hallway and begins walking toward them.

CHAPTER 24
COHASSETT BEACH: DAY 6

Sarah looks out the window toward the highway, where the sky is beginning to brighten from the rising sun in the east, but she's still unable to see any signs of people through the thick fog that's rolling in over the dunes behind her. Aside from the much welcomed light outside though, the wind and rain continue to pelt the small house, even more than yesterday it seems. The night inside the house was silent for the most part, with only a brief moment of commotion coming from the front porch as one of the infected tried unsuccessfully to open the door — but there was absolutely no sign of Jake, either on the highway or the perimeter road in back of the house. Hearing the rumbling stomachs of the boys behind her, she turns around and faces Curtis, who looks exhausted and defeated, but he's still wide-awake.

"Did you get any sleep?" Sarah whispers.

"I think I got a few minutes."

"If you wanna watch the road, I'm gonna search the house for anything else that's edible."

He stands up painfully, hearing and feeling his joints cracking as they protest any further activity. His legs feel like dead weights after the stress of last night, not to mention being tied up for so long — but he manages to make it to the chair next to Sarah, his eyes still adjusting to the washed out color of gray mist outside the window.

When she stands up and grabs her side, wincing in pain, Curtis stops her and lifts up her sweatshirt, revealing a large bruise just above her hip. "Did he do that to you?"

"No, I got it in the cabin, trying to get that trap door open."

"What happened when I was knocked out? We haven't really talked about it. Did he hurt you?"

She stays silent for a moment, wishing that the last two days could be forgotten entirely. "There was some pushing and shoving, but it was mostly just threats and intimidation. The worst part of it was leaving you guys." She leans in close, whispering as quietly as possible. "Matt was so scared that he wet himself, I felt horrible for him."

"What about Ben?"

"He didn't really react, not until I started to leave."

"Well, he's been through a lot lately — I'm just sorry I couldn't be there for you..."

"You couldn't have done anything anyway. We're alive, that's all that matters." She pulls away from him and walks to the door, then turns around. "If I don't find any food, we should really think about moving once this fog clears."

"We should be able to find something around here. I don't think we ever searched any of these houses."

"That doesn't mean that somebody else didn't."

"Like Amanda?"

"Or Jake... We know that he's been around for a while."

The house outside of the bedroom is still fairly dark, with cheap, fake mahogany paneling darkening the walls and ceiling, and curtains over most of the windows. After opening the curtains in the living room to let more light in, she discovers that the glass is covered with so much dust and mildew that it would be nearly impossible for anyone to see them from the outside. Unfortunately, the illumination does little to improve the looks of the room, with trash and clutter obscuring much of the worn-out and stained carpet beneath it. When she walks into the kitchen, which is only marginally cleaner, she sees boxes of belongings packed up and left on the table and counter, some of them only partially full. She checks each of the boxes, dumping the contents onto the floor and sifting through everything, but the only food she finds is a can of powdered cocoa mix shoved deep into the corner of one of the cupboards. Not caring to even check the expiration date, she slips it into her bag and walks into the next room — pausing for a moment when she smells the air inside, a horrible mixture of perfume and foulness. The moment she enters, she knows there's something different about it, aside from the odor. The room is clean and tidy, with toys and dolls lined up perfectly on the shelves along the far wall. Lying on the bed, still wrapped tightly in a pink-colored blanket that seems much too large for the mattress, is a small skeleton that looks to be a few years younger than Ben. On the nightstand next to it is an empty glass and pill bottles, and a bag of potato chips leaned against the lamp.

"Find anything useful?" Curtis asks from behind her.

"Half of a can of cocoa mix, a bag of potato chips..." She checks the bag, relieved to find that it's still sealed up — then she looks at the bed again. "...and this little girl."

"Any sign of her parents?"

"No, they must have left after she died. Can you imagine what that would've been like?"

Curtis sits down in a small child-sized chair in the corner of the room, looking at the mummified remains on the bed. "What's really strange is that all of this was happening right down the road from us, and we had absolutely no idea."

She looks out the window, seeing the dense fog continuing to move into the area — then she looks back at the girl, noticing a ribbon tied in her light blond hair. "No one will ever know what her name was — do you know how incredibly sad that is?"

"There might be something around here that..."

"And the worst part is, nobody would care even if they did know — including us." she says, cutting him off. She sits down on the floor, afraid to sit on the bed. "What are we gonna do, Curtis?"

"I think we're gonna have to brave the fog and search the next house, since it's apparently not lifting today."

"I don't mean today, I mean after today."

From the look on her face, he can tell that her stress level is reaching the breaking point, and that his own face probably doesn't look much better. "Whatever we do, we have to stay together, no matter what."

"We can't stay around here anymore, not until these people are gone."

"We need food, and medicine, and weapons — we can't go wandering into the wilderness without supplies."

Sarah stands up and opens the bag of chips, savoring the salty taste of the slightly stale crisps. "We had all of that, and it still didn't do us any good."

Wearing dry clothes that they took from the house, the Lockwoods walk north on the perimeter road, all of them painfully aware that they're getting close to Westport once again — and that Jake could still be looking for them. Although they can't see very far through the fog, one advantage is that sound travels extraordinarily well, and twice now they've heard somebody toward the highway talking to themselves. Mindful of that, the four of them walk in silence from house to house, looking for something that's remained relatively untouched. When they come to a newer double-wide mobile, Curtis notices two cars parked in the driveway, and boarded up windows across the front.

"These guys didn't leave," he says, his voice low. "Which means they didn't take anything out of the house."

"How do we get in?" Matt asks.

After trying the handle on the front door first, they walk around to the back where there's a tall chain-link fence around the backyard. Curtis taps his hand on it before opening the gate, looking around for a dog that might still be around. They see another line of secured windows along the back wall, and a sliding glass door that's covered in scraps of wood that are put into place from the inside. There's also a small animal door beside it, with either an arm or leg bone sticking out of it. Curtis kicks the bones aside, then lies down in front of it and looks inside, seeing mostly complete darkness, and a few more human bones scattered across the kitchen floor.

"There's no way you can fit in there..." Sarah tells him.

He tries squeezing through in every possible way, but she's right, there's no way his shoulders could possibly fit. He stands up and looks the rest of the place over, hoping to find another way in.

"Let's keep moving," Sarah says. "I don't feel comfortable staying in one place for too long."

"There's food inside, and bottles of water — I can see them on the counter."

"What if there's still people in there?"

"Judging from the bones, I'd say there probably isn't."

"I can fit," Ben says.

Curtis pats him on the shoulder, looking up at the roof. "That's okay, buddy, I think I can get in through the skylight up there." Seeing no ladder anywhere in sight, he starts climbing the fence where it attaches to the side of the mobile, his ascent more awkward than he anticipated. "Wait for me out front. Just hide in front of those cars."

When he gets to the top and sees his wife and sons make their way around the corner, he walks along the roof to the skylight on the other side. Looking through it, he sees a master bedroom below, and a bed directly under him. First checking to see how secure it is to the roof, he stomps his foot onto it a few times, each time harder than the last — but it doesn't budge. After another series of repeated blows, he finally puts everything he has into it, making more noise than he intended to, but the plastic skylight gradually begins to breakdown and crack. When it gets to the point that he can reach down and remove most of the window, he stands back up and looks over the edge at his family. Behind them, perhaps a hundred feet away, is a group of six people looking back at him, and even more moving slowly through the fog from the north. He motions for Sarah to stay quiet, indicating that there's something behind her, then he scrambles through the broken window and onto the dusty mattress below.

There's enough light in the bedroom to see most everything, and besides being dusty it's actually in decent shape. Opening the door into the living room though, is a completely different story. Through the darkness he can still make out the battered walls and tossed furniture, and in his mad rush to the front door he can feel his feet tripping over bones scattered across the floor. Reaching the front wall, he desperately searches for the handle, but finds what feels like a skull instead. As his eyes adjust to the darkness, he manages to spot the doorknob, directly behind the remains of someone that's leaned up against the door. The moment he unlocks and turns the handle, Sarah and the boys come crashing through.

"Close the door!" Sarah screams, falling onto the carpeted floor behind him.

Curtis slams the door shut just as somebody tries pushing it open. He locks it, then notices a board next to him that he slides down into two crudely made brackets on either side of the doorway —

someone's obvious attempt at a barricade that he hopes will hold up.

Sarah stands up, still shaking, and checks Ben out the best she can in the dark.

"What happened?" Curtis asks her.

"They came running up behind us. One of them grabbed Ben's jacket, but I don't see any marks."

"I'm fine, she didn't hurt me," Ben responds.

"Do you see a flashlight anywhere?" Sarah asks.

Curtis and Matt spread out and begin searching the living room, both of them careful not to touch anything. The only light is coming through a small window in the top of the front door, and some from the broken skylight in the next room. The carpeting under their feet is crunchy in places, and when Matt picks up a flashlight that's sitting in a recliner and turns it on, they find out exactly why. There's a streak of dried blood soaked into the carpeting that runs from the front entrance all the way to the kitchen, where the stain widens out and covers a large portion of the room. Curtis takes the light from Matt and helps Sarah search Ben's body for any wounds or scratches, and when they're satisfied that he wasn't harmed, he takes the pocketknife out and begins looking around the place more thoroughly.

"You guys stay here, we still don't know if the house is empty."

"Curtis, shine the light on the door," Sarah says.

As soon as the beam hits the doorway, the mood in the room darkens even further. Not only are there scratch marks on the door itself, but the carpet in front of it is torn to shreds, leaving the subfloor beneath it exposed, with fingernails still deeply embedded into the wood. The wall next to the door is damaged as well, with part of the drywall ripped away and the insulation partway pulled out from behind it.

"The door was just locked, wasn't it?" Sarah asks Curtis.

"Yeah, it opened fine — they must have been sick." He walks into the next room, leaving his wife and sons still staring at the skeleton crumpled at their feet.

Between the master bedroom and the kitchen is another bedroom, and other than having a door nearly ripped off of it's hinges, there doesn't seem to be anything out of the ordinary inside — just a typical mixture of video games, baseballs and clothing, all once belonging to an older boy by the looks of everything. Seeing the baseballs and catcher's mitt on the window sill, Curtis looks around a bit closer for a bat, but doesn't see one anywhere. On the other side of the kitchen is a laundry room, and yet another exterior door that's secured with plywood and boards. When he walks back into the kitchen, he finds the baseball bat lying on the floor — or what's left of it anyway. The end of it is broken off, leaving a sharp splintered edge that's stained red with blood.

"What the hell happened in here?" Sarah asks, joining him.

"I don't know, but there's a lot of food in here." He shines the light around at the counters, which are completely covered with dry goods and cans of vegetables and meat. "They were obviously planning on staying here for the duration."

Sarah picks up some boxes of cereal from the stove-top and sets them on the table in the middle of the room, which is already covered with various canned food and bottled water. Bending down with her ear to the stove, she turns a knob and then listens closely to the burner before shutting it off again. "The gas is still on."

"It must be propane. Let's hope there's still plenty left in the tank."

"Dad, I think they're at the window now!" Matt yells, terrified by the rattling glass panes.

"I know Matt, but they can't get in through the plywood. This place is pretty secure."

Sarah leans in close to him and whispers... "We got in..."

"Most of those things aren't coordinated enough to open a door, let alone climb a fence." He opens up a bottle of water and takes a drink, handing the rest of it to Sarah, then walks into the living room and gives the flashlight to Matt. "I want you two to search the place, every box and drawer."

"What are we searching for?" Ben asks.

"Batteries, weapons, medicine, flashlights, whatever you think might be useful — and bags, something we can take with us."

"We aren't staying?"

"No, we need to get away from town, at least for a while."

"I'll check the boxes in the kitchen, you guys look everywhere else." Sarah tells them, as she drags a gallon of bleach from under the sink.

"Disinfecting everything?" Curtis asks.

"As much as I can." Pouring some of the bleach into a pot, she looks around for something to dilute it, but she doesn't want to waste their limited supply of bottled water on something they can't drink. "Check the toilet tanks, see if they have any water in them," she tells Curtis.

Just as he turns to leave the room, the banging on the front door suddenly stops, leaving the house eerily quiet. They both stay silent, listening carefully as a new sound comes from the backyard — the distinctive rattling of a chain link fence. Curtis looks out through the thin spaces between the boards that cover the sliding door, and sees a man and a woman attempting to climb up onto the roof in the same spot that he did. He watches them for a for a moment, convinced that they're incapable of making it to the top — and then he hears something overhead, stomping across the length of the roof toward the skylight. He runs toward the open master bedroom door, almost slipping on the trash-covered floor as he passes through the kitchen, then grabs the doorknob and waits, watching the hole in the ceiling as raindrops continue to fall onto the mattress below. As soon as he sees a shadow appear in the opening, he slams the door shut and braces his body against the jam.

"Find something to hold this shut!" he shouts to Sarah.

"Like what?" she responds, her voice panicked.

"Rope, chain, anything...!" he screams, hearing something drop onto the bed inside the room. Watching as his family desperately searches for something useful, he looks at the front door and realizes that it's their one and only exit out of the house, and for a moment he considers the possibility that they could just make a run for it if necessary — but then Sarah returns from the laundry room with a small spool of yellow rope in her hands. As the people begin slamming their fists against the front entrance again, the sound of someone laughing can be heard through the thin, hollow door between him and the bedroom.

CHAPTER 25
GRAYLAND: DAY 6

Still pretending to be asleep, Christine can feel a strong, damp wind blowing across the hayloft floor, and when she opens her eyes she sees the hint of actual daylight coming from the doors at the end of the barn. The screaming and yelling from next door stopped a while ago, right after the hunters were apparently driven back into seclusion by the sun. They've been replaced by the tranquil sound of birds chirping in the trees, and the wind rattling the wooden rafters and roofing over her head. The entire time that she's been lying here, she's been asking herself what her father might do if he were in this situation — or what advice he might have for her. All of the scenarios running through her head, however, whether she tries to escape or not, end in the same gruesome way — with Amanda eventually killing her.

She turns her head, just far enough to see the girl holding her hostage — but instead of staring at her like she was earlier, Amanda is standing up, looking at the top of the stairs that lead into main aisle of the barn below. Watching her walk slowly across the floor, Christine sits up when she hears the creaking sound of door hinges downstairs.

"Stay here, and don't move," Amanda says firmly, still looking straight ahead.

Christine sits up further, but stays seated as the noises downstairs become even louder. As soon as Amanda disappears around the corner, she considers making a run for it, but it's impossible to tell exactly where the girl is — it's almost as if she floats across the floor, making virtually no sound whatsoever. She slowly climbs off of the pile of hay and stands still for a moment, listening to someone talking downstairs. Part of her hopes that it might be Larry and Beth, but she knows they wouldn't be foolish enough to make a racket like that, and they certainly would've checked the entire place out by now to eliminate any danger. Bending down to pick up a loose board on the floor, she sneaks closer to the top of the stairs, then peeks around the corner into the filtered light below. There's two men standing just inside a pedestrian door beside the main doors, one of them talking nearly non-stop, and the other seemingly ignoring him — then something appears out of nowhere behind the talker, emerging from the shadows so quickly that Christine lets out a gasp. In one fluid motion, Amanda's knife reaches up behind the man and slices through his throat, dropping him to his knees, and giving the young girl an opportunity to drive the knife deep into his back several times before disappearing once again. The other man just stands there, watching as his companion bleeds out in front of him. He smiles as she steps into the light once more, and as he begins walking toward her, she backs up in the direction of the stairs, then stops suddenly when yet another man cuts her off. Although quite certain that she's completely hidden from view, Christine carefully backs away from the top of the staircase as a third man appears, all three of them surrounding Amanda.

Once she's back in the hayloft, she looks around for another way out, one that doesn't involve jumping straight down to the ground. When she hears a loud commotion downstairs though, and the cries of a girl fighting for her life, she panics and climbs out onto the metal roof of the lean-to on the side of the barn. She carefully walks down one of the panels, which are covered in slick mildew and algae — and right before reaching the bottom, her foot slips out from underneath her and sends her sliding the rest of the way down to the ground. Landing on her butt and twisting her ankle, she struggles to catch her breath for a moment, then tries to stand up in the mud-covered paddock beside the barn — a task that would be far easier if she wasn't being pelted by a wind-driven rain.

As she limps along the path leading toward the bog, she passes right next to the neighboring building where she heard the screams the night before. The door is still open, but she can only see a few feet inside of it — the rest being obscured by darkness. There's a stream of blood, however, running from inside the building and down into the swamp below it. She can smell the death and decay coming from the building and the bog as she hurries across the bridge, looking back at the open barn doors only briefly before moving out of sight completely — but she doesn't see either the men or Amanda.

Crouching down, she hides behind some planters next to a trailer in the 'Gentle Breeze' park, the pots overflowing with dead or dying flowers and bushes. She takes a moment to catch her breath and look around, but the only movement around is the fog blowing quickly through the air from the beach. Her mind is spinning in circles trying to figure out what to do next, and she can feel herself trembling as the panic finally sets in. Finding Larry and Beth shouldn't be a problem, or at least that's what she hopes — but the real problem is staying alive long enough to get to their cabin, especially without any weapons. The only guns that she knows of are the ones in the house on the other side of the park, still inside of the bags that they left on the floor — if they're still there that is. Knowing that she'll be exposed once she starts down the sidewalk that winds through the mobile park, she grabs a shovel from out of a nearby shed and then jogs down the path as quickly as she can. With her ankle swelling uncomfortably in her shoe, she finally reaches the house and approaches the front door, a little surprised to see it open, and even more surprised that the curtains on the windows are open as well. The bags are still visible, lying in the exact same spot as they left them — and although one of them appears to be open, she can see at least two pistols on the floor next to it. She climbs the few steps onto the porch, one at a time, then checks to see if the room is empty before entering. Just as she starts to bend down to pick up one of the guns, she hears the floor squeaking in the hallway beside her.

"I wouldn't do that," comes a man's voice.

Christine turns her head and sees a man wearing filthy clothes, probably in his thirties, and holding a rifle that's aimed directly at her head. She stands up and starts to back away toward the doorway, but the man takes the barrel of the gun and closes the door behind her, motioning for her to sit down on the couch. "I'm not armed..." she pleads, with tears running down her cheeks.

"Let's keep it that way for now, okay?" He sits down across from her in an old recliner, then points his gun at the floor instead of her head. "How old are you? You look like you're still a kid."

"Fifteen."

"Yeah, that's what I figured. Are you from around here?"

"No, I'm from Adna."

"Never heard of it."

"It's near Chehalis, east of here."

"And you're alone, all this way from home?"

She nods, afraid of saying too much. He looks friendly enough, but she's heard more than a few of the infected speaking almost normally in the past. Besides, there's something about his eyes, and the way he keeps shifting from side to side that doesn't sit well with her instincts.

"Listen, I'm not gonna hurt you, but I also can't have you running around with a gun either — understand?"

She nods again, noticing that most of his clothes are dry — except his shirt, which is soaked in what must be sweat.

"Have you been in this town for very long?" he asks.

"Two nights I think, it's hard to keep it straight."

"Yeah, I know how that is. I noticed a lot of people when I came into town, and they didn't look all that friendly..."

"They're hunters."

"Hunters?"

"They kill everything in sight, even each other."

"I don't know, they didn't look all that dangerous to me."

He stands up, then aims the rifle at her again, kneeling down to place the pistols back into the bag.

"You look like you're soaking wet," he says, looking her up and down. "There's some clothes in the back bedroom, why don't you go change..."

He motions again with the barrel of the gun for her to get up, then follows her down the hallway. Shivering from the cold and fear, she opens a dresser and pulls out some jeans and a sweatshirt that reek of mildew, but they still smell better than the ones she has on. She turns around and starts to close the door, but he holds it open with his hand, then stands in the hallway watching her.

"Sorry, I can't let you out of my sight. I still don't know you."

"Can I at least cover myself up with a blanket while I change?"

"It's a rough world, sweetheart — just change your fucking clothes so we can get out of here."

Feeling absolutely humiliated and violated, Christine starts taking her clothes off while the man watches her with a smirk on his face. When she's done, he gestures for her to lead the way back out into the living room, then smacks her on the butt as she passes by. Instead of following her, he picks up her clothes and starts searching through them, checking every pocket carefully. It completely slipped her mind that she still had a pocketknife in her pants.

"Mind explaining this?" he asks, unfolding the blade and showing it to her.

"I forgot about it, I didn't..."

"Right, let's go," he says, interrupting her.

"Where are we going?"

"A church, which can't be too hard to find in this town. There doesn't seem to be much to it."

He points to the back door, which she opens and then steps outside, then immediately backs up when she spots an old man coming around the corner of the house. Her captor pushes her out of the way and stands on the back porch, aiming his rifle at the man. As soon as the first shot is fired, she crouches down to the floor and places her hands over her ears as he continues to shoot. Then she sees something reflecting under a piece of broken drywall, the same drywall she broke the day before when she fell out of the ceiling. She glances up at him, then grabs her old revolver from under the debris and slips it into the pocket of her sweatshirt.

"Come on, he's dead."

She stands up again, wondering if her saw her — then she follows him down the steps and into the parking area outside.

"What's your name by the way?" he asks.

"Christine."

"You got a last name, Christine?"

"Not anymore."

The man laughs. "Okay, fair enough. My name is Jake."

"Jake Wilson?"

The man turns around, and from the expression on his face, Christine knows immediately that she shouldn't have said that.

CHAPTER 26
GRAYLAND: DAY 6

Hearing gunshots in the distance, Larry's heart is racing as he begins to back away from the man approaching him in the hallway, his finger lightly squeezing the trigger of his gun. He can already hear that the guy is breathing heavily as they back up past a window, but when the sun appears on his face, Larry can see bruises covering his face and arms, and large, dark open sores. When another man appears from the kitchen behind him, carrying a hatchet in his hand, Larry can see the same grotesque features on his skin as well.

"Drop your gun buddy, we're not gonna hurt you..." the man says, his voice filled with sarcasm. "We just wanna talk..."

"Stop, or I'll shoot you!" Larry responds.

Still moving forward, the man tilts his head to look at Beth, who's staying behind Larry. "There were three of you earlier, where is the other one?"

"Listen, if you stop, we can talk about everything..."

"Oh, you're gonna talk, I'm not worried about that."

Larry can't see a weapon anywhere on the closest man, but his hands are bruised and bloody. "Beth, keep an eye behind us, they might be leading us into a trap."

"Why don't you just shoot them?" she asks quietly.

"He doesn't wanna wake up the entire town, honey, he's not that stupid." the man replies, motioning for the guy behind him to circle around next to him, blocking that end of the hallway off completely.

"This is your last warning, back off!" Larry screams.

"What do you think, Nate, do you think he'll shoot?" the man asks his companion, who looks back and forth between Larry and Beth, with bloodshot eyes that look glazed over and dead. The unarmed man looks back at Larry and smiles. "I call him Nate, but in reality I have no idea what the hell his name is. The crazy fucker hasn't said one single word the entire time I've known him. Then again, not a lot of people around here do."

Larry jumps back as the man takes two quick steps toward him, then he fires three shots into his chest and shoulder, sending him back against the wall. The guy with the hatchet immediately lunges at Larry, but Beth manages to empty her entire clip in his direction, hitting him in the torso and legs and knocking him to the floor. "Beth, reload!" Larry yells at her, keeping his gun aimed at the man he shot, who's still standing upright. Waiting until she finishes loading another clip into her gun, Larry fires one more shot into the man's forehead, then another one into the back of his friend's head before reloading his own pistol. "We need to find someplace to hide before the others come looking."

Beth grabs Larry's arm and pulls him into a classroom behind them, just as more footsteps are heard coming from the cafeteria. After making their way into the room and closing the door behind them, they discreetly look out through a window in the upper half of the door, and see several more dark shadows passing by. They watch for a few more minutes, and then Larry takes a seat at the teacher's desk and tries to catch his breath. "How many did you see?"

"I think there were eight, but I'm not sure." Taking her eyes off of the hallway, she starts reading something on the wall instead.

"What is that?"

"It's an emergency escape map, in case there's a fire."

He pulls himself back to his feet again and joins her, feeling light-headed and tired. "Where is the closest exit?"

"It looks like there's one in the classroom across the hall — which is the north side of the building."

Larry looks out at the hall again, seeing no signs of movement in either direction. "Okay, we'll move straight to the room, then barricade the door behind us — that way they won't be able to follow us."

"Okay, I'm ready when you are."

They push the door open slowly, and the dry hinges fill the silent hallway with a faint creaking sound as they move quickly across the corridor, seeing no sign of the group that passed by only a few minutes before. Larry wedges one of the student chairs underneath the handle, testing the door as quietly as possible to see if it holds.

"Will that work?" Beth asks him.

"Let's hope so, there's no locks on these doors." He takes another look out into the hallway, then sits down in one of the chairs, laying his head onto the desk in front of him.

"We should get out of here as soon as possible."

"I need to rest for a few minutes — we might have to run like hell once we're outside."

She sits down next to him, looking out of the windows at the trailer park beyond. The sun is now up, but the rain is still coming down in buckets, and is blowing against the glass and partially obscuring the view. The tall fir trees that are scattered throughout the mobile park are bending over from the storm, dropping large branches onto the homes below.

"It's getting bad out there again, worse than yesterday," Beth says, hoping to keep him awake.

"At least the fog will cover us."

"That guy was talking, coherently — we haven't seen any of them that can speak like that."

"Amanda does."

"Did you notice the scratches on his arms? They didn't look self-inflicted, they looked like somebody else's defense wounds."

"They must've killed everyone else in town."

"He had bruises all over his body too — didn't Jennifer have those right before she died?"

"On her chest, yeah, but they weren't open sores like theirs — they were more like purple bruises. She said they didn't hurt though."

"Did she ever say anything... odd?"

"She wasn't one of these people, Beth."

"I know she wasn't, I was just wondering if..." she looks at him, seeing the look of detachment growing on his face. "Never mind. Are you about ready?"

"Yeah, ready as I'm gonna be." He stands up, feeling the weight in his arms and legs as he grabs his bag again. Between two wide windows on the outside wall is a door leading to the parking lot. Larry unlocks it, then pushes through and holds it open for Beth to follow him, and as he turns around and faces the empty parking lot next to the building, the window next to him shatters as the sound of a gunshot echos through the air from somewhere nearby.

Beth jumps back inside and pulls Larry in with her as another three shots hit the door beside him, and then the two of them scramble on their hands and knees into the corner and away from the windows. "Did you see where that came from?" she asks.

"I saw a muzzle flash from the last shots — in a trailer across the way," Larry replies, scared and out of breath.

Beth looks up at the exit map on the other side of the room and tries to read what it says, but the graphics are too small to see. "Stay here, I'm gonna sneak across the room and see where the other exits are."

"Stay down and out of sight..."

"I know, I'll be careful." Crawling on her stomach to the opposite wall, she grabs a chair from behind a desk and uses it to knock the framed map off of it's hook, then barely catches it before it hits the floor. She looks behind her, making sure that somebody wasn't standing there, then crawls back to Larry.

"What does it say?" he asks.

"There's only two exits on the south side. One is the main entrance on the other end of the building, and the other one is through the kitchen."

"We can't risk running through that kitchen."

"They could be keeping an eye on the entrance though, maybe the kitchen is the safer bet..."

"Okay, but if we see anybody, don't hesitate to shoot them — and keep some extra clips handy."

The two crawl around the edge of the room, Larry leading the way. When they get to the door, they both rush into the hallway without looking, hearing yet another gunshot hit somewhere in the classroom. As they get to their feet and start running down the hall, they hear a voice coming from behind them, moving quickly. With the kitchen still too far away to reach in time, Larry finds a dark place to stand, then turns around and takes in a deep breath, aiming his gun down the corridor with Beth right beside him. It takes only seconds before the group comes into sight, and before any of them even realize they're standing there, they both open fire into the crowd. Empty their clips at almost the same time, they immediately start reloading as they watch for any activity.

"Shine a light down there, I'll cover you..." Larry says, pointing his gun in their direction again.

Holstering her pistol, she aims the flashlight at the group and sees most of them lying motionless on the floor. Two others are writhing around in pain and coughing up blood. "Do you wanna finish them off?"

"Why bother?" he says, walking back toward the kitchen. "It's just a waste of ammunition."

CHAPTER 27
COHASSETT BEACH: DAY 6

Curtis closes his eyes for a few seconds, trying to stay as calm as possible while Sarah attempts to tie a loop into the end of a rope. The guy on the other side of the door is surprisingly strong, and Curtis isn't sure exactly how long he can hold it shut — especially as his hands become covered in sweat.

"Sarah, you need to hurry it up…"

"I'm working as fast as I can — it's not like you're any better at tying knots."

Although grateful that the handle is a lever-type instead of a knob, he can still feel his fingers beginning to slip on the polished brass surface. The man is violently twisting the handle and pulling at the same time, and occasionally tugging at it so forcefully that Curtis isn't sure that the hinges will be able to hold it — even if he can.

"Here, try this…" Sarah says, slipping the looped end of the rope over the door lever beside Curtis' hands.

With both of them pulling on the rope, Curtis guides the other end of it around the wood stove in the center of the room, then tightens the slack.

"Okay, slowly let go," he tells her, as she carefully releases the rope and backs away. He starts easing up on his grip too, waiting for the man to pull hard before finally letting go completely. When he's convinced that the wood stove will hold the man back, he collapses onto the couch behind him and watches as the assault on the door becomes even more aggressive. Before long though, the man begins to scream and kick at the hinged side, eventually causing a crack to appear on the surface as the door begins to split apart. Curtis rushes back and leans against it with all of his weight, but he can feel the wood beginning to give way as the kicks keep coming. "Sarah, find some kitchen knives, I don't think this thing is gonna hold together much longer."

"Dad...!" Matt says from the kitchen. "Come here, quick!"

"I'm a little busy Matt..."

"Someone is trying to get in through the pet door."

"Are they a full-grown adult?"

"I think so."

"Then they can wait, they can't fit through. Just stay out of the kitchen for now, okay?" Curtis turns his attention back to Sarah, who has just returned with two large kitchen knives in her hands. He takes one of them from her, then holds the blade against the rope.

"What are you doing?" Sarah asks, baffled as to why he would suddenly release the man.

"Take the boys into the other room and close the door."

"No, I'm not going anywhere — and don't cut that fucking rope! I can hold onto it and open the door just a crack."

"Okay, just brace yourself against something, this guy is strong as hell." Curtis holds onto the rope, then waits for Sarah to untie it, using the wood stove to secure herself. Little by little, he gives it some slack, watching the door slowly open a few inches. With a few feet of distance from the room still, he leans over to see if the man is visible through the small opening, when a hand suddenly reaches out and nearly grabs him by the forearm. He pulls back hard on the rope and pins the man's arm in the door, then takes hold of it and bends it backward against the jam in an attempt to break it. He hears Sarah scream something at him, and a split second later the man grips his coat sleeve and pulls his arm into the bedroom, biting him just above his wrist as he desperately tries to free himself. He turns around, seeing the rope fall to the floor as Sarah slams herself against the door, breaking it completely free from it's hinges. The guy, who stands nearly a foot taller than Curtis, let's go of his arm and turns to face Sarah — but just as he reaches for her, she lunges forward at him, piercing the tip of her blade into the middle of his throat. He falls back onto the bed and tries to pull the blade out, but Curtis already has his hands wrapped around the handle, pushing the knife further into his flesh as the man thrashes around underneath him.

Feeling the cold drops of rainwater run down his face from the broken skylight above, Curtis finally lets go when the intruder stops breathing. He sits back for a minute, suddenly aware of how much his body is shaking all over, then he gets up and sits in a chair in the corner of the room.

"Is your arm okay?" Sarah asks, as she tries to get his coat off.

"I don't know, it hurts like hell."

She examines the sleeve closely as she slips it off of him, seeing marks in the fabric, but no holes. His skin, already marked from being tied up in their cabin, has some nasty bruising appearing on the surface of the skin — but to her relief, there are no punctures visible. "It looks okay, he didn't actually get his teeth into you."

Curtis can feel his heart racing and breathing becoming rapid as the stress begins to sink in, "I thought he was gonna kill us..."

"He didn't though, and we're all still okay... Just sit here for a minute and calm down." She kneels down in front of him, waiting for his breathing to settle down before standing up again. "I'm gonna check on the kids, okay?" Seeing him nod back, she walks out of the room and finds the boys standing on the couch, both of them looking into the kitchen. Wedged in the pet door, with one arm and a head stuck, is a young girl that can't be any older than about ten.

"She can't move," Ben tells her. "She tried to back out a minute ago, but she couldn't."

Sarah pulls a chair out from the table and places it several feet away from the girl, then sits down and stares at her. "Can you speak?"

"I don't think she can — but she cried when she got stuck," Matt says.

"Do you have a name?" Sarah continues. The girl looks up at her with tears in her eyes, then attempts to free herself again by wriggling her body, but it doesn't do any good. She settles down and rests her head on the floor, then starts whimpering as she makes eye contact again.

"What's going on?" Curtis asks, coming in from the bedroom and standing behind her.

"This girl tried to climb through the pet door, and I'm trying to figure out if she's sick."

"Of course she's sick, just look at her..."

"I don't see any symptoms — aside from the fact that she won't talk."

"Her skin is dark around the eyes."

"And her hands are blue..." Matt adds.

Curtis picks up a broom from the laundry room, then stands over her.

"Don't hurt her!" Sarah yells.

"I'm not gonna hurt her." He lowers the handle down next to her face, then moves it to within only a couple of inches. In an instant, the girl stretches her neck out and tries to bite the broom handle, then lets out a blood-curdling scream when Curtis drops it and backs away. He feels a nudge against his side, and looks over to see Sarah handing him a blanket.

"Throw it over her, I don't wanna have to look at her."

CHAPTER 28
GRAYLAND: DAY 6

Nestled in the shadows of a covered porch, curled up in the fetal position with tears running down her face, Christine listens to shot after shot as Jake fires his gun at the school across the parking lot. She knows who he's shooting at, and that he's aware of it as well, but for the life of her she can't figure out why he's doing it. She watched him fire the first bullet, and could tell from the reaction on his face that he missed his target. Whether it was Larry or Beth that he was aiming at she didn't know, but the desperate determination in his eyes as he kept firing was the most terrifying thing she's ever witnessed. After that, she sat down on the floor and placed her hands over her ears, trying to drown out the senseless violence in front of her.

"Hey!"

She feels something kick her leg, and looks up to find Jake staring at her.

"Get ready to move, they're probably headed to the other side of the building."

She closes her eyes again and begins to cry, her mind overwhelmed with emotions — then she feels another kick, this time much harder than before.

"Hey, look at me!"

She lifts her head up, and then finally opens her eyes after being kicked once more. His gun is aimed directly at her now, the barrel so close to her skin that she can feel the heat coming from it. "Why are you doing this?" she asks tearfully, as she pulls herself to her feet.

He takes his aim away from her, then gestures toward the door. "Come on, they're gonna get away if we don't move now."

"Beth loves you so much…"

He stops and turns around, pushing her against the wall — then he grabs his jacket sleeve and pulls it up, exposing a gruesome wound on his arm that looks gangrenous. "Do you see this?" he says maniacally, his voice rapid and angry. "I got this last fall, killing a doctor that saved my life." She tries to look away from it, and he grabs her head and shoves her even closer. "Ask me why I killed him…"

Feeling nauseous from the odor, she forces herself to speak. "Why…?"

"Because he was already dead, just like all the others. None of us were meant to live through this, not me, or you, or Beth or Larry."

"Beth is alive, and so is Larry…" she cries out.

"The entire world is dying, Christine. We've been stripped of our souls while we await our final judgment, and I'm the executioner."

Christine can see the insanity raging in his eyes, and the breathing that gets worse the more excited he becomes. Part of her was hoping that Jake was simply having a nervous breakdown, which would be completely understandable considering everything that he's been through — but his behavior and symptoms are exactly the same as David's were, right before he tried to kill both her and George.

He turns around and looks back at the school through the scope on his rifle, and for a moment Christine considers reaching for her gun to shoot him — but just as her hand begins to move into her pocket, he takes hold of her arm and pushes her out the door in front of him.

"Head southwest, that way…" he orders her, pointing toward the front of the school.

She steps down into the muddy ground that sits between the trailer park and the school, then begins walking slowly through the ankle-high puddles of water.

"Hurry up!" Jake yells at her, kicking her in the butt and sending her face-first into the water. He reaches down as he walks by and grabs her by the collar, lifting her onto her feet again. "If you're no use to me, I'll end you right now — understand?"

Already cold from the pouring rain and wind, Christine shivers as she tries to stay ahead of him. In the distance to her right, she can see someone walking south along the highway, limping badly as they fight to stay upright in the strong winds. She wants to scream for help, or somehow get their attention as Jake continues to push her from behind — but in this one instance, his delusional beliefs are more true than not. These people aren't dead, but they might as well be.

When they come around the corner of the building, they see another entrance to the school about two hundred feet away — this one with the door propped open with a concrete block. Seeing no movement yet, Jake stands under the cover of the eaves and forces Christine to sit down on the pavement in front of him, then he aims his rifle over her head toward the door.

"I used to work at a prison, did Beth tell you that?" he asks, his voice strangely calm and relaxed.

"Yeah, I think she told me about it."

"We had this one inmate who shot up a school when he was a teen — and we got him when he turned eighteen. The idiot drove his own fucking car to the front of the school, parked right in front of the camera, then opened fire. Guess what day it was?"

"I don't know."

"Saturday." He starts laughing, then coughs so hard that he almost loses his balance. "The stupid bastard had it pretty rough on the inside though. Two weeks after landing in our unit, someone shanked him in the shower."

"They killed him?"

"No, I think he actually lived long enough to die from the virus, just like everyone else. How is that for karma?"

"Jake, please think about what you're doing..." she cries, breaking down in tears again.

He ignores her, choosing to focus his attention on whatever comes out of the doorway instead. He's spent the last four months obsessing over this exact moment, seeing the situation play out in his head every time he closes his eyes at night.

She can hear commotion in the school behind her, but she can also see the same crippled man she saw earlier, still limping down the highway. When the guy sees her as well, he stands in the middle of the road and watches her for a moment, then begins stumbling toward them slowly, dragging his left foot across the asphalt parking lot.

"There's a guy walking this way..." she says, pointing toward the highway.

"Is he close?"

"He just left the highway..."

"Then shut up and let me concentrate, he'll have to wait his turn."

Without even glancing back at the door, she can tell that Beth is about to come walking through it — and Jake knows it too. When her voice can be heard from somewhere inside, sounding frantic and scared, Christine watches as he holds his breath and stares through the rifle scope. She looks back at the door and sees Beth emerge, then struggles to her feet and pulls the revolver out of her pocket.

"Jake, I'll shoot if you don't drop your gun — I mean it!" she screams, pointing the gun at his body as her hands shake violently. He lets out a sigh and smiles, then slowly drops his aim to the ground. "Drop the gun, then kick it to me!"

Almost in slow motion, he gently lays the rifle on the pavement, then looks up at her with a slight smirk on his face. "We're full of surprises, aren't we?"

"Jake, is that you?" Beth yells out, dropping her bag and running toward them. When she sees the gun in Christine's hands though, she stops and pulls her own pistol out, then motions for Larry to stay back.

"Beth, stay away from him, he's trying to kill you..." Christine tells her.

"That's not true, hon, she's crazy," Jake argues.

Beth raises her pistol and aims it at the teen, then starts walking carefully toward Jake. "Drop your gun, sweety, he's not hurting anyone, okay?"

"You have to kill him, he's sick!" she yells back, her voice becoming hysterical with fear.

"Christine, drop your gun and move away from him, I won't ask you again," Beth says more forcefully than before, moving between the girl and Jake. "I'm gonna put a bullet in your head if you don't do what I say, do you understand?"

Her entire body trembling, Christine bends down and sets the revolver onto the asphalt, then stands up just in time to see Jake holding a handgun to the back of Beth's head. A split second later she feels the spray of blood as Beth falls to the ground, her body hitting the pavement only a few feet in front of her. Christine crouches down to pick her gun up again, but then collapses instead as the sound of more gunfire fills the air. When it finally ends, and the only thing she can hear is the sound of her own sobbing, she lifts her head up and sees three bodies lying on the ground. Jake is right beside Beth's body, still gasping for breath as his lungs fill up with blood. Larry is a short distance away, perhaps ten feet — moaning loudly as he clutches his left leg.

"Larry...?" Her voice is shaky and weak as she grabs her gun and stands up.

"Is he dead?" Larry answers back.

"Almost — he's still breathing a little bit."

"I need you to shoot him in the head, okay?"

"I... I don't..."

"Christine, don't think about it, just aim it at his head and pull the trigger."

She passes by Beth, trying not to look at her, then stands over Jake — kicking the pistol next to him out of his reach. He's staring directly at her, his eyes looking kind and full of remorse as he tries to extend his hand out to her.

"Take a deep breath and relax, you're doing him a favor," Larry says, as he tries to lean against the brick wall of the school behind him.

She closes her eyes, trying to remember what her father had said about moments like this, where you might be forced to do something that you despise. Without thinking about anything at all, she opens her eyes again and pulls the trigger, shooting him in the forehead twice. Remembering the man that was approaching from the highway, she turns around and finds him just staring back at her. When his feet begin to move again, she fires a round at him, missing wildly — then she fires her two remaining shots, but those miss as well. She bends down and picks up Jake's gun, wiping the blood from the handle and taking her time to carefully aim it. The next two shots hit the guy, knocking him to the ground and out of harm's way. She looks around at the rest of the town, expecting to see crowds of people coming out of the shadows and fog — but the town looks empty once again, and the only sign of life that she can see is Larry's bedraggled body trying desperately to sit up.

"Can I get some help?" he asks her.

She helps to lift him up, then examines his leg as he winces in pain. "Were you shot?"

"I don't think so. I fell back and landed on my hip — I might have broken something."

"We need to find someplace to hide for the night, before those people show up again."

"I'll find someplace, don't worry about me — but you have to get out of town before it's too late."

"I'm not leaving you..."

"We're gonna die if we both stay here. At least you might stand a chance on the road if you leave now."

"What about you?"

"I'll have to take my chances." He points at his bag that's still lying on the ground where he dropped it. "Hand me my bag, I'll give you some supplies to take with you."

She sets the bag at his feet, then unzips all of the compartments. "Where should I go?"

He takes a smaller bag that was inside and starts loading it with pistols, ammunition, food, water and medicine, saving almost none of the latter three for himself. "Just follow the beach to Cohassett, then take the highway to Olympia. That family said that everyone there was dead, and right now that sounds like a pretty good place to be. Whatever you do, don't walk into Westport — and try to stay as far away from Cosmopolis as possible, that jackass that brought his wife and son here told me that it was overrun." He hands the small bag to her, then pops two painkillers into his mouth as he rests his head against the wall behind him. "If you happen to come across a family named the Lockwoods, see if you can stay with them — they're good people."

"That's what you said about Jake..."

"I know, and there's a pretty good chance that Jake already killed all of them, but they're still your best chance at staying alive."

She stands up and looks at the sun, guessing that it must be just after noon. "Larry, if I..."

"I'll catch up if I can," he interrupts. "You'd better get going." She hesitates at first, but then turns around and starts walking away. "Hey, Christine!" he hollers out.

"Yeah?"

"Did you ever see any sign of Amanda?"

"Yeah, she found me."

"What happened to her?"

"She was killed, by those people."

She turns again and heads back to the highway, walking north through the wind and rain that's still beating down around her. When she gets to the last house along the road, she looks back at the town, seeing the same abandoned and desolate scene that she saw when they first arrived. Ahead of her, there's a sign alongside the road. 'Westport: 6 Miles, Aberdeen: 23 Miles, Olympia: 72 Miles'

She shudders at the thought of traveling that kind of distance — especially alone. Her father, David, Larry, Beth — everyone in her life had protected her for months, making sure that she was never in any serious danger. Even Amanda, in her own twisted way, had saved her more than once over the last couple of days.

The dark road that lies ahead only adds to the loneliness — but the true feeling of despair is really only felt when she reaches a small, winding driveway that leads into the woods, where she can see the remnants of a smoldering cabin that's nestled amongst the trees.

CHAPTER 29
COHASSETT BEACH: DAY 7

As old as it is, Curtis doesn't really have any memories of this neighborhood as a child. He remembers riding past the old farm houses on their way to town, and how it seemed strange to see cows and horses right across the street from the ocean — but whatever it looked like all those years ago, he's quite certain that it looked nothing like it does today. Peering out through cracks in the plywood barricades that cover the windows, he's noticing a sudden and drastic change in the behavior of the infected, one that's making him leery of walking among them — even in the daylight.

When they first ventured into Westport, nearly five months ago now, most of the people were actually relatively harmless. They mostly wandered aimlessly around town, apparently oblivious to the fact that you even existed, and only a few of them showed any hint of hostility or even intelligence. Today, however, the same people that used to stumble around without a shred of coordination seem to be regaining much of their strength and agility. As their physical abilities improve though, their mental stability appears to be permanently damaged. Last night the neighborhood was filled with the sounds of screaming and pleas for help as Curtis watched the mayhem taking place in front of their temporary home. People were being assaulted and murdered at a frenetic pace, their bodies tossed aside when they were done as if they were killed by animals.

Inside the mobile home, things were finally calm for the time being. While they had a few visitors during the night, they're almost positive that none of them knew of the family's existence. The young girl in the kitchen disappeared early in the morning, while Matt was standing guard. He said the girl began to struggle and cry out, and then someone ripped her out of the pet door that she was trapped in, then dragged her across the yard and into the woods behind the property. As much as the thought of it bothered all of them though, none of them actually miss her presence.

Smelling the rich aroma of food cooking on the stove, he turns around and sees Sarah dishing macaroni and cheese onto paper plates, while Matt and Ben both work on setting the table for a proper meal. As much as he'd love for things to stay like this for a while, he also knows that it's imperative that they distance themselves from people as much as possible. Sooner, rather than later, they have to find another place to hide, somewhere secluded enough to keep them isolated from the madness around them — and before somebody on the outside discovers them.

"Dinner is almost ready," Sarah says from the kitchen.

"Okay, I'll be there in a minute." He goes back to watching a house just a few doors down the road, where someone has been standing on the rooftop and tearing off the metal panels that cover the house since the night before. A few more people are on the ground, ripping pieces of lap siding from the walls and tossing them into the street. He keeps expecting them to run out of energy or to lose interest, especially considering how little they've actually accomplished in all of that time, but they've been working non-stop for nearly eighteen hours now, and are showing absolutely no signs of slowing down.

"It's gonna get cold, Curtis."

"Yeah, I'm coming." He sits down across from his wife and says a prayer before he begins dishing up his food, drawing a look of confusion from Sarah, since she's never heard him sound the least bit religious in all the years she's known him. He notices the expression on her face, and simply shrugs. "I don't know why I did that — it just seemed like the right thing to do."

"I'm not complaining, we could use all the help we can get."

The meal is the first real food they've been able to eat for days, and might be the last decent thing they'll be eating for some time. Besides the macaroni and cheese, Sarah also fixed corn, beans and beef stew, which were all prepared straight out of their cans and heated on the stove top.

"What were you watching out there?" Sarah asks him. "You look worried."

"The same people down the street."

"You're afraid they're gonna find the hole in our roof?"

"No, it's not that. I mean, yeah, I'm afraid of that, but I'm not sure anything is safe anymore. I really think we should leave first thing in the morning if the road is empty."

"And go where?"

"We need to find a place away from everybody, like we talked about — away from any town or neighborhood where people might have survived, like a farmhouse or something."

"We can't take all of this food."

"No, but we can take some of it — enough to last us for a while if we ration it." He can see the doubt in her eyes as she starts picking at her food instead of eating it. "We just can't stay here forever, it doesn't even have a decent source of clean water."

"I know, but we're safe, and comfortable — and I hate the idea of traveling without any protection, where we have no idea what to expect around the next bend in the road."

Curtis looks into the corner of the room, where the boys worked for much of the afternoon shoveling human remains off of the floor where they won't trip on them. He wants to point out how incredibly low her threshold of 'comfortable' is these days, but he decides it's probably best to keep quiet. "In three or four days we're gonna run out of bottled water, and then we'll have to either go search for more in town, or move locations and start drinking rainwater again. If we go now we'll at least have some to take with us."

She nods her head in polite disagreement, still troubled at the thought of leaving themselves vulnerable to the world outside these walls.

"We'll stay away from the highway. There's just too many people on it anymore, even in the daytime."

"That leaves what — the beach?"

"There's a swamp to the east, and woods on the other side of it. Hardly anybody lives out there, and I doubt anybody is out there now."

"Where would we sleep?"

"There's a few houses tucked back into the woods, or at least there used to be."

Sarah stops eating altogether and stares down at her half-eaten plate, her mind coming up with a thousand reasons why this is a bad idea. "I don't like the thought of wandering around in the middle of a swamp, Curtis, not when those things out there are getting stronger."

"It's either that, or we take the roads — and it's for certain that we'll run into people that way."

She looks at Matt and Ben sitting next to her at the table, knowing that whatever decision they come to will likely save, or kill, both of them. Despite having no appetite, she forces herself to continue eating, trying to savor what might be their last meal for a long while.

"Did you hear that?" Matt asks, standing up from his chair and looking toward the front window.

"I didn't hear anything," Curtis replies, following Matt across the room to the window with a limited view of the street.

"I heard someone yelling."

Curtis gently pushes him away from the small crack in the plywood barricade, trying to see for himself what might be going on out there. He still can't hear anybody talking, but he soon spots a young girl walking down the highway with a bag in her hand, aiming a gun at three men that are following her.

"Do you see someone?" Matt asks.

"Yeah, it's a girl." She starts to walk faster, then trips on some debris in the road and almost falls down. After she regains her balance, she drops her bag onto the ground and fires several shots at each of the men, then reaches into her pocket and slaps another clip into the gun.

"What the hell is going on out there?" Sarah asks him.

"Here, take a look..." he says, backing away from the window.

Looking through the narrow field of vision, Sarah sees the girl walking down the road in front of their house. Suddenly, she stops in their driveway, looking ahead at the people tearing the neighboring house apart. She expects to see her try to go around the place, especially when it becomes obvious that the people on the ground have spotted her. Instead, she stands in a shooting stance in the middle of the highway and begins firing rounds at them, being careful and deliberate with every shot. After unloading one clip, she reloads and fires two more before holstering the gun again and continuing on. "She just killed those people down the road."

"The people on the house?"

"Yeah, she even got the one on the roof."

"Does she look sick?"

"I don't know, I can't tell, but she looks dangerous."

Sarah steps away from the window and sits back down at the table with Curtis and Ben, while Matt continues to watch the girl until she disappears from sight. "We should catch up to her, she might be able to help us..." Matt says.

"From now on, it's just the four of us — no exceptions," Curtis says.

CHAPTER 30
HIGHWAY 105: DAY 10

Throughout her young life, Christine can't ever remember a time when she complained about being alone. She's been an introvert since she was a little girl, preferring to spend time in her own company instead of spending it with anyone else, which is a trait that used to worry her parents when she refused to make friends at school. Whether she was shut inside of her room at home, or in some quiet corner of a coffee shop in town, she had always thought of herself as being completely alone in those moments — but until right now, she never realized how wrong she was. It didn't really matter if she actually communicated with the people around her or not, subconsciously she still felt their presence. She could listen to their conversations, feel their footsteps, she could even hear the sounds of lawn mowers and airplanes in the distance and know that people were nearby.

Today, however, as she sits on a park bench eating a package of stale processed cheese and crackers, overlooking the dark waters of Grays Harbor, she feels entirely and utterly alone for the first time in her life. She can see the ruined remains of Aberdeen and Hoquiam on the other side of the water, the buildings blackened and crumbling to pieces after the massive fire that spread throughout both cities. Unlike when Larry saw it last, there's no smoke visible anywhere, which she figures is probably because there's really nothing left to burn.

Although she's too far away to see whether there's any people across the harbor, she can't imagine that anyone survived the inferno.

It's been three days since she's seen another person, and that was nearly ten miles away after leaving Cohassett. After staying much of that time at a gas station alongside the road in Markham, waiting for the torrential rainfall to ease up enough to walk, she thought it was only a matter of time before one of the infected residents of the area would come along, looking for something to kill or destroy — but nobody ever came, and the road after that has remained empty ever since. Since both of her parents are dead, along with David, Beth, and likely Larry by now — every single person that she's ever known appears to be gone — and she's wondered more than a few times during the past couple of days if she might be the last surviving person in Grays Harbor, but something in her mind keeps pushing the bleak thought from her consciousness.

Glancing down at her watch and realizing that the sun will be down in a few hours, she grabs her bag and heads down the road again, studying the map of the area that she swiped from the gas station. Larry had told her to bypass Cosmopolis, but the only way to do that is to cross the river and head straight through the heart of Aberdeen. She considers the idea of staying on this side of the bridge for the night, then crossing over into what's left of the city in the morning — but it takes her less than an hour to make it to the crossing, giving her plenty of time to find something on the other side.

Approaching the entrance to the bridge over the Chehalis River, she can smell the scent of something burning on the wind, and as she climbs to the top of the road, she can see the true scope of the devastation to the city. Because of prevailing wind, the south side of the harbor was spared any of the ash from the fire, but the north side of the bridge is still covered in large clumps of slick ash, dampened by the rainfall of winter. She can see burned out cars everywhere, and a few of the buildings in downtown that have collapsed entirely, but most of the older brick and stone structures are still standing — or at least the outside shell is anyway. Several skeletons are scattered on the streets and sidewalks too, but all of them have burn marks that suggest that they've been here for quite some time.

Unlike the last crossing, which looked relatively untouched by the fire, the two bridges over the Wishkaw River in the center of the city appear to be severely damaged by the intense heat. After looking over the first one, and seeing that large sections of the roadway had fallen into the river, she decides to take her chances on the next one — despite the fact that the metal structure shows signs of twisting on the western end. She stays close to the railing along the side, seeing a few small places where the asphalt has given way on this one as well. Ahead of her, most of the buildings appear to be in far better shape, and the first building that looks even somewhat livable is a drug store shortly after the bridge.

"Hello?" Christine yells out, after pushing the unlocked front door open. "If anybody is in here, I have a gun, so don't try any shit with me..." She steps through the door, leaving it unlocked just in case she needs to make a quick exit, then takes out her flashlight and aims it around the store, seeing no sign of anyone around. After making a check of the perimeter, she goes ahead and locks all of the doors in the front and back, then closes the security gates that cover the windows along the street as well. Sitting down behind one of the check stands, she props her sore legs and feet up onto the counter, then closes her eyes and begins to drift off — but then a thought crosses her mind, one that she should have been paying attention to if she weren't so exhausted. She opens her eyes again and looks around with the flashlight, and sees aisle after aisle of merchandise still sitting on the shelves. Forcing herself up again, she walks down each aisle of the store, her frazzled mind trying to keep track of what she can carry with her. There's food, personal hygiene products, batteries, extra flashlights, and more medication than she could ever use in a lifetime. As she throws a blanket down on the pharmacy waiting bench, then opens a candy bar that she took from the snack aisle, she wonders why a place like this wouldn't be picked clean by either survivors like her, or even the infected scavengers that tore every other town apart. Eventually she starts to nod off, keeping her gun and flashlight close to her side as she listens to the rain start to fall on the roof once again. If another storm is coming in from the ocean, she can certainly think of worse places to have to stay.

Hearing a loud rattling, Christine wakes up to a pitch-black room, and for a moment she forgets where she is. She sits up and grabs her gun, then listens for a moment as the rattling continues. Then the noise stops, leaving the store completely silent except for the rain. She tells herself that it must be the wind, but deep down she knows better — the wind was blowing even harder earlier in the evening, and yet it didn't make a sound. Getting to her feet, and leaving her flashlight turned off for the moment, she walks quietly down one of the aisles, then freezes as something crashes in the front of the store. She continues, crouching down low as she peers around the corner and aims her gun toward the noise. Standing at one of the front shelves, someone with a light is flipping through a selection of chips and candy, stuffing some of them into their pockets. When they turn around and start shining their light down each of the aisles, Christine steps into the open and aims her pistol at their chest, the way her father had taught her.

"Don't move! Put your hands up where I can see them!"

The person drops a bag of chips onto the floor, then places their hands up. "You know, you might wanna make sure the door actually locks before going to sleep…"

Christine instantly recognizes the voice, and shines her flashlight onto his face just to make sure. "Larry? Is that really you?"

"Yeah, it's me, what's left of me anyway. Can I put my hands down now?"

Placing her gun back into the holster, she runs and nearly knocks him down as she wraps her arms around him.

"Whoa, easy now, my hip still hurts like hell," he says as he hugs her back.

"Oh, sorry! There's a bench in the back that's pretty comfortable…"

"I think I'll just sit for a while." He pulls a chair out from behind a check stand as Christine sits down on the counter. "I was afraid I wouldn't catch up to you."

"I got held up for a while."

"Have you seen anybody in the city?"

"No, not a sign of anyone."

"I saw one — a light up on the hill." He gets up and limps to the front of the store, where they can barely make out something illuminating the fog on the top of the hill to the west. "I'm pretty sure it must be the hospital."

"You mean the one where Jake was?"

"Yeah, it's the only one in the area."

"Jake told me he killed the doctor there, right after the guy saved his life."

"Well, someone is living there." Larry hobbles away from the window and heads toward the back of the store, picking his bag up along the way. "You said there's a bench back here?"

"Yeah, back by the pharmacy. You don't look like you're getting around very well…"

"No, I'm not, and all of this damn walking doesn't help it any." He sits down on the bench, then grimaces as he swings his feet onto the other side. "What about you?"

"I'll sleep on the floor — there's a bunch of lawn chair cushions for sale on aisle eight."

"Lucky for you that the apocalypse happened during the summer, huh?"

Christine smiles, thankful that he can find humor in all of this misery. "Larry, I'm really sorry about Beth, I feel horrible about what happened."

"Thanks, but it's not your fault, it's not anyone's fault."

"I should have just killed him when I had the chance."

"Try not to dwell on what could've been. Trust me, it's just a waste of your time."

"Thanks." She hugs him again, and then sits down in an uncomfortable chair next to the bench. "Maybe we should stick around here for a while — let your body heal up before moving on."

"Is there water?"

"Tons of it."

"What about painkillers?"

"In this town? There's gotta be."

Larry laughs, for the first time in a long while. "You're not even from around here, are you? That doesn't say much about Aberdeen."

"I've never actually been here before, but when we left, my dad talked about coming here. He said the world ending could only be an improvement."

"Well, I'm sure there's something to like about it," he replies sleepily.

"Larry, are you still awake?"

"Yeah, I'm still awake."

"My dad told me that most of the cars won't run because of the explosion — is that true?"

"You mean the EMP? Yeah, that's probably true. I also saw some older cars that were ruined by some of these infected assholes though."

"But some of them run, right?"

"Some probably do, but most of the roads are blocked anyway, so they're probably not worth the trouble. Why?"

"I'm just tired of walking, that's all."

Larry laughs again, then turns over onto his side. "That makes two of us."

After listening to him begin to snore, Christine hears something faint coming from his bag. When she bends down to unzip it, a loud static buzz startles her, and sits Larry straight up on the bench.

"...on this midnight check. It's been three days since your last contact — is everything okay over there, Shelton?"

Larry grabs the handheld radio from his bag and holds it so that they can both hear it. It's a man's voice, clear as day, as if they were in the next room.

Then another voice comes on, a man that sounds much older. *"Sorry, Aberdeen, this might be our last transmission for a while. The entire town is burning — we've been overrun."*

"Copy that, Shelton. Are you safe?"

"Nobody is, Aberdeen."

"I hear you. May God be with you..."

"I have to switch off, they're right outside. Over and out, and thanks."

The radio goes silent, leaving Larry and Christine staring at one another in the dim light of her flashlight.

"I left the radio on, just in case you contacted me," Larry says. "I forgot all about it."

"Do you think they're the ones at the hospital?"

Larry holds the radio to his mouth and presses the button, then pauses as he tries to figure out what to say. "Aberdeen, do you copy?" He waits several seconds for a reply, then tries it again. "Aberdeen, if you can hear me, please respond."

"*Who is this?*"

"My name is Larry, I just arrived in the city. Are you at the hospital? I can see a..."

"*Contact me again at noon tomorrow.*" the radio voice says abruptly, cutting him off.

Christine walks up front, looking once again at the light still flickering in the distance. The rest of the neighborhood is mostly obscured by darkness, except for a few shops directly across the parking lot from the pharmacy. As she looks around for movement, which has become both a tiring and necessary habit these days, she spots something shimmering in front of one of the small buildings across from them. The longer she watches it, the more she's convinced that it's moving toward her — and as her eyes adjust to the lack of light and color outside, she suddenly realizes what it is. "Larry, come here, quick..."

Stumbling across the floor, feeling somewhat sick to his stomach from exhaustion, Larry stands next to her and looks in the direction that she's pointing. "What is it?."

"She's right in front of us, halfway across the parking lot."

He stares into the darkness even closer, finally seeing something moving very slowly through the fog, her head barely visible over the top of the mist. "Is that...?"

"Yeah, I think it is."

He pulls a pair of binoculars out of his pocket and scans the parking lot again, barely catching a glimpse her before she ducks down and disappears into the low-lying fog.

"You know, the entire time I was with her, I never even asked her what her last name is," Larry says, checking that the lock on the front door is secure.

"Williams — her name is Amanda Williams."

CHAPTER 31
COHASSETT BEACH: DAY 11

Stepping out into the crisp morning air, Sarah breathes in deeply to cleanse her lungs of the mildew and rot that was trapped inside of the house. As much as she enjoyed the security and safety of its walls, she also knew that it was probably only a matter of time before one of them ended up sick from exposure to the filth. Once they made the decision that they were leaving, those same walls that once seemed so safe and comforting, started to feel more and more like a prison instead. At the first sign of daylight they began packing whatever provisions they could carry, all of them stuffed into dusty suitcases that they found in the garage. They had absolutely no idea where they were headed, but they were determined to find something better than this. They were homeless for the first time in their lives, and yet surrounded by an endless supply of vacant houses and condominiums — none of which were now safe from the local residents.

The four of them make their way down the highway, each carrying bags or suitcases, and passing by the oldest houses on the outskirts of Westport — houses that have been damaged over the last few nights by an unruly group of the infected.

"Wanna walk on the beach instead?" Curtis asks, stopping at a road that leads to a public access to the ocean.

"I think I've had my fill of dunes for a while," Sarah responds.

"We won't walk on the dunes, we'll stick close to the shore where it's easier to walk."

She looks at both of the boys, and can tell by their faces that she's already been outvoted. "Fine, but just for a while."

The access road is covered with potholes, which are still full of water from the night before, but otherwise it's quiet and empty until they reach a small parking area at the very end. A newer gold-colored Honda sedan is sitting by itself in the middle of the lot, facing a short sand dune that's positioned between the car and the beach. On top of the dune, Curtis can see something lying on the ground.

"Follow me, but don't get too close," he says, leaving his suitcase on the pavement as he heads up the path with a golf club that he found along the road. He motions for the others to stay put as he approaches the top, seeing what's left of a person spread out on the ground. Sitting on the sand next to the body is a piece of paper that's sealed inside of a mason jar, and a .38 revolver that still looks to be in decent condition — despite being exposed to the elements.

Walking up behind him, Sarah kneels down and looks closely at the skeletal remains, then she picks up the jar and reads enough of the handwritten note through the side to confirm her suspicions.

"What does it say, Mom?" Ben asks.

"It's not for us, sweety, it's private." Laying the jar back down in the same place, she sees Curtis pick up the gun and open the chamber. "Does it have anything in it?"

"It's full, except for the one round."

"Four shots, then?"

"Yeah, we'd better make them count."

They walk back down the path, where Curtis grabs his suitcase again before heading down to the beach. As they cross the last of the dunes and view the ocean for the first time in quite a while, they all stop in their tracks when they discover the immense collection of ship-wrecked boxes and debris that's been washed up on the shore.

"Can we look in some of them?" Matt asks.

"A few, but be careful, we don't know what kind of a ship it was," Sarah answers.

Watching the two boys run down to the high-water mark where most of the packages have ended up, he looks up and down the beach in search of any people, but thankfully, he sees nothing. "You know, we haven't seen a single person all day."

"I know, it's almost creepy. I'm just afraid we're gonna run into Jake somewhere out here."

"We can't live our lives worrying about where he might be."

"If we have to worry about something, it might as well be him." She sees the kids about fifty feet ahead of them, taking computers and cell phones out of the boxes, then tossing them to the side. "It's peaceful out here, isn't it?"

"Yeah, it is. I forgot how much it takes your mind off of everything." He turns around and sees Matt and Ben running back, both of them empty-handed. "You didn't find any hidden treasures?"

"It's just a bunch of electronics," Matt explains. "It's all wet anyway."

"Well, I'm sure there's still more ships out there that haven't sunk. Maybe one of them will have a bunch of footballs or something."

Hearing something down toward the water, Matt grabs his dad's jacket and forces him to stop. "Dad, there's somebody down there."

With everyone staring at the mountain of broken shipping containers and boxes, Curtis takes his gun out and carefully inches his way down to the debris field. "Is anyone there?"

A woman, who's nothing more than skin and bones, jumps out from behind one of the containers, then starts running quickly along the surf.

"Wow, she's really fast!" Ben exclaims.

"Yeah, too fast," Curtis says.

"Could you tell if she was sick?" Sarah asks him, still watching the woman as she runs north.

"Yeah, she was definitely sick. She had those purple marks all over her face."

"If they keep getting faster like that, they're gonna be that much harder to get away from."

"Or kill..."

Moving further down the beach, they come across a few smaller boats and a life raft that have washed up sometime recently, but there's no signs of any footprints surrounding them. What they don't see, partly buried just ahead of them, is a mass grave with only a few appendages visible through the sand. Instead, Curtis stops and points at a house that's sitting just beyond the dunes.

"That's quite a house, isn't it?"

"It looks like a castle." Matt answers.

Curtis can see where he gets that. It has a normal metal roof, just like most of the other houses in the area, but the rest of it looks like blocks of stone or concrete, and it has a tall concrete wall surrounding the property, with only a small wrought iron gate visible, leading down to the beach. He turns to Sarah, who's looking up at the sun, conscious of the time and how vulnerable they could all be after sundown. "What do you think?"

"I think it's worth checking out — but let's be careful," she replies.

Getting closer to the house, they can hear the subtle sounds of the wind chimes on the wrap-around porch, and the creaking of the iron gate as it sways back and forth in the wind current. Up close, the house doesn't look nearly as big as it did on the beach, but it's still in better shape than anything they've seen today. Inside the wall, the yard is full of flower beds and fruit trees, and in one corner there's a woodshed that looks like it's almost filled to capacity.

"This place looks too good to be true," Sarah says, as she walks up onto the porch and peeks through a window.

"Yeah, but good would be a nice change of pace." With his gun still in his hand, Curtis quietly turns the handle on the front door and opens it, surprised at how clean and fresh the air is inside. "Anybody home?" he yells, but he gets no response. As Sarah looks the kitchen and living room over, he quickly checks the bedrooms and bathrooms out, making sure the house is entirely empty.

"Nobody is home?" she asks.

"Nope, just us. Is there any food?"

"Not much, it looks like they evacuated everything. What's that door over there?" she asks, pointing a narrow door in the living room.

"I think it's a basement, I can feel a cold draft coming through it."

"Maybe we should check it out..."

"The door is locked, from this side. We can probably find a key somewhere around here."

"Are we gonna stay the night?" Matt asks.

Curtis looks around, seeing a wood stove in the corner of the living room, and a water cooler sitting in the kitchen that's still half full. "I think so, at least for tonight."

"Should we close the gate outside?"

He looks out the kitchen window and sees the open gate swinging slightly in the wind, and a chain and lock hooked to it. "Okay, but only to the gate and back. Make sure we can see you, and don't lock it until we find a key."

Sarah wraps her arm around Curtis' back, then looks out at the ocean view. She can picture herself standing here, watching a sunset on a warm summer evening, while the others scour the beach for clams for supper. She notices that two of the fruit trees already have buds on them, and with a little pruning and thinning, the yard could be perfect. "I have to admit, I'm getting a little excited about this place."

"Yeah, me too. It has just about everything we need — except maybe some more food and guns."

"Are we near a town?"

"Yeah, maybe a little too close for my liking."

"Which town is this?"

"Grayland."

ACKNOWLEDGMENTS

I'd like to thank everyone for supporting this series — those of you who know me personally (and now question my sanity), and those of you who have sent so many kind words of encouragement in reviews and emails. The first book, Westport, was started a few years before publication, and was delayed by both procrastination and a fight with cancer — the latter of which proved to be a cure for the former. Now that I'm healthy again (at least physically), I'm looking forward to writing more novels in the years to come.

I've been asked on numerous occasions how many books will ultimately be in the series, and to be honest, I really have no idea. I'm currently working on the third book, titled 'Aberdeen', which will be out in early 2019, followed by a stand-alone book named 'The Regency', which tells the story of the hotel that was featured in 'Westport'.

You can find updates on my website, jamesbierce.com, along with information on where you can find my books for sale.

Again, thanks for reading, and I hope you enjoy the next story...

Sincerely,
James Bierce

Made in the USA
Middletown, DE
23 December 2020